Patrick Lee is the author of *Runner*, the first Sam Dryden novel, as well as three previous novels: *The Breach*, *Ghost Country* and *Deep Sky*. Both *Runner* and *The Breach* are currently in production as major motion pictures. He lives in Hudsonville, Michigan.

Only to Die Again

PATRICK LEE

PENGUIN BOOKS

PENGUIN BOOKS

UK | USA | Canada | Ireland | Australia
India | New Zealand | South Africa

Penguin Books is part of the Penguin Random House group of companies
whose addresses can be found at global.penguinrandomhouse.com.

First published in the USA by Minotaur 2015
First published in Great Britain in Penguin Books 2015

001

Set in 12.5/14.75 pt Garamond MT Std
Typeset by Jouve (UK), Milton Keynes
Printed in Great Britain by Clays Ltd, St Ives plc

A CIP catalogue record for this book is available from the British Library

ISBN: 978–1–405–91502–1

www.greenpenguin.co.uk

MIX
Paper from
responsible sources
FSC® C018179

Penguin Random House is committed to a
sustainable future for our business, our readers
and our planet. This book is made from Forest
Stewardship Council® certified paper.

For Thom and Judy Sharp

PART ONE
Saturday, August 8, 2015

Chapter One

The smell hit Marnie Calvert even before she got out of the car. The vents sucked it in from outside: a mix of charred wood and oxidized metal and melted plastic – maybe from linoleum or carpet backing. Then there was the other smell, beneath all those. That smell reminded her of backyard gatherings and nice days at the park. It made her want to throw up.

She wasn't going to throw up. She never had, in eight years with the Bureau. She killed the engine and shoved open the door and stood up into the desert night.

There were already ten or twelve vehicles at the crime scene. State Police, San Bernardino County sheriff's cruisers, three fire trucks out of Palmdale. Most of the units were idling, their flashers strobing and their headlights aimed inward on a focal point: the burned-out husk of a mobile home, all by itself next to a gravel road in the middle of the Mojave.

Outside the car, the smells were all stronger. Marnie gave her stomach ten seconds to relax; she turned in place and took in the landscape. Far to the west, the lights of Edwards Air Force Base dotted the plain before the foothills of the San Gabriels. The mountains stood in faint contrast against the lit-up haze above Los Angeles, maybe seventy miles away. The only nearer light was Barstow, a dim smudge off to the north. Everywhere else, the desert was black and empty and baking hot – four in the morning, early August.

'Agent Calvert?'

Marnie turned. A sheriff's deputy came toward her, out of the glare of the scene. He was fifty, give or take, a stocky guy just going soft. The nameplate above his badge read HILLER. Marnie had spoken to him on the phone.

She shut the door of her Crown Vic and crossed to him. Her shoes crunched on the hardpan.

'My forensics people are on their way,' she said.

Hiller nodded and led her between the nearest cruisers. Past their stabbing light, Marnie got her first full look at the ruin of the trailer. The hand she'd been shielding her eyes with fell away, and she stood staring.

There was almost nothing left of the thing. The walls and roof were gone, and even much of the base had collapsed between the cinder-block stacks that'd supported the place. A few structural metal uprights still stood, connected by shallow roof arches, like blackened ribs.

There were four body bags arrayed on the ground beside one of the fire trucks. Nothing in them yet.

Marnie knew the whole story already. She'd heard the first details in her office, at the federal building in Santa Monica. The rest had come by phone while she'd driven out here, including an audio file sent to her by e-mail: a recording of a 9-1-1 call that had come from this trailer, just about two hours ago now. She had listened to it three times, then opened the Crown Vic's windows and let the oven air of the desert rush in around her. As far as she could remember, her thoughts had simply gone blank for the few minutes after that.

9-1-1 Emergency —

Can you trace this? A girl's voice. Almost whispering.

What's the nature of the emergency —

I'm on a cell phone. Can you trace where I am?

Are you in danger right now?

No answer.

Miss, are you in danger?

Three more seconds of silence.

Then: *My name is Leah Swain. I'm here with three other —*

The girl cut herself off with a rush of breath, high-pitched and scared.

Miss?

We didn't call anyone! the girl screamed. It sounded like she had the phone away from her mouth, her voice aimed at someone in the room. *We didn't call anyone! I promise —*

That was it. The line went dead on that word, at 2.04 a.m. and 20 seconds, by the time stamp on the dispatcher's computer screen. Also on the screen were the caller's GPS coordinates; the phone had sent them by default, in response to 9-1-1 being dialed. Within the next thirty seconds, a state patrol unit on I-15 had been routed toward the location. Five minutes later, when the trooper was still two miles out, he reported seeing the flames. The trailer was an inferno by the time he arrived, and its listed owner, Harold Heeley Shannon, white male, age sixty-two, history of criminal sexual misconduct, was nowhere to be seen. Only tire impressions remained where his car, a red Ford Fiesta, had been.

Marnie crossed the empty space of the trailer's dirt yard. She tracked around the wreckage clockwise until she was no longer downwind. She was close enough now to see the collapsed debris that had settled into the structure's footprint. The soggy remnants of the walls and ceiling and floor, and all that they'd enclosed.

Only one thing had held its shape: a cage with thick metal bars, forming a cube maybe six feet on each side. Marnie covered the last few yards and stopped at the boundary where the trailer's end wall had been. The cage stood just inside, canted atop the burned rubble of the floor it had rested on.

Marnie had been to bad scenes before. She'd found a body in a plastic drum once, decomposed after being sealed inside for two years. The bones had lain cluttered like discarded hand tools, submerged in a soup of fluids that'd leaked and separated and settled. Another time she'd seen a crawl space where a woman, thirty-one years old, had been kept for a weekend before her captor strangled and buried her. On a pine beam in the corner, where she must've hoped the police would someday see it, the woman had written with her fingernail, *Becca I love you, grow up to be happy no matter what happens.* With a child counselor's help, Marnie had delivered that message in person. Days like that one usually ended in her basement in West Hills. She had an old catcher's mitt from her days in Little League, twenty years back, and she would sit in the dark down there for an hour or more, feeling the stitching and the worn-smooth leather. She didn't know why she did it. Didn't care why, either, on those kinds of nights.

There were four bodies in the metal cage. They were blackened, with only shreds of clothing stuck to them. All lay pressed flat to the barred floor of the cage, positioned the way they'd died: trying to breathe the last air in the room.

Marnie became aware of Hiller standing next to her.

'All kids,' he said softly. 'Not even in their teens, that size.'

The wind shifted, just for a second. It was long enough to send the smell at Marnie again before she could think to exhale – the smell that was awful because it was familiar, even pleasant. The smell of cooked meat.

Leah Swain had disappeared from a playground in Irvine just over three years ago, when she was eight. Marnie had put in time on the case back then, along with a dozen other agents in L.A. and San Diego. The girl's parents had done interviews on local and national news, begging whoever had their daughter to return her. Maybe those interviews had played on a TV set here in this trailer, where Leah had sat in her cage. Where she had lived for these past three years. Where, tonight, she had somehow gotten hold of Harold Shannon's cell phone. Where she had burned.

'We've got the plate and vehicle description out to every cruiser in California and Nevada,' Hiller said. 'Shannon's DMV photo, too.'

Marnie had seen the man's picture herself, on her

phone. It looked like a mug shot. Gaunt face, sunk-in eyes, long hair and beard the texture of steel wool.

At the edge of Marnie's vision, distant headlights appeared. She watched them come in. They were half a mile out, taking it slow on the washboard ruts of the gravel road. Probably her forensics guys. She walked back to her car to wait for them, but by the time she got there she saw that it wasn't an FBI vehicle arriving. Just an uplink truck for ABC7 News out of L.A.

She leaned against her Crown Vic and rubbed her eyes. When she opened them again, some of the cops nearby were watching her. Maybe they thought she was crying. Maybe they thought she looked too soft for the job. That was fine. Their thoughts were their business. She stood upright again and walked away from the scene, out into the pitch black, where it would be okay to let her hands shake. She wasn't going to throw up, wasn't going to cry, either, but her hands were going to shake like hell as soon as she let them. The rage had to go somewhere, that was all.

A hundred yards west of the trailer, she stopped – there was a deep, wide arroyo channel carved into the desert floor there, running south from a culvert under the road. The arroyo's depth was filled with years' worth of trash: jagged metal engine parts, broken appliances, plastic garbage bags torn open by animals. All of it lay in shadow beneath the plane of the surface, leaving the arroyo nearly invisible in the dark. Even with the lit-up crime scene casting its glow over the desert, Marnie had almost walked right into it.

She sank to a crouch and sat on the channel's edge. In the faint light, the strewn trash made her think of a lion's den scattered with bones. Leah Swain had ended up in a lion's den because she'd gone to a playground during the wrong ten minutes. There would never be any better answer than that.

Marnie turned her gaze up to the horizon and watched for the forensics team, and felt the first tremors in her hands coming on.

Chapter Two

Four hours earlier, when Leah Swain was alive and waiting for Harold Shannon to go to bed, when she was staring at the cell phone he'd left on the coffee table, just reachable with the strip of quarter-round wood molding she'd pried off the base of the wall behind the cage, Sam Dryden was staring at the ocean.

He was two miles inland, in the hills above El Sedero, California. He could see the lights of the shore road and the marina; beyond those, the ocean was a vast black nothing. Closer in, the town was buttoned down and quiet, a few minutes after midnight at the end of a Friday.

Dryden stood on the balcony of a cottage, its yard boxed in on the sides by hundred-year-old evergreens. The air was saturated with the smells of pine and cedar, the boughs wet from the rain shower that had come through an hour before. Now the stars were showing, sharp as pinpricks on the black sky.

The cottage wasn't his home; he could see his home from here, way down on the waterfront. This cottage was a second place he'd bought to fix up and sell – the third such purchase in the past two years, each one a little bigger as he got more comfortable with the work. It was far from the skill set his background had given him, but that was fine. He never wanted to use any of those skills again.

The wind picked up. Droplets of water shook loose from the trees and pattered the ground. Dryden stood listening for a while, then turned and went back inside.

The cottage's living room was gutted to the studs. When he'd bought the place, it had still had its original wiring from probably the 1930s: push-button switches, knob-and-tube wires sheathed with fabric, not a ground wire to be found in the house. It was a miracle it hadn't burned down fifty years ago. Dryden had torn everything out and redone it to code. Same story for the plumbing.

He'd reshaped the cottage's layout while he was at it. Opened the kitchen up to the living room. Made the doorways and the windows bigger. More light. More airflow.

Tonight he'd finished putting in fiberglass insulation throughout the place. He'd worn a respirator mask and goggles, but his hair and skin had been coated with the stuff by the time he was finished. Half an hour ago he'd showered – the bathroom was gutted, too, but the new clawfoot tub was in place, with a blue tarp hung around it for a makeshift curtain – and now he was clean again, walking the rooms of the cottage, taking in the day's effort. This morning his footsteps had echoed through the house; now they were dampened and muted, the reverb all soaked up by the fiberglass. Difference. Progress.

He wondered sometimes why more people didn't do this kind of work. It could be a pain in the ass, no doubt – you might tear the plaster off a wall and find the uprights inside rotted, and just like that you were looking at days and days of added labor – but even so, the job had every-thing going for it. It had tangibility. You could see your work take shape as you went. And when you got dirty, getting clean was a literal thing. Sawdust and insulation and drywall mud on your skin – all those things came off in shower spray and went down the drain, simple as that. Not every line of work offered that kind of clarity.

He came to the master bedroom. Some of the finish material for the closet had been delivered this week: shelving and a big framed wall mirror. It was all leaning in the corner for now. He caught his reflection from the doorway. He'd been in good shape even before taking up construction, but the physical work had done him some good all the same. He liked the way he looked. Not bad for thirty-eight.

He switched off the bedroom lights and returned to the balcony. He stared away at the town again, and the ocean. He could see the strobing lights of an airliner way out over the water, probably coming in toward LAX, an hour down the coast from El Sedero. He was still watching it when his phone rang in his pocket. He took it out and looked at the display: The number was unfamiliar. Dryden tapped the answer button, forgoing cleverness for a simple hello.

A woman responded. 'Are you at your place?'

Dryden recognized the voice instantly – it belonged to a friend: Claire Dunham.

Something in her tone. Urgency and adrenaline.

'I'm close to it,' Dryden said. 'Why?'

'You're in El Sedero?'

'Yeah. Why?'

For the second time, Claire seemed not to hear the question. She said, 'How fast can you get to Barstow? Two hours?'

Dryden thought about it. The straightest route came to mind easily enough, and this time of night there would be hardly any traffic.

'Something like that,' Dryden said.

'I need you to meet me near there. You have to go right now. Meet me south of Barstow on the Fifteen. There's a town called Arrowhead, just an off-ramp with a gas station. Park there and wait.'

Over the call, Dryden heard a sound fade in: the drone of heavy tires on pavement. It swelled and then tailed off to nothing in the space of a few seconds. He got the impression of Claire in her car, passing a semi on a freeway at high speed. If she was coming from her own home, up in the Bay Area, and hoping to be in Barstow by two in the morning, then she must be halfway there already.

'What the hell is this about?' Dryden asked.

When Claire answered, Dryden realized there was more than just stress in her voice. There was fear – deep and real.

'Tell you when I see you,' Claire said. 'Don't bring your phone. Thanks, Sam.'

The call ended. Dryden stood there a moment longer, replaying it in his head. The instruction about the phone implied nothing good. A cell phone had built-in GPS and was constantly updating the network with its current location. Whatever Claire Dunham had going on near Barstow, she didn't seem to want an official record of their presence there.

Claire was not the sort of person who sought out trouble for no reason. Far from it: She was one of the few people on earth Dryden fully trusted.

You have to go right now.

Dryden stepped in off the balcony, closed the sliding door behind him, and was at the wheel of his Explorer twenty seconds later.

Chapter Three

Arrowhead was exactly what Claire had described. An off-ramp to a crumbling two-lane that ran west to east, out of the desert and back into it. Pitch-black emptiness in both directions. Northeast, where the freeway led, the near edge of Barstow was ten miles out.

Close to the off-ramp stood a shabby diner and a Sunoco station. Only the latter was open for business, casting a milky pool of light over the scrubland around it.

Dryden took the exit at 1.58 a.m. He rolled into the darkened lot of the diner and parked. Except for the attendant inside the station, there was no sign of life anywhere.

Dryden watched the road and the freeway, and waited.

Claire Dunham.

What could she be caught up in?

Dryden had met her ten years before, back in the life he mostly tried to forget these days. Claire had been a technician, an expert with the electronic hardware Dryden and his people had used all over the world, and in many cases she'd been right there in harm's way with him and the others.

Lots of those who had known her – men, especially – had found her nearly impossible to read. They assumed she was cold, indifferent to others. Dryden had assumed it, too, early on, but he'd understood later that he was wrong about that. The truth was that Claire Dunham's unreadability was a two-way street. She could make no sense of people, a fact she must have come to terms with long ago, probably way back in childhood, and at some point she'd stopped trying. Probably anyone would have, in her shoes. But she wasn't cold. Once a stray dog had wandered into the visiting officers' quarters at Bagram Airfield, and Claire had taken to it. The thing had looked like a burlap sack full of wrenches, its fur matted and its ribs showing. Dryden had expected it to die, despite Claire's efforts – not just feeding it, but tracking down meds for three or four different afflictions the thing was riddled with – but he'd been wrong about that, too: The dog had lived another eight years, mostly lying around by the pool at Claire's place up in San Jose, soaking up the sun.

A mile or more west of the freeway interchange, headlights crested a rise, coming in fast.

Dryden killed his engine and got out. He could hear the hiss of tires and the whine of a powerful vehicle running in high gear. A moment later it passed into the halo of light from the Sunoco, and Dryden recognized the outline of Claire Dunham's Land Rover. It braked hard and came to a stop in the road close by. Claire leaned over and shoved the passenger door open and gestured fast for Dryden to get in.

Dryden had hardly done so when Claire gunned it again; within seconds they were beyond the overpass and into the darkness, following the two-lane out into the empty desert east of I-15. Claire pushed the engine to 95 miles per hour.

She didn't look good. In the light from the instrument panel, her face gleamed with sweat, though the A/C was blasting. Her eyes – large and green, normally expressing nothing but calm – kept going to the digital clock on the console, which now showed 2.01.

Dryden could think of only a handful of times he'd ever seen her look rattled before, and those had always been awkward social situations. To see her off-balance like this bordered on unthinkable.

'What's happening?' Dryden asked.

Claire ran a hand over her forehead, wiped it on her shirt, and gripped the wheel again.

'I couldn't explain it right now. You'll know pretty soon.' Her eyes went to the clock once more. *'Fuck.'*

'Why don't you give it a try?'

Instead of answering, Claire reached into the backseat and hauled a black duffel bag forward into her lap. It was already open. She reached in and withdrew a Beretta 9mm and held it out to Dryden.

'Loaded, one in the chamber,' she said.

Dryden took the weapon, checked that its safety was on, and rested it on his thigh. He glanced over and saw that Claire had a Beretta of her own already holstered in a shoulder harness.

She reached into the duffel again and took out something larger than a pistol. It was a squat black instrument the size of a lunchbox, with a minitripod folded up beneath it. Dryden recognized the thing at once; he and

Claire had used them often, back in their old lives. It was a laser microphone. Its beam could measure sound vibrations on a pane of glass – you pointed it at the outside of a window, and you could hear noises from inside the building.

It was no surprise Claire owned one; she had gone into the private security business after the two of them had left the military, eight years before. She was well sought after these days, working for tech firms in Silicon Valley, securing company sites and even the homes of executives. As Dryden understood it, corporations also sometimes hired her to snoop on employees they didn't trust, and very often their mistrust turned out to be well placed.

Claire snapped the tripod's legs into position with one hand, getting the machine ready. At that moment the pavement gave way to gravel, and the Land Rover, doing just under 100 miles per hour, rattled and slewed violently. Stretches of chatterbumps came and went, making the whole vehicle shudder like a washing machine with a brick in it.

'Goddammit,' Claire hissed.

They came over a shallow ripple in the landscape, and Dryden saw a single point of light far ahead in the dark. A bare bulb over somebody's porch, he guessed, maybe a mile ahead.

'There,' Claire said. Her eyes were locked on the distant light. She eased off the gas, slowing to 70 and then 50. The Land Rover's engine scream fell away to a low growl, and Dryden understood: Claire didn't want their approach to be heard.

Taking a hand off the wheel again, she opened a compartment on the side of the laser mic. Inside were half a dozen wireless earpieces; she gave one to Dryden, then took another for herself and fixed it to her ear. Dryden did the same.

The porch light was half a mile away now. Dryden could just make out the shape of the building it was attached to, low-slung and boxy. A mobile home. A red compact car sat in front of it.

Claire kept the Land Rover at 50 until they were three hundred yards out, then killed the headlights. Any closer and the lights' glow might have been visible from inside the trailer, even if there were curtains over the windows.

With the beams off, the desert became ink black. It was impossible to see even the road. Claire cursed softly, took her foot off the gas, and rolled to a stop. She didn't bother shutting off the engine; she just dumped it into park and was out the door half a second later, stepping around it and setting the microphone on the hood. Dryden got out on his own side. Already he could see the red laser dot jittering back and forth in the trailer's distant yard, as Claire steered it.

She leaned over and sighted down the length of the instrument and brought the beam to rest on a window near the trailer's north end. She steadied it and let go, then drew her sidearm and advanced toward the trailer at just shy of a full run. Dryden followed. Their footfalls were almost silent. They had learned long ago how to move quietly and quickly on desert ground.

Through his earpiece, Dryden began to hear noises

from inside the trailer. Strange noises. A kind of softened clicking sound – it made him think of a cat's claw tearing at upholstery, catching and slipping, again and again.

Then the noise stopped.

For the next few seconds there was no sound at all.

He and Claire were two hundred fifty yards from the trailer now. The bare porch bulb cast a weak yellow light, sixty watts if that. It left the terrain pitch black between the two of them and the trailer's dooryard.

All at once, over the earpiece, Dryden heard something unmistakable: the digital click of an iPhone being switched on. To his left, he saw Claire react to it, picking up her speed.

Three tones came over the earpiece in rapid succession, the first one high-pitched, the next two lower and identical to each other.

Someone in the trailer had just dialed 9-1-1.

Two hundred yards to go.

The ringing of the outgoing call was just perceptible. It trilled once, and then a tinny voice answered on the other end. Dryden couldn't make out the words, though he could guess them well enough.

Then came another voice, almost whispering, but much easier to discern. A young girl's voice, inside the trailer. 'Can you trace this?'

The 9-1-1 operator started to respond, but the girl cut her off.

'I'm on a cell phone. Can you trace where I am?'

A quick spill of words from the dispatcher. One of them sounded like *danger*.

This time the girl made no reply.

The dispatcher spoke again, but still there was no answer from inside the mobile home. Seconds passed.

Then the girl said, 'My name is Leah Swain. I'm here with three other –'

She broke off, exhaling hard, the sound full of fear.

Dryden thought he heard one last syllable from the dispatcher, and then the girl began screaming, high and terrified.

'We didn't call anyone! We didn't call anyone! I promise, it's okay! We didn't call anyone!'

For a moment it sounded like the girl was somehow talking and screaming at the same time. Then Dryden realized what he was actually hearing: There was another girl inside the trailer. Maybe several.

Even as he registered that fact, a man began shouting over the girls. *'What did you do? What the fuck did you do?'*

Next to Dryden in the dark, Claire swore and broke into a full sprint. Dryden matched her. Though Claire had told him nothing about the people in the trailer, the key points of the situation were as clearly defined as razorwire tips.

The man's screaming became almost indiscernible over the girls' cries, but the phrase *kill you* stuck out more than once. The man's shrieks sounded more animal than human. That was the last thought that crossed Dryden's mind before the ground dropped out from under him.

His feet had been pounding the desert surface, and suddenly one of them came down on empty space. He pitched forward and threw his arms ahead of him, aware of Claire doing the same thing to his left. For a sickening half second he imagined there was nothing beneath him but a hundred-foot drop, and then one knee smashed hard against a metal edge and pain exploded through his leg. His hands landed amid trash bags and scattered pieces of plastic – broken casings of machinery and who knew what else. He heard Claire crash down into similar debris, five feet away, already fighting to climb up the other side of the trench they'd fallen in – an arroyo strewn with garbage.

Dryden moved his leg and found it wasn't injured. He'd banged the kneecap badly, but nothing was broken.

In the trailer, the man's screams continued. '– *gonna fucking kill you, do you understand that?*'

Dryden was still holding the Beretta Claire had given him. With his free hand he pushed himself upright and scrambled toward the far side of the arroyo –

And found himself yanked to a halt by his other leg.

The calf of his jeans was hung up on something. Some jagged metal corner that'd pierced the fabric and now held like a barbed hook.

Five feet away, Claire was struggling to move, too. Dryden could hear something like rusted bedsprings warping and straining under her exertion, the whole mass shifting amid clutter as she fought to free herself.

Inside the trailer, the man's voice had taken on a lunatic chanting quality – '*Kill you . . . kill you . . .*' – as if he were speaking only to himself now. There came a wooden banging noise over the audio: cabinet doors being flung open, it sounded like, one after the next. Cans and boxes being shoved aside in a mad search for something.

Dryden yanked his trapped leg toward himself with all his force, meaning to rip the fabric free. It was no good; the trash simply shifted beneath him, giving him no purchase from which to pull.

'*Kill you . . . kill you . . . HERE!*'

The slamming of the cabinet doors ceased, along with the voice. All that followed was the sound of the girls screaming.

Dryden jammed the pistol into his waistband and groped in the darkness for any solid handhold. One elbow thumped lightly against a metal surface, the sound of the impact blunt and reverberant. A washer or dryer, half-sunk into the dirt wall of the arroyo. He wrapped both his hands around an edge of the appliance, as if it were the lip of a cliff he meant to scale. He wrenched his body upward and felt the jean fabric tear and give way. Both legs came up fast; he drew them up to his chest, braced his feet where his hands had been, and exploded from the crouch like a runner out of the blocks. Half a second later he was on the surface again, landing on all fours, coming up and sprinting as fast as his body could move.

One hundred yards to the trailer.

Seventy-five.

Fifty.

'*Want to see what you get?*' the man inside screamed. '*This is what you fucking get!*'

Dryden drew the Beretta and covered the last fifty yards in an adrenalized surge that felt more like flying than running.

There was a low wooden porch in front of the trailer's door – two steps and a shallow platform. The door was hinged to swing outward, but it was also rusted and damn near falling off its frame. Dryden vaulted onto the porch without slowing and hit the door with his shoulder; the cheap frame buckled and the door burst inward, and just like that he was inside, the details of the space coming at him all at once.

A big steel cage with four young girls in it, screaming and holding on to each other.

A skeletal man with long gray hair and a long gray beard, holding a bottle of lighter fluid and picking at the cap with his fingertips. Trying to open it.

The man jerked around at the crash of the door. His face seemed caught between expressions – rage and surprise. As the guy's voice had done over the earpiece, that face gave Dryden the impression of something not quite human. Some predatory thing, instinctive and feral.

The man's eyes darted away from Dryden, to the filthy countertop that separated the living room from the kitchen. Amid the clutter there, five feet away, lay a twelve-inch hunting knife.

The guy's attention came back to Dryden, the eyes narrowing in fast calculation. Dryden didn't wait for him to finish it. He centered the guy up and put two shots through his forehead. The man spasmed and fell back, collapsing at the base of the wall.

The bottle of lighter fluid landed beside him.

Still sealed.

Near silence fell over the room. The girls had stopped screaming. They were only staring now, eyes huge, their breath hitching.

Running footsteps outside. Claire landed on the porch, crossed the threshold, and came to a stop just behind Dryden. The girls' eyes went back and forth between the two of them.

All four were just kids, somewhere between eight and twelve years old. They wore simple T-shirts and sweatpants. They had long hair brushed straight, and trimmed nails, and clean skin.

Groomed pets, Dryden thought, and felt like emptying the rest of the Beretta into the dead man's face.

He saw an iPhone lying on the floor inside the cage, and a long strip of quarter-round molding just sticking out through the bars. A single nail remained at one end of the molding – the end that lay outside the cage. Dryden considered the nail and the phone, and thought of the cat's-claw-on-upholstery sound he'd heard before the 9-1-1 call: the sound of the nail catching on the carpeting, as the girls dragged the phone toward them from wherever it'd been. They had made the call the moment they had the phone in hand.

'We need to go,' Claire said.

Dryden turned to her. Claire's anxiety was gone – most of it, anyway. Dryden pictured her during the last minutes of the drive, constantly checking the clock, keenly aware that time was running out.

'How the hell could you have known?' Dryden asked.

'Later,' Claire said. 'It's time to leave.'

Dryden made no move. He looked from Claire to the girls, and then to the phone on the ground, trying to make any of it fit.

'I'll explain,' Claire said. 'I'll show you. But not now.'

Dryden continued staring at her. It was the first time tonight that he'd seen her in bright light. Though the immediate tension was gone, in other ways she looked far worse than Dryden had realized earlier. She had dark hollows beneath her eyes, and her skin was pale. She hadn't lost any weight – she was the same lean-framed five foot eight she'd always been – yet she seemed diminished in some way. She looked physically exhausted, far more than a long drive and a short sprint could account for.

'I'll explain,' Claire said again. She made as if to leave, then seemed to catch herself. She turned and scanned the carpet to Dryden's right, stooped and picked up the two spent shell casings from the Beretta. She pocketed them and moved past Dryden, out onto the wooden porch.

Dryden turned his attention back to the cage. Steel bars welded roughly together. A crude door, made of the same bars, latched with a heavy padlock.

The whole situation still landing on him, one miserable piece after another.

The four girls stared out through the bars, their eyes still wet from crying.

From outside, Claire said, 'They'll be fine when the cops get here. We won't. Come on.'

Dryden hesitated a moment longer, then turned and stepped through the doorway. Claire was already running for the gravel road and the Land Rover. From far away in the night, in the direction of the freeway, came the keening of a police siren. Dryden stepped off the porch and sprinted after Claire.

Chapter Four

The smell hit Marnie Calvert even before she got out of the car. The vents sucked it in from outside: a mix of alkaline dust and aviation fuel exhaust. A helicopter had just touched down close by; she'd watched it descend as she covered the last half mile of the drive.

She killed the engine and shoved open the door and stood up into the desert night.

There were already ten or twelve vehicles at the crime scene. State Police, San Bernardino County sheriff's cruisers, three ambulances out of Palmdale. Most of the units were idling, their flashers strobing and their headlights aimed inward on a focal point: a decrepit old trailer with a red Ford Fiesta parked in front of it, all by itself next to a gravel road in the middle of the Mojave.

Outside the car, the kicked-up dust was thicker, but it was already drifting away into the scrublands. The desert was black and empty and baking hot – four in the morning, early August.

'Agent Calvert?'

A sheriff's deputy came toward her, out of the glare of the scene. He was fifty, give or take, a stocky guy just going soft. The nameplate above his badge read HILLER. Marnie had spoken to him on the phone.

She shut the door of her Crown Vic and crossed to him. Her shoes crunched on the hardpan.

'The kids are right this way,' Hiller said.

The four girls were sitting on a metal bench the paramedics had set up beside one of the ambulances. Each looked dazed, certainly scared, but it was clear at a glance there was no immediate medical trauma. The EMTs were as relaxed as such people could be at a crime scene, crouching beside the girls and simply talking to them. No doubt they'd done some basic physical assessments, and the girls would still be taken to a hospital, but those were formalities.

Marnie crossed the dirt yard and knelt down to eye level with the girl on the left end of the bench. The girl whose face had stared at her from her office bulletin board for six months, back when she'd disappeared. Even in the years since then, Marnie had revisited the case file often.

'Leah?' Marnie said.

The girl had been looking at her own hands in her lap. Now she lifted her gaze and met Marnie's eyes. She'd been eight the last time Marnie – or anyone else outside this trailer – had seen her. She was eleven now.

Her eyes looked older than that. A lot older. She nodded and said nothing.

'Hi, Leah. My name's Marnie. I'm an FBI agent.'

'Are my mom and dad coming?'

'They're going to be at the hospital when you get there, and that'll be soon. The police are going to drive you there.'

28

'I don't want to go to the hospital. I want to go home.'

Leah's voice cracked, but she kept her composure. She looked practiced at doing so.

'Hey,' Marnie said softly. 'You're going to be home before you know it. And guess what. Pretzel's still there.'

At the mention of that name, a trace of happiness flickered through the girl's eyes. The emotion seemed to surprise her.

Pretzel, a golden retriever, had been a three-month-old puppy when Leah Swain disappeared in the summer of 2012. Marnie had seen the dog herself when she'd interviewed the parents back then. Half an hour ago, speaking to Mr Swain on the phone, Marnie had heard the retriever barking like hell in the background, the wife calling its name and telling it to sit. Dogs were emotional antennas – it was hard to imagine the vibe it must be picking up in that house tonight.

Leah blinked repeatedly. Her eyes were just noticeably moist now.

'I promise I won't bother you with too many questions,' Marnie said, 'but can I ask you just three or four? They might be important.'

Leah nodded.

Off at the far edge of the lit-up scene, Marnie heard men's voices greeting someone. She turned and saw a man she recognized: the chief of the LAPD, walking in from where the chopper had touched down. She was pretty sure the desert south of Barstow was hell and gone from the guy's jurisdiction, but this was one of those cases where all the boundaries were sure to get blurred. And it had ended happily, which meant politicians would want their faces associated with it. Marnie wondered whether the guy would have flown out here if the night had turned out differently.

For a moment that image forced itself into her head: the scene she might have rolled up to, if Harold Heeley Shannon had gotten his way. The awful picture was unusually vivid in her thoughts.

Marnie pushed it away and turned back to Leah.

'You told the police two people came into the trailer and stopped Mr Shannon from starting a fire,' Marnie said. 'A man and a woman. Is that right?'

Leah nodded.

'Did you ever see those people before?' Marnie asked. 'Did Mr Shannon know them?'

The girl shook her head.

'Did they say anything to you or the other girls?'

Another head shake.

'What about names?' Marnie asked. 'Did they call each other anything?'

Leah thought about it. Her eyebrows drew closer together. 'I don't think so.'

'Can you remember anything they did say?'

'They were in a hurry to go. The lady kept saying they had to leave before the police came. So they did.'

The girl thought about it a moment longer, then simply shook her head again. Even through the mask of shock and suppressed emotion on her face, it was clear the girl was keeping nothing back. She had no idea who the man and woman had been, or how they'd managed to arrive at that exact moment, seconds after a 9-1-1 call nobody on earth could have anticipated.

Two minutes later, in a caravan of police SUVs and cruisers, the girls left the scene. Hiller waved Marnie into the trailer, where the cops had so far treaded lightly; an FBI forensics team from Santa Monica was still en route to process the place.

Inside, the cage held Marnie's attention for a full ten seconds. Then her gaze fell on Harold Shannon, his eyes open and pointed at the ceiling, his brains and most of his blood soaking the carpet in a tacky puddle. The first responders had noted that the exit wounds suggested hollow points and that the shooter must have taken the shell casings. So much for ballistics evidence – fragmented scraps of bullets weren't going to tell them anything.

Hiller was standing at the mouth of a hallway leading off to the trailer's back rooms.

'You got a strong stomach?' he asked.

'I've seen worse corpses,' Marnie said.

'I wasn't talking about the body.' Hiller nodded behind himself, down the hall. 'There's something back here I guess you'll need to see. Or . . . know about, anyway.'

She wondered at the odd choice of words but followed him as he led the way out of the living room.

There were only two rooms off the hall: a tiny bathroom, and then Shannon's bedroom.

There was nothing special about the bathroom, beyond that it was filthy. Marnie gave it a glance and continued along the hall. She found Hiller standing just inside the doorway to the bedroom, yet keeping his gaze pointed back into the hallway. He didn't want to look at the room. Marnie stepped past him and saw why.

The furniture was basic enough: a bed and a nightstand, both about as disgusting as the rest of the trailer. The bedsheets appeared to have never been washed. The nightstand was covered with beer bottles full of cigarette butts, and paper plates and bowls caked with rotted food scraps. There was a single window, with dark green curtains pulled over it. There was a bare bulb hanging from the ceiling. Marnie saw all those things and forgot them in the same half second, as she took in the reason Hiller had his eyes pointed away from the room.

The space was wallpapered with photographs. Digital shots, home printed on 8½"-by-11" sheets of high-gloss paper. The pictures were lined up on the walls in a grid that covered them floor to ceiling, corner to corner. Their edges met with absurd precision, though not a scrap of tape was visible anywhere. Maybe the paper sheets were spray-glued to the wall. A labor of obsession.

Marnie realized she was keeping her viewpoint moving. Unwilling to let it stop on any single image. All the same, she saw them. Saw what they were. After a few seconds she blinked and aimed her gaze at the doorway. Hiller was still standing there. Marnie could hear his breath hissing in and out through his teeth.

Her own breathing stayed quiet, but she could feel her hands wanting to shake.

*

When she stepped back out onto the porch she saw an uplink truck for ABC7 News parked at the edge of the scene. No sign yet of the forensics team.

She walked to her car, then went past it into the darkness, away from all the eyes. A hundred yards west of the trailer she came upon an arroyo channel – almost walked into it, in the trace light. The thing was strewn with garbage and broken machinery. She sat on its edge, her gaze fixed on the horizon, and let the tremors in her hands set in.

She was still sitting there five minutes later when headlights topped a rise to the west, her team rolling in at last. She squinted and turned away – her eyes had adjusted to the darkness – and found herself staring at the arroyo's edge beside her.

Where she could just make out what she'd been unable to see a few minutes before: scuff marks and scrapes from hands and shoes. Like someone had landed on all fours here, maybe after vaulting over the arroyo. Or out of it.

Marnie took a miniflashlight from her pocket and switched it on. She studied the scour marks on the desert hardpan, then swung the beam to the far side of the arroyo. Nothing in particular jumped out at her over there, but in the beam's peripheral light something else did.

A scrap of fabric, caught on jagged metal in the arroyo's depth.

She shone the light down onto it. It was a torn piece of denim, hanging from the spearlike point of a broken axle.

In almost the same moment, something closer drew

Marnie's attention. She adjusted the light again and blinked in surprise.

Three feet below her, an old washing machine lay half-submerged in the arroyo's dirt wall. Along the nearest edge of the washer were two shapes stamped with desert dust: the impressions of a pair of shoe soles, from the balls of the feet forward.

And maybe something else.

Marnie lit up the channel's wall beneath her, dug one of her feet into it, and slid carefully down to the washing machine. She crouched over the thing, putting the flashlight and her eyes three inches from the shoe impressions.

They were flanked by handprints, just visible in the light glare. Eight fingers, pressed to the metal. Eight fingerprints.

Chapter Five

The man who called himself Mangouste stepped out the back door of his home and closed it behind him. The night was cool and moist, unseasonable for this part of California. He crossed the rear yard to a gate at the back, opened it, and stepped through into the forest beyond. Here the air was thicker still, the undergrowth looming out of a ground fog that had settled into the lowest parts of the wood.

There was a way through the brush – not quite a trail, but close enough. Mangouste followed it a hundred yards, to where it opened to a clearing fifty feet across.

In the center of the clearing was a place where the ground hummed with a vibration from below. He could only just feel it; a person who didn't know better could walk over this spot a dozen times and not notice.

Mangouste moved in small steps until he found the place where the hum was strongest, then sat down there, on the damp leaves. He spoke under his breath in French and ran a hand through his hair. His fingertips passed over the faint remnant of a scar hidden there. He'd had it since childhood, more than thirty years back – the result of a brick swung by another child who had probably meant to kill him.

He had lived in France then, in Caen, eleven years old,

long since orphaned. There were places for orphans in the city, but those places were worse than being alone on the street, so he had stayed away from them whenever possible. Being on your own was dangerous, of course, but danger could be adapted to. He had been homeless for nearly two years when the incident with the brick happened. He remembered it almost perfectly, even now – how quietly the attack had come, how nothing more than stupid luck had made him turn his head just then, taking a glancing blow instead of a dead-on impact. He recalled how instinctively he'd reacted. What it had felt like to put the blade of his knife into the other boy's throat. How that strange moment had been intimate, in its own way: holding the boy down on top of the trash bags, pinning his arms and listening to him whimper as the blood came from his neck in hot little spurts. When the police found him there, an hour later, he was sitting with the dead boy's hand in his lap, moving the digits one by one, mesmerized by the absence of life in them.

He had expected to go away to prison, but it didn't happen that way. What happened was that he spent two days in a jail cell, and then in the middle of the night a policeman woke him up and took him out through the back door. The man put him into a van and drove him away; he rode for hours, lying on the backseat, truly afraid for the first time – he simply did not know what would happen to him at the end of the ride.

What happened was that he fell asleep in the van, and woke in a very comfortable bed in a room overlooking a resort town of some kind – a hillside full of enormous villas sweeping down to a lakefront. It turned out to be Lake Como in Italy. There was no sign of the policeman when he woke, but there were plenty of other people in the giant house – grown-ups and children, too. They were kind to him. They understood his mistrust and allowed him to come slowly out of his shell. They knew where he had come from, and how he had lived. They knew more than that, actually.

Your father was a soldier, they said. *Did you know?*

He nodded. Yes, he knew. It was just about all he knew of his parents – that one sentence.

Your father was a very good soldier. A loyal one, who helped us. You're here because we owe it to him to look after you. This is your home now.

This had seemed too good to be the whole truth, and it hadn't been. He had learned the rest of it in time: Yes, his father had done something for these people, but he himself would also be expected to do something for them, years down the road. He would be expected to do a great many things, as it would turn out. That was why they had taken him in.

But that was fine.

It was more than fine, in fact. By the time he understood the whole picture, he had come to agree with it. He had lived among those people for years by then, in their beautiful homes all over Europe, and their view of the world had persuaded him.

Some people call us a movement, they said, *but that's the wrong word. We're something purer than that. We're an idea – the most important idea in the world. We came very close to* changing *the world, once upon a time. What we want now is another chance to try.*

Toward that end they were using all their power, which was considerable. They had what must have been billions of dollars. They had their own airliners, done up inside like yachts. They had powerful friends who visited sometimes and stayed up late into the night, sitting around the table, talking about what might have been, had things gone differently all those years ago. And talking about what might still be, somewhere down the road.

If we're patient. If we can bide our time and stay low.

Some of their powerful friends were minor politicians from countries in Europe and even the United States. A few were not minor. There was even a famous American actor who came around now and again to pledge his financial support to the cause; he would drink Grey Goose and sit poking the embers in the giant fireplace in the den. *Think of what the world could be,* he would say, his eyes reflecting the guttering flames. *Think how beautiful it could be.*

The boy was in his teens by then. He spoke five languages and had developed a gift for regional accents capable of fooling native speakers. His American English was especially good – midwestern, the way all the newscasters talked. He was tall and lean and fair-haired, the scar from the brick long since buried away. He was shaping up to be everything his caretakers had dreamed of.

By then, they had given him his nickname: *Mangouste.* Mongoose. He'd liked the sound of it, and insisted on it whenever he was among friends. He chose to believe it had always been his name, even when he had lived alone on the streets – especially then. The name was like a heart-beat, like something real and true at the center of him, a thing to remain constant across the years and miles and lies that would make up his life.

All this time later, half a world away, Mangouste leaned back and pressed his hands to the forest floor behind himself. He felt the vibration in his palms. The thrum of heavy machinery, deep in the ground.

If we're patient.

If we can bide our time.

Mangouste closed his eyes. The time for patience was over.

Chapter Six

Highway 395 was empty. This stretch of it, far north and west of Barstow, lay nowhere near any inhabited place. Dryden was in his Explorer, following Claire. They passed an old billboard positioned at ground level, its face just blank wood, baked white by years of exposure in the desert. A quarter mile farther on, the Land Rover braked and turned off onto the flat hardpan. In the sweep of its headlights, Dryden saw nothing but open country and a few low hills.

He followed the Land Rover. It rolled another two hundred feet and then Claire killed its headlights. Dryden pulled up beside her and did the same. The Mojave was pitch black, one horizon glowing faintly red in the predawn like a heated blade.

When they'd left the trailer they'd gone east, away from the incoming police units, then made a wide backroad loop to reach Arrowhead from the other side and retrieve Dryden's Explorer; now they were an hour's drive away from the crime scene.

Claire opened the Land Rover's door and got out. In the glow of the dome light, she walked forward and crouched at the base of a Joshua tree and came back up with a cell phone in her hand. It looked like a cheap pay-as-you-go model, the kind you could use a few times and throw away, without leaving any trail that led back to your real name. No doubt it was the same phone she had used to call Dryden earlier, before reaching this spot and stowing it here.

A disposable phone, and still Claire had felt the need to leave it behind when she went to the trailer. Dryden considered the degree of paranoia that would inform such precautions.

Claire pocketed the phone and returned to the SUV, waving for Dryden to join her. Dryden shut off the Explorer, stepped out, and got into the Land Rover on the passenger side.

Even in the near dark, Dryden could sense the condition Claire was in: the same exhaustion she'd shown in the trailer. Her breathing sounded wrong. In silhouette against the dim horizon, she sat slumped at the wheel, all but holding on to it for support.

'I've barely slept for the past three days,' she said. 'Couple hours total, maybe.'

'Tell me what this is,' Dryden said. 'All of it.'

Claire nodded but didn't speak for a long time. Dryden had the impression that only stress had been propping her up earlier. She took a deep breath, then let go of the wheel and turned in her seat. She reached down behind the seatback, took something from the floor in front of the middle bench seat, and set it on the console between herself and Dryden. In the dark it sounded like a hard plastic case.

Claire opened it and reached inside, and a second later the screen of a tablet computer flared to life, bathing the Land Rover's interior with pale light.

The plastic container was the size of a briefcase, its interior and lid both padded with gray foam. The tablet computer was strapped to the lid's underside, facing upward now because the lid lay fully open.

The other half of the case contained a machine Dryden couldn't identify. It was the size of a small cereal box, lying in its padded indentation. The machine was made of black plastic, with ventilation slats on its top and sides. Faint red light shone through the slats, from an LED somewhere inside. The machine emitted a deep, just-audible hum that rose and fell in its pitch. A slender wire, probably a USB cable, connected the device to the tablet computer.

For the moment Claire ignored the strange machine. She tapped an icon on the tablet's screen, labeled ARCHIVE. A file window opened, displaying a long list of what looked like audio clips – the icons were all tiny speaker symbols. Claire scrolled to the bottom of the list and tapped the second-from-last file.

An audio program opened and the file began to play.

Dryden heard a woman's voice speaking, indiscernible beneath a wash of static. It stayed like that for five seconds or more, and then it cleared just enough that he could make out most of the words.

'. . . *have said they will not release any names until the families have been notified. A spokesperson for the San Bernardino Sheriff's Department told us they know the identity of only one of the victims, based on the 9-1-1 call that came in just after two in the morning. Medical examiners will attempt to identify the other three by dental* records. I'm going to go back to Richard Amis, who's still out at the scene. Richard.'

A second of hissing silence followed, and then a man began to speak.

'Tamryn, it's still a very active scene out here. Any normal day, you could drive past this place and not see another car for miles, but this morning there are upward of a dozen vehicles on-site, local and federal officials, including arson investigators. Based on what I'm hearing, the evidence supports what the first responders assumed. The trailer's owner, Harold Heeley Shannon, was keeping the four victims in a cage, and when he discovered they'd called the police, he set fire to the trailer and fled, leaving them locked inside. Tamryn, I have to tell you, I've seen a number of investigators at this site become outwardly emotional. It's unlike anything I've seen in more than ten years of reporting.'

Another pause, and the woman's voice came back.

'I want to give our listeners the description of the perpetrator again, Harold Heeley Shannon, he's a white male, age sixty-two, long gray hair, gray beard, there's a red Ford Fiesta registered in his –'

A burst of static drowned out her words for a few seconds.

'– come back to you with any developments on that story as we get them. For ABC7-FM, I'm Tamryn Bell. It's eleven minutes past eight o'clock.'

The first notes of a commercial came through the static; Claire tapped the stop button and closed the audio player.

Dryden stared at the tablet screen, unblinking. All that he'd heard – and all that he'd seen at the trailer – felt both real and intangible at the same time. Like thumbtacks stuck to empty space where a wall should have been.

His thoughts went to the specifics: The woman on the radio had said it was eleven minutes past eight, and the reporter at the scene had described it as morning – 8.11 in the morning. It wasn't even 4.30 in the morning yet. The stars were still out over the Mojave.

Dryden stared at the time stamp on the file: *09.47 p.m. – 08/07/2015.*

That was last night, around a quarter to ten, a couple of hours before Claire had called him.

Dryden looked up from the screen and found Claire watching him, gauging his response. Dryden met her gaze for a moment, then simply shook his head.

I'm lost. Explain it.

Claire seemed about to speak but stopped. She shut her eyes, leaned back into her headrest. Then she opened them again and closed the list of audio recordings.

On the tablet's screen, she tapped a program icon labeled simply MACHINE. It seemed to be the only other application the computer had. When it opened, Dryden saw a bare-bones program window featuring four labeled buttons: ON, OFF, RECORD, and STOP.

At the moment, OFF was highlighted in bold. Claire tapped ON.

For a second or two, nothing happened. Then the red glow inside the black plastic box disappeared, and a green glow replaced it. The deep, cyclic hum sped up, rising and falling through its frequency range at two or three times its earlier speed.

44

Like something waking up, Dryden thought.

Then, from the computer's speakers, came static. Steady, hissing, like an aerated faucet.

'Give it a minute,' Claire said.

But it took only ten or fifteen seconds for the static to recede. A song faded in: ZZ Top's 'La Grange.' Almost at once it sank back into the hiss. Gone.

For more than a minute after that, there was nothing to hear. Claire kept tilting her head, as if picking up subtle changes in the static.

Then the distortion faded again, and a man's voice came through, deep and measured, speaking calmly about something. Within seconds his words became discernible.

'*. . . two and two on Almodovar, who has a four-game hitting streak coming into this one. Curve ball outside, that'll make it three balls, two strikes. We've got one out and one runner on, top of the second, score is one-nothing San Diego.*'

'Think the Padres are playing at four thirty in the morning?' Claire asked.

Dryden stared at her, waiting for more. Between them, the play-by-play continued.

'*Fastball, Almodovar gets a piece of it, pop-up foul left, still three and two.*'

Claire touched the clock display on the Land Rover's instrument panel. Ran her fingertip across the glowing numbers: 4.27.

'Give or take a minute,' she said, 'I'm gonna say Almodovar hits that pop-up around two fifty-one this afternoon.'

45

Dryden understood and didn't. The thumbtacks were still stuck to nothing. He shook his head again.

Claire countered by nodding.

'You're listening to something that hasn't happened yet,' she said.

Chapter Seven

Dryden had stopped shaking his head. He was only staring now. At Claire, then at the black box, then at the tablet computer. From its speakers the announcer was still talking. Almodovar got a fourth ball and walked.

'Ten hours, twenty-four minutes,' Claire said. She rested her hand on the black box, the green light through the slats silhouetting her fingers. 'It picks up radio signals ten hours and twenty-four minutes before they're transmitted.'

Dryden stared and tried to see how it could be a joke. The trailer had been real. The man he'd killed there had been real. This part, though – no. It had to be some kind of joke, hard as it was to imagine Claire Dunham doing that. It was a hundred eighty degrees from her character.

'You're reacting the same way I did,' Claire said, 'when I first saw it. Anyone would.'

'What you're talking about isn't possible,' Dryden said.

'You said it yourself in the trailer: How could I have known? No one in the world, outside that metal cage, could have expected that 9-1-1 call.'

Dryden's mind went back to the recorded news broadcast. He said, 'That audio clip, the reporters talking about the girls being dead –'

'I recorded it last night at nine forty-seven,' Claire said, 'when this machine received it.'

'And you're saying that report will actually be on the radio at eight eleven this morning?'

Dark amusement crossed Claire's face. 'Not now it won't be.'

Dryden looked away into the night. The red edge of the horizon was brighter than before, but the faint light smudge of Barstow was still visible to the south of it.

Static crept back in over the baseball game, washing it out to nothing. Dryden's thoughts seemed to go with it. Out into the ether.

'I don't know how it works,' Claire said. 'No one does, exactly – not even the people who built it. The way I understand it, they stumbled onto this effect.'

'What people?'

'A company I started working for, just over a month ago. It's called Bayliss Labs. They're a spin-off from a big defense contractor, up in the Valley. They were separated off for security reasons – Bayliss works on really sensitive technology. Bleeding-edge stuff.'

Dryden realized most of her words were going right past him. He was stuck on what she'd already said. He was stuck on the machine.

Claire opened her mouth to go on, but Dryden shook his head. 'It's just not possible,' he said. 'What you're saying this thing can do . . . it's not possible. This isn't something you stumble onto.'

'It is. They did.'

Dryden could only shake his head again.

Claire started to say something, then stopped. She seemed to be marshaling what she wanted to tell him.

Finally she looked up. 'Do you remember a story in the news, a few years ago, about a kind of particle called a neutrino?'

'I've heard that word. I don't remember any news about it.'

'There was a big dustup in the scientific community, all over the world. There was an experiment that seemed to suggest neutrinos can travel faster than light. Remember now?'

Dryden thought about it. He nodded. 'Vaguely.'

'It wasn't exactly front-page stuff, but it was kind of everywhere. It would have been a very big deal if later experiments proved it was true, but there was no slam dunk in either direction. A lot of people wrote it off. A lot of other people kept working on it. Bayliss had a few minor projects devoted to the concept, using novel materials to try interacting with neutrinos – that in itself was tricky; neutrinos are strange, even to physicists who are used to strange things, like quantum mechanics. Neutrinos barely interact with most other matter; they're emitted by the sun, and the ones that hit the earth usually pass through it without striking so much as an atom. Think about that – they slip right through the planet without touching it. The projects at Bayliss were aimed at finding materials that would capture neutrinos like an antenna. They were using sheets of graphene layered with other materials I couldn't name now if I tried. They started seeing results after about a year of working at it.'

'What would be the point of that?' Dryden asked. 'What would they gain by capturing these things?'

'Who knows? Usually discoveries come first, and applications follow. People always think of some use for a new toy. I know they weren't expecting *this* outcome, though.' She indicated the machine.

Dryden stared at the thing again. 'But how could it do what you're talking about? How could it pick up radio signals that don't even exist yet?'

'I can only explain it the way I heard it, and all I heard were educated guesses.'

'Like what?'

'Did you ever read Stephen Hawking? *A Brief History of Time*?'

'I gave it a shot. That was probably twenty years ago. I don't remember any of it now.'

'I'm probably going to mangle some of this,' Claire said, 'but the main parts are about time itself. What time actually *is*. It's a physical thing; it's not just some human construct to measure hours and years. Time is something tangible, like gravity and light. And it's not just *like* those things – it's *tied* to those things. People like Einstein and Lorentz worked out the basics a hundred years ago. Things like time dilation – how the closer you get to the speed of light, the more time slows down for you. That's a nailed-down fact. No one disputes it.'

'Okay,' Dryden said.

'The guys at Bayliss came to believe neutrinos – some of them, at least – really do travel faster than light, and when they do, they actually move against the direction of time.'

Dryden stared at her. 'You mean *back* in time.'

Claire nodded. 'And it's possible they can carry information with them. It's possible they're absorbing the energy of radio waves in the future, and releasing that same energy when this machine picks them up in the present. If they absorbed *enough* of it – a pattern of it, the kind of pattern that makes up a radio signal – then that pattern could show up when this machine absorbs the neutrinos. Those particles would just be acting like a relay. Like a booster.'

Dryden let the idea sink into him. His eyes dropped to the black box, the ghostly light from inside it seeming to ripple with the deep hum.

'I told you,' Claire said, 'those are guesses. It's the best they could come up with. Maybe it doesn't work like that at all, but it *does work*. And once the people at Bayliss realized what they had, it scared the shit out of them.'

She was looking his way. Dryden raised his eyes and met her gaze, and when she spoke again, her exhaustion was palpable. 'I need you to believe me.'

Dryden was quiet for a moment. Then he spoke, almost surprising himself.

'Alright. Jesus . . . alright.'

He saw relief rise in Claire's expression.

'They hired your firm to handle their security?' Dryden asked. 'When they got scared?'

Claire shook her head. 'Not my firm. Me personally. They hired me to be their internal security chief. The executive in charge at Bayliss was a friend of mine, Dale Whitcomb. He and I met a few years ago, when I did home security for him – I saved his life, probably his family's lives, too. He asked me to come on board at Bayliss last month because he trusted me, and because I was an outsider to the company. He wanted someone like that. Someone he could be sure didn't have hidden loyalties to anyone else there.'

Dryden thought he saw where she was going. He waited for her to continue.

For a moment it looked like she wouldn't be able to. Another wave of fatigue seemed to pass through her – not so much tiredness as simply emptiness. Then she blinked and took a breath and made herself continue the story.

'Dale said he was terrified from the moment they realized what this thing did. That very first afternoon, he and a few of the techs in the lab, listening to the first signals coming through, putting it all together. He said you could see the goosebumps on their arms. He said the moment that finally broke the spell for him was just a weather report. That night's weather – ten and a half hours in the future, but not a prediction of it. Just a present-tense rundown. He said just like that, it finally hit him in full. The power of the thing, and what it meant, and everyone who would come out of the woodwork to claim it, if he and the others weren't careful. He said he felt like he was in that Steinbeck book, *The Pearl*.'

After a moment, Claire went on.

Dale Whitcomb had seen the machine's potential for good right away, she said. It was so obvious: ten hours' notice about airline crashes, say, or any kind of disaster that came without warning. It would change the world.

Its potential for bad was every bit as clear. The wrong people could create all kinds of misery with a machine like this. What they could do with financial markets was easy to imagine, but that was probably just scratching the surface.

The first unnerving question showed up immediately: Whom to tell about this thing?

On paper there was an easy answer to that. There were proper channels to go through – certain people at the Defense Department that Bayliss Labs was supposed to report to, when they came upon any kind of breakthrough.

'And that would've been fine if all they'd created was a better radar system for drones,' Claire said. 'But *this* stuff ... For God's sake, Bayliss's official contact at Defense was a man who'd been investigated for fraud less than a year before. What was the right move? Tell that guy everything and hope for the best? Or go over his head to someone else, and basically still just cross their fingers?'

Whitcomb had settled on a different route, she said. He had personal connections in DC, people he'd had lunches and dinners with, time and time again during his long career in the gray space between business and government. At least some of them were decent people, he believed, beneath all the politics. Whitcomb decided the safest move was to set up a meeting with several of them all at once and demonstrate the technology for them. Show it to those hand-picked safe bets and enlist their help and guidance on how to proceed.

He would need prep time to line it all up. Time to be

sure he had the right people in mind, then more time to get them all together without telling them anything in advance. Given the schedules of people like that, it would take some number of weeks to arrange. Maybe as much as a month.

Which scared him just a bit.

A month was a long time for a whole company to keep a secret.

Bayliss Labs wasn't large by any count: fewer than twenty people, the whole enterprise housed at a single site in Palo Alto. The lab space, the offices – everything under one roof. But even with so few in the loop, Whitcomb was terrified of leaks. He had good reasons for that. Some of his employees were on close terms with powerful outsiders. One of the financial guys had gotten his job because he was a nephew of a major shareholder. It was hard not to picture the guy telling his uncle at least some of the big news. There were half a dozen other weak spots like that, mostly connections back to the original company, the big defense contractor.

'Dale asked me to come on board within the first three days after the breakthrough,' Claire said. 'I guess he just wanted an ally there with him. At least one person he could absolutely trust.'

'What happened when you hired on?' Dryden asked.

'For a while, nothing. Everyone was saying all the right things. They agreed with Dale's ideas on how to approach the government, and in the meantime the research continued. They built other prototypes of the machine. They tried tweaks in the design, but always got the same results. The time difference is always ten hours and twenty-four minutes. And there's no way to tune it – you can't go up and down the dial or anything. You just hear what you hear. But anyway, yes, everything seemed fine at the beginning.'

'Seemed,' Dryden said.

Claire nodded. 'And then it didn't.'

Dryden waited.

Claire leaned forward and folded her arms atop the steering wheel. She rested her forehead on them. Enough time went by that Dryden thought she might have passed out. Then she began speaking again.

She and Dale had done their best to be vigilant for leaks, she said. To the point of being paranoid. They'd enlisted one of the computer techs, a guy named Curtis whom Dale had known longer than anyone else in the company, to help snoop on all the rest. The snooping included personal communications in employees' homes, illegal as it was. There was just so much at stake.

But for nearly four weeks, nothing struck the three of them as suspicious. Nothing seemed wrong. Until three days ago.

Claire's phone had rung at five minutes before six, Wednesday morning. Dale calling, sounding panicked.

Get out of your house right now. Get in your car and go somewhere.

What is it? Dale, what's happening?

Curtis found something. Evidence of something going on.

What do you mean?

We think there are people at Bayliss who've been working with

55

someone on the outside, sharing the designs for these machines, maybe since the first days after the breakthrough. Someone out there with high-level resources, we don't know who it is yet.

Dale —

Jesus, Claire, just get in your car —

I'm going right now.

Do you remember the safe location you picked out, when you protected my family? The place we'd all meet up if something happened?

Yes.

I'm going to hide one of the machines there. I want you to pick it up later today.

Dale, what are you going to do?

Nothing too risky if I can help it.

Where's Curtis?

He's going to meet me later. He says he copied a huge amount of data from these people — some kind of secure server they were using for all their communication. He already told me some of what he found. It's scary stuff, Claire.

Like what?

They've built their own copies of the machine, but there's more to it than that. They've got some kind of system they created, to exploit this technology in ways we never thought of.

Exploit it how?

Claire raised her head from her forearms and met Dryden's eyes. Hers looked haunted.

'Dale told me some of what Curtis had told him,' she said. 'Details about this system these people built, who-ever the hell they were. It scared the shit out of me, just hearing about it. It's . . . brilliant. And horrible. Dale told

56

me that much, and then he said he had to go. He told me to ditch my phone and get a throwaway. He said he'd get one, too, and he'd leave the number with the machine I was supposed to pick up.'

Her gaze dropped to the open case. The tablet computer and the strange black box.

'This machine was there when I got to the place,' she said. 'And the phone number. But when I called it, thirty seconds later, there was no answer. I gave it a minute and tried again, and then I ditched that phone, too, and got out of there. Six hours later, on the news, I found out what had happened. Maybe you heard about it, too, in a way.'

Dryden thought about it. Three days ago, the Bay Area – some memory flickered but didn't quite light up. Some big story he'd just caught the end of, flipping past the news.

'Chemical fire and explosion,' Claire said. 'A company called Empire Services. All employees dead or simply unidentifiable. Empire Services was the public name of Bayliss Labs. The building that was destroyed was Bayliss's entire facility. I have no idea if Dale or Curtis is still alive somewhere. I don't have any safe way of looking for either of them, and I guess they could say the same for me.'

For a long time she just sat there, holding the wheel again. Like it was the gunwale of a lifeboat. Like her own weariness would drag her into the deep if she let go.

'Whatever you need help with,' Dryden said, 'I'm in. You know that. You had to know that before you even called me.'

She looked at him. An edge of sadness twisted her features.

'What?' Dryden said.

'I had no intention to involve you in all this,' Claire said softly. 'Not for something random like the guy in the trailer, and not for the rest of this, either. I never meant to drag you into it at all.'

'Then why did you?'

Claire's eyes went back to the machine.

'I didn't, actually,' she said.

'What do you mean?'

Claire started to respond, but stopped. A pair of headlights broke into view to the south, coming up 395 in the same direction Dryden and Claire had driven a few minutes before. The vehicle's outline was just visible against the dim sky – a low shape with a light-bar on its roof. A police cruiser.

None of its flashers were on. The car was going the speed limit, maybe a little faster. Nothing about it suggested urgency or purpose. Just a random patrol.

'Shit,' Claire whispered.

She closed the plastic case, blacking out the glow of the tablet screen and plunging the Land Rover's cab into darkness. Already its headlights and instrument panel were off. Along with Dryden's Explorer, the Land Rover sat two hundred feet off the road where the cop would pass. The two vehicles were unlikely to be visible to the officer, though they would have to arouse suspicion if they were spotted.

Closing in now, the cruiser passed through a long,

gentle curve where the road skirted some shallow rise in the desert. Dryden had hardly noticed the curve when he'd driven it himself. He noticed it now because it sent the police cruiser's high beams swinging ten degrees west of the highway, out into the darkness where he and Claire were parked. An unwitting searchlight.

The brightest portion of the beams came nowhere near the two parked vehicles, but the beams' periphery cast a faint glow through the nearby scrub, setting shadows beneath each chaparral bush. Dryden instinctively looked down to keep his eyes from shining. Claire did the same. Nothing could be done about the reflective metal and glass of the two SUVs.

Claire's fingertips drummed on the wheel, the uncharacteristic tension running through her again.

'It's not a problem if he sees us,' Dryden said.

'It's a big problem.'

'We're seventy miles from the trailer. There's nothing to connect us to it.'

'That's not what I'm worried about.'

'What, then?' Dryden asked.

Claire didn't answer. She raised her eyes just enough to watch the cruiser coming on. It was a few hundred yards south now, its headlights finally swinging back onto the road as it moved beyond the curve. A few seconds later, without slowing, it blasted by and continued north into the darkness.

Then its brake lights came on.

Claire's breath hissed out like air from a ruptured pneumatic line.

The cruiser came to a stop. For five seconds it just sat there in the road, maybe three hundred yards to the north, its taillights glowing. Like the officer was weighing the decision. Wondering if he'd really seen something.

In the same moment, Claire did something Dryden couldn't understand. She ignored the cruiser entirely and turned her gaze on the surrounding desert. She scanned the darkness, her eyes going everywhere, as if she suddenly believed something dangerous was out there. It made no sense – she had shown no such fear until now, after all the minutes they'd been parked here.

The cruiser's brake lights stayed on. Like a tossed coin, tumbling in the air. Stay or go.

The brake lights went out.

The officer goosed the vehicle forward.

And brought it around in a tight U-turn.

Its headlights lit up the world, filling the Land Rover's cab with harsh glare that made Dryden squint.

The effect on Claire was immediate. She turned the key in the ignition and shoved the selector into drive.

'What are you doing?' Dryden shouted.

Claire had not taken her foot off the brake yet. She turned to Dryden, and when she spoke, her voice was saturated with fear. 'Get back in your vehicle and go. Now.'

'Claire, this is –'

'I can't explain it! Go! Please!'

The way she screamed the words, it sounded like she was begging. Like she was kneeling beside a ditch with a pistol to her head. The sound of it pierced Dryden – a needle into the deepest part of his brain, the reptile complex where fight-or-flight decisions were made in thousandths of a second.

He decided.

He reached for the door handle.

But before he could pull it, everything changed.

A hundred yards away off the vehicle's left side, far from both the Land Rover and the police cruiser, a pin-prick of light flared. A millisecond pop, like a flashbulb – but it wasn't a flashbulb.

The windows on both sides of the Land Rover's middle bench seat shattered, and Dryden heard the buzzing whine of a bullet cutting the air, passing through the vehicle maybe a foot behind him.

On instinct, Claire took her foot off the brake and shoved the accelerator to the floor. The Land Rover lurched forward into the dark, its headlights still doused.

Way out in the night, the muzzle flash came again, followed by others in unison, like spastic fireflies. Three shooters, maybe four, clustered tightly together, all firing at once.

Claire had the SUV doing 40 now, jostling over the scrubland. She was driving by the indirect glow from the police cruiser, still a couple hundred yards behind them. All at once the cruiser's beams swung sharply away. Dryden turned in the passenger seat and looked back. The patrol car had jerked sideways and stopped. In the faint interior glow of its dashboard equipment, Dryden could see that its windows had all been blown out. As he watched, one of its headlights burst. The cruiser was taking the brunt of the rifle fire; the cop was almost certainly dead.

Claire cursed under her breath, pushing the Land Rover to 50. Without the patrol car's headlights, the desert surface was nearly pitch black. The only visible detail was the road, a faint asphalt ribbon reflecting the predawn sky. Claire veered toward it across the hardpan but had gone only a few hundred feet when another bullet hit the Land Rover, punching through metal somewhere toward the back. A second later the concentrated fire from all the shooters began to rain against the vehicle, blowing out the rear windows, punching through the panels of the body. Clearly the shooters had night-vision scopes of one kind or another.

A tire blew; the vehicle slewed violently to the left before Claire got it back under control. The road was close now, fifty feet away as she angled toward it.

Then the driver's-side window shattered, and Claire gasped, losing hold of the wheel. The Land Rover pulled hard left again, much too sharply for this speed. Dryden reached for the steering wheel, got his hands on it in the darkness –

Too late. The world heaved sickeningly beneath him as the big vehicle pitched onto its side and then its roof, tumbling hard enough that he had to hang on to keep from being thrown clear. He felt the strange machine in its plastic case, his own body pinning it to the console as he leaned across and clung to the steering wheel. Then the rolling vehicle came down on its roof for a second time, and Dryden's head smacked against something, and all sensation switched off.

Chapter Eight

She's breathing. I think she's good.'

A man's voice, somewhere in the dark and the choking dust. No concern in his tone. Just flat assessment.

Dryden cracked his eyes. He was lying in the half-crushed cab of the Land Rover, which lay on its roof. Claire's midsection was beside him; someone had dragged her halfway out of the wreck. Flashlight beams cut through the dust – a talc-like powder in the air, probably from the air bags. Ragged scraps of plastic hung from the blown-open steering wheel and the passenger-side dashboard.

The hard plastic case with the strange machine inside it lay next to him. Through the closed lid he could faintly hear it still working, the static hissing out through the seam.

'Wake up,' the man outside said.

A slapping sound followed, a hand to a face, over and over. A different man laughed, high and jittery.

Claire murmured in response to the slapping. She took a sharp breath. The laughter continued another few seconds.

Dryden's head cleared the rest of the way.

The Berettas. Where were they? Claire had stowed them behind the seat after they left the trailer, but now –

The answer came by way of a metallic clatter, someone fishing something out of the crushed vehicle, just behind Dryden.

'That's two weapons,' a man said. 'I don't see anything else.'

'He awake in there?'

'He's coming around.'

'Who the hell is he?'

'Get him out of there, let's see.'

Four different voices – two on each side of the vehicle. A second later, hands gripped Dryden's ankles and pulled. He slid out into the clear air and the darkness, the flashlight beams blinding him. Through their glare he saw a rifle aimed down on him, far enough out of reach that he could make no move against it. Smart men. Well-trained men, anyway.

Someone rolled him over and patted his pockets. Found his wallet and then his keys, and took both. One of the light beams swung away as the man flipped open the wallet and studied his ID.

Dryden turned and stared through the blown-out window frames of the flipped SUV. The dust inside had mostly cleared. He could see all the way through and out the far side, where Claire was now fully conscious. It looked like she had a bullet graze across the back of one hand – the one she'd had on the steering wheel – but no other visible injury.

'I got his name,' the man above Dryden said. 'Want me to call it in?'

'Not out here.' This voice belonged to the first man who'd

spoken, standing over Claire on the other side of the Land Rover. He seemed to be in charge. 'Throwaway phones or not, they don't want the cops tracking anything at this site. Keep them switched off until you're on a freeway.'

'What do we do with him?' the man with Dryden's wallet asked.

The leader was silent for a few seconds, thinking. Then: 'They want the girl taken to the interrogation site, but they want the thing in the hardcase brought directly to them. So we'll take the girl, and you take the case. Take the man with you; they can decide what to do with him. Use his vehicle, it's not damaged.'

A third man spoke up. 'We need to go. Dispatch keeps trying to raise that cop. Every minute we spend out here –'

'We're set,' the leader said. 'Move.'

The man crouched down over Claire, wrenched her arms behind her back, and zip-tied her wrists. Then he and the other man on that side of the Land Rover hoisted her up by her arms and dragged her away toward a vehicle Dryden could just make out: an open-top Jeep Wrangler.

The man standing over Dryden pocketed his wallet, then squatted down and grabbed his forearms; he shoved them together behind Dryden's back. Five feet away, the man with the rifle repositioned, keeping his friend out of the line of fire and the barrel squarely on Dryden's center of mass. Dryden felt a zip-tie encircle his wrists and pull tight enough to dig into the skin. Finally the second man lowered the gun. He crouched at the Land Rover's passenger window and pulled the hard plastic case out into the light.

*

They marched him back toward his Explorer at nearly a jog, keeping one of the Berettas tight against his rib cage. The Jeep Wrangler started up before they'd gone even ten paces; Dryden craned his neck and watched it go. It pulled around in a tight arc and raced away southbound on 395.

The pistol barrel dug into him like a spur. 'Move, goddammit.'

He picked up his speed. He had his own reasons to go as fast as possible, but it was just fine to let them think he was compliant.

As they neared the Explorer, his eyes picked out the police cruiser. It sat dark and steaming a hundred yards farther back, its windows shattered and its radio squawking. A woman's voice, clear and urgent. The word *respond* kept coming through the hiss.

They covered the last stretch at a run. The man with the Beretta gripped Dryden's arm tighter; the second opened the Explorer's back door on the passenger side. Together they shoved him through, headfirst, onto the floor behind the front seats. For maybe two seconds, one of them stood staring down on him, studying the vehicle's interior in the dome-light glow. There were scraps of construction materials everywhere in back: lengths of two-by-four lumber, spools of sheathed electrical cable, PVC piping.

'Who is this guy?'

'Who gives a shit? Come on.'

They slammed the door and climbed into the front seats. In the seconds it took them to do that, Dryden positioned himself so that his hands, bound behind him, were pointed back into the space beneath the middle bench seat. He could feel the bottom of the seat's cushion pressing against his side, the whole length of his torso. Which meant his hands would be blocked from the passenger's view – and free to grope for anything he might reach beneath the seat.

A second later the vehicle roared to life. Dryden expected it to veer only slightly as it made for the road; it had been parked already facing south.

Instead it took a hard turn, a hundred eighty degrees, the movement sliding his body roughly on the matted carpet. Then the vehicle straightened out and accelerated.

They were going north on 395, not south.

Opposite the direction of the men who'd taken Claire.

Chapter Nine

'You see flashers ahead, get off the road,' the man in the passenger seat said. 'Kill the lights and get out into the scrub – slow, no dust trail.'

'I know.'

Tension in their voices. From his viewpoint down behind the driver's seat, Dryden could see the passenger looking forward and backward every few seconds, watching for distant police units, but also watching Dryden, his eyes dropping to take stock of him on every pass from front to back.

Dryden still had his bound wrists under the bench seat behind him. He kept his shoulders dead still, except for the rhythmic movement of his breathing, which he exaggerated. The best things to project now were fear and defeat. He let his head sag to the carpet and clenched his teeth. He blinked rapidly. He made his breath hiss in and out, just perceptibly shuddering. *I'm cowed. I'm not going to be any trouble. Go ahead and relax.*

Some of this stuff was pretty basic – psy-ops 101. The man in the passenger seat seemed to eat it up. The evidence was subtle, but it was there. Longer glances out the front and back windows, shorter glances down at Dryden. On some passes he didn't look down at all. The guy was relaxing.

Maybe thirty seconds had gone by since they'd left the scene – maybe ninety since the Jeep with Claire in it had departed. Two vehicles doing 60 or 70 in opposite directions. The math got uglier by the second.

Dryden kept his shoulders moving steadily with his breathing. Kept his head sagging. And moved his wrists.

His hands could feel plenty of things beneath the bench seat. A slip of paper that was probably a Home Depot receipt. One end of a short length of two-by-four lying sideways under the seat. A six-inch scrap of wire sheathing he'd stripped from a cable, last week when he rewired the cottage.

And the trailing edge of a plastic bag. Again, from Home Depot.

Not an empty bag. What was in it? He thought he could remember stowing it here, a few weeks back, before the wiring and before the plumbing, too. Back when he'd still been doing framing work, putting in the new closet in the master bedroom.

He got his fingertips around the plastic and pulled it closer, the crinkling sound lost under the roar of the engine and the drone of the tires.

Something heavy in the bag. He knew what it was – a tight stack of one particular item he'd bought in bulk: framing brackets. Little L-shaped pieces of galvanized steel, stamped out and press-bent and sold with the factory grease and metal shavings still clinging to them. They were practical and unfancy and cheap. And sharp, at least to a degree. Dryden could think of a dozen things that would have been better to find under the seat – a drywall knife would have been nice. But the brackets might do.

He worked the stack out of the bag. Contorted his wrists, gripping the stack, feeling for how best to position the thing to slide it against the zip-tie.

There was no good angle. No way to work the stack against the plastic band without also cutting the hell out of his skin.

So be it.

'I think this thing's on,' the passenger said.

Two minutes now, since they'd left the scene. Three since Claire had been taken south.

Dryden could feel blood slicking his wrists. He thought he could feel the zip-tie beginning to give, too. He hoped.

'Don't open it,' the driver said.

The passenger was no longer sparing any attention for Dryden. The guy was glancing up occasionally through the windshield, but mostly his focus was on something down near his own feet.

'It's on,' the passenger said. 'I can hear something. Static, I think.'

'Doesn't matter. Don't open it.'

The zip-tie broke with a *snick* – louder than Dryden had wanted. He tensed and watched the passenger for a reaction.

Nothing.

He separated his hands. Groped in the dark again, beneath the seat, and got hold of the two-by-four. It was at least two feet long; he could feel the far end of it resting against the back of his knee.

He glanced up at the passenger. The man was only staring forward now, chewing on his lower lip. Maybe he was stewing about being shut down by the driver. Maybe there was an ongoing dynamic between them, alpha and beta, aggressive and passive-aggressive. No doubt it was fascinating.

Dryden pulled the two-by-four tight against himself, then raised his hip upward just an inch or two, his body forming a long, shallow arch with his feet at one end and his shoulder at the other. He eased the two-by-four through the gap until it lay in front of him, then brought his hands around to his front side.

His head was still resting on the floor. He directed his gaze forward, at the space beneath the driver's seat. The Explorer was fairly new, just two years old, but it was the base model for the most part. No special electronics under the seat cushions. No motorized adjustments, no warming coils. Nothing but steel supports set in glide tracks, and a release bar to let the driver scoot the seat forward or back.

And empty space. Four vertical inches of it. Enough to admit the two-by-four, along with his forearm. Dryden could see all the way through to the footwell in front of the driver. Could see the man's foot on the gas, and the brake pedal beside it.

The man at the wheel was named Richard Conklin, at least as far as his current employer was concerned. It was not his real name, but he'd used it often enough that he sometimes slipped into thinking of it as a kind of alter ego. Under his real identity, he was twice divorced and paying out a great deal of money in child support for kids who hated him, and toward whom the feeling was very nearly mutual.

Richard Conklin, though. Richard Conklin was a killer. He was a killer when the job called for it, anyway.

Other times, the job might be to break into a house and steal something – some piece of paperwork, say – or simply drive a vehicle from one location to another and not look in the trunk. Above all, Richard Conklin did precisely what he was paid to do, and never asked why. He never even knew who he was actually working for. There were always go-betweens. Double-blind connections. One-time-use phones and carefully couched language for instructions. Paranoia was everybody's friend. That was how Richard Conklin had always done business.

Until last month. Until the meeting up in Silicon Valley, with the people he was working for now. The people who wanted what they called a *rapid response team,* a term that sounded like *private army* to Richard Conklin's ears.

The work had begun right away, sometimes solo jobs, other times team efforts like tonight. It was steady work, which was nice, and the pay was excellent, which was even nicer.

Richard Conklin was thinking that very thing when something collided with the side of his foot – not painfully, more like a solid thump from a mallet. It smacked his foot sideways, right off the accelerator; he jerked his head down to see what was happening. He never got the chance.

In the next instant the vehicle's brakes locked up as if he'd jammed his heel on them. The tires bit the road and shrieked, the whole chassis dipping at the nose as if its back end had lifted half a foot off the pavement. He and the passenger were slammed forward against their seat belts. He felt the air compress out of his lungs, and then the awful rubber screech finally halted and the world went still.

He couldn't breathe. Couldn't get the air back into his chest. Couldn't –

Movement, a blur of it, right between the front seats. The guy they'd tied up. Richard turned in time to see the stranger throw a hard punch into the passenger's temple, about as savage a hit as he'd ever seen. The passenger's head snapped sideways and cracked against the side window – unconscious, just like that. Richard forgot about getting his breath back; his focus jumped to the two Berettas he'd taken from the wrecked Land Rover. One of the handguns was tucked into his partner's waistband, the other in his own. Richard's hand darted for it even as the stranger turned to him.

Dryden saw the hand moving. Saw what it was moving toward. In the fraction of a second he had to work with, he considered what he had seen in the previous instant: The now-unconscious passenger had Claire's other Beretta, and the man's rifle was leaning upright in the footwell, against the door. Neither gun was a useful option – not in the time it would take the driver to draw his own gun, at which point everything was going to get messy. Grappling for a firearm, especially in a confined space, was clumsy as hell at the best of times. Too many variables. Too much luck involved.

The driver's hand reached the Beretta. Closed around it. Dryden gave up on grabbing for it himself.

He reached for the driver's head instead. He looped his left arm around it and got a grip on the guy's chin. He braced his other hand on the back of the skull. He twisted the head counterclockwise, facing it toward the driver's-side window, as far as it would turn before the neck stopped it. He tightened his grip, locked his elbows to his own sides, and pivoted explosively at the waist, wrenching the head through another forty-five degrees of turn. He heard a vertebra crack like a walnut shell, and the man's hand went slack around the Beretta. Dead, or within seconds of it. Good enough.

Dryden thought of the Jeep Wrangler, probably five miles south now, doing 70. He could feel the seconds draining away. There were no more to spare.

He swept the Beretta forward off the seat, into the footwell, then unclipped the driver's seat belt. He grabbed the guy by the waistband of his pants and hauled the body over the console into the middle bench seat. A second later he'd clambered behind the wheel himself. The engine was still running; the Explorer was, in fact, rolling gently forward at idle.

Ten seconds since he'd stopped the vehicle.

Dryden glanced at the passenger. The man was still breathing but showed no sign of waking anytime soon.

Dryden took the second Beretta from the man's waist-band, then cranked the wheel and made a tight U-turn. When the Explorer was pointing south, he floored it, pushing the speed up through 50, 70, 90. The needle edged past 110 and hovered there, the engine screaming like it might blow something if he pushed it any harder.

The man in the passenger seat shuddered. Dryden glanced at him again, considering the layout of the situation.

He had a decent chance of catching the Jeep. The desert was big and mostly flat, and still mostly dark – he would see the Jeep's taillights if he got within even a couple of miles.

But if he didn't . . .

Dryden kept one hand on the wheel and kept the other poised to backhand the passenger if he woke. If he didn't catch the Jeep, he would need the man alive for questioning.

He kept the speedometer near 110 and divided his attention between the passenger and the road blurring by.

He passed the shot-up police cruiser ninety seconds later. The eastern sky was just bright enough now to cast a bit of light over the desert. The cruiser was still steaming, hunkered in the dark like a smashed insect.

He watched the road to the south, though he didn't expect to see the Jeep's taillights for another couple of minutes at best.

The needle wavered up and down near 110. The yellow lines on the highway looked unnatural, sliding by at this speed. Like a bad special effect in a movie.

Thirty seconds past the cruiser.

Sixty.

Nothing ahead but darkness.

Ninety seconds.

Then he topped a rise and saw a light. Not red. Pale yellow, a single pinpoint in the black landscape.

Half a mile later he knew what it was. He felt his chest tighten. He let off the accelerator.

The keening whine of the Explorer's engine cycled down – 80 miles per hour, 60, 40.

He rolled to a stop twenty feet shy of the white light. It hung high above the roadbed on a rusty arm sticking out from a wooden post. In its glow, a second paved road bisected 395, running east and west into the desert.

The men in the Jeep Wrangler would have had every reason to get off 395 as soon as possible. There were sure to be police coming up the highway any time now, closing in on the stricken cruiser with the unresponsive driver.

The Jeep could have gone east or west from here.

West seemed more likely. It would lead toward the coast, and eventually Silicon Valley, several hours north, if that was where they were going.

But the men in the Jeep weren't necessarily going straight back to wherever they'd been sent out from. They were taking Claire to the interrogation site, wherever that was.

Dryden put the Explorer in park and shoved open his door. He reached across the unconscious passenger and took hold of the man's rifle, a Remington 700 with a scope the size of a small coffee can.

A night-vision scope.

Dryden got out and clambered onto the Explorer's hood, then onto its roof. He stood upright and first scanned the three directions with his own eyes. East. South. West. Nothing out there. Just black country under a brightening sky.

He found the power switch for the scope and turned it on. It was a Zeiss, a little newer than the hardware he'd used back in the day, but familiar enough in its operation.

He found the selector switch for its thermal-vision setting, and the optical magnification ring. He twisted the ring to its most powerful zoom, 12x, then shouldered the rifle and put his eye to the lens.

He glassed the southern route first – 395 running down toward Barstow.

The landscape looked ghostly in the blue-white false-color image. Even now, after hours of night air, the road held a different temperature than the surrounding land. Maybe an effect of humidity or soil acidity. Whatever the case, Dryden could see the road easily, snaking away for miles.

There was no vehicle to be seen on it.

He turned in place and studied the western stretch of the crossroad.

Nothing there.

And nothing to the east.

He'd just lowered the rifle when he felt the Explorer rock lightly on its shocks – movement in the cab, beneath his feet.

'Goddammit,' he hissed.

He slung the weapon on his shoulder, vaulted down to the hood and then the asphalt, and drew the Beretta from his waistband.

But he saw at once there would be no need for it.

The man in the passenger seat wasn't coming around. He was seizing. His shoulders jerked forward and back; his head hung to one side, a pencil-thick line of blood coming from his nose and one ear.

Dryden thought of the punch he had hit the man with, seconds after freeing himself and locking up the brakes.

He had thrown the punch too hard. Had centered the impact too much on the temple. In that moment, he had been in no frame of mind for restraint. His only thought had been to immobilize both men as quickly as possible.

Careless. Too many years past his training – even a couple of years back, he would've reined in his emotions better than that.

All at once the seizure stopped. Dryden was pretty sure he knew why. He tracked around to the open driver's-side door, leaned in, and pressed a finger to the man's carotid artery pulse point. For a second or two he thought he felt something, weak and fluttering. Then nothing.

He withdrew his hand. Stared at the dead man in front, and the dead man in back, and then at the darkness and the three roads leading into it.

Three choices. A shell game.

He slid behind the wheel again, slammed the door, and shoved the selector into drive. He turned hard right and floored it, skidding and then accelerating west on the crossroad – the best bet of the three, though not by much.

For the next four minutes he kept the vehicle's speed above 100 miles per hour. He passed another crossroad but didn't stop. A mile farther on, he passed another. He crested a rise and at last saw a pair of taillights far ahead, like cat's eyes in the near-dark. He overtook the vehicle within sixty seconds: an old pickup with a gray-haired man at the wheel. Nothing ahead of it but wide open miles of nothing.

He kept the needle over 100 for another five miles. Until long after the math had become undeniable. He denied it anyway and kept going, mile upon mile.

Nothing. Just empty road and empty land. Nothing else to see.

Dryden let off the gas. He coasted to a stop on the shoulder. He rolled the window down and sat gripping the wheel, his palms slick and his breath coming in fast surges. He could hear the low, rhythmic chorus of insect noises in the desert scrub.

And beneath that, another sound: the hiss of static from the passenger footwell.

Chapter Ten

It was twenty minutes later. Dryden was parked at an overlook in the foothills; he had come to it by way of a two-track that probably hadn't seen traffic in weeks.

The overlook faced east across the desert, into the sunrise. Ten miles out on the plain, Highway 395 gleamed dully in the light. There had been a steady procession of emergency vehicles moving north on it, the whole time Dryden had been watching. Farther up in that direction, he could see them clustered at the place where he and Claire had been attacked.

He opened his door and got out. He went around to the passenger side, opened both doors there, and dragged the dead men into the weeds. He went through their clothes and found three wallets – one of them his own. In the other two he found a combined two hundred thirty-one dollars in cash, and no IDs. He pocketed the money, wiped his prints from the wallets, and tossed them after their owners.

Each dead man had a phone on him, the models identical and cheap. Throwaways, for sure, though they'd been modified with some add-on software. When Dryden pulled up the recent call logs, all the phone numbers were simply lines of asterisks. Only the time stamps remained visible. Neither man had made or received a call in more than an hour – long before the attack on Claire and himself.

Dryden pulled the phones' batteries, wiped his prints as he'd done with the wallets, and left the phones with the dead men. He got back behind the wheel but left the engine off. He sat staring at the distant crime scene, thinking.

What kept coming back to him was Claire's behavior right before the shooting started. The way she had suddenly scrutinized the darkness around them, seconds before the first shots were fired. She had somehow known those men were out there – had known *someone* was out there, anyway – but she had only known it once the cop arrived.

Before that, she hadn't seemed concerned at all that someone might be watching them.

It made no sense.

How had the random arrival of a patrol car, one that had damn near driven past without incident, tipped her off to the ambush?

It wasn't as if the cruiser's headlights had given the attackers away. Claire had not turned her attention to any one spot. She had seemed to respond on a more fundamental level: The very fact that the cop car had shown up, that the officer was about to stop and question them, had somehow *told her* those men were out there.

Dryden considered it, and got nowhere.

After a minute he turned his attention to a more basic question: How had those men set up the ambush in the first place?

How had they found the spot where Claire had left that phone? There was zero chance they had tracked the phone itself. If Claire Dunham wanted to be electronically invisible, she could do it in her sleep. Data security was her world. Big companies – *tech* companies – paid her large sums to teach them about it.

She had purchased the disposable phone so she could be untrackable. She would have paid cash for it in some store she'd chosen at random. And before she stashed the phone near that tree in the desert, she would have detached its battery to keep it from pinging nearby towers. She would have done that before she got within thirty miles of the place where she hid the thing.

The shooters hadn't found that spot by tracking the phone.

So how had they done it?

Dryden thought about it as the minutes passed. Nothing came to him.

The plastic case still lay in the passenger footwell. The machine was still turned on inside it, hissing.

Dryden stared at it. Something about it nagged at him. Some loose thread, trailing from the tangle of things Claire had shown him, though he couldn't seem to place it.

He picked up the case, set it on the console, and opened it.

The tablet computer's display was still lit up, showing the bare-bones program that controlled the strange machine.

Ten seconds passed. The static faltered. A twangy voice and a steel guitar faded in, then back out.

Dryden tapped the OFF button on the screen, and the hissing cut out. He closed the program and tapped the only other icon he could see: the file folder of audio clips.

As soon as the list of files opened, he saw the loose end that had been bugging him.

Right below the clip Claire had played earlier, about the burned trailer and the dead girls, there was one last audio file.

Something she must have recorded later on.

Dryden traced his finger over the time stamps for each file; they were displayed on the right side of the screen.

Claire had recorded the news clip about the girls at 9.47 last night. That was a little over two hours before she had called Dryden.

The time stamp on the final clip read 11.56.

Ten minutes before she'd dialed his number.

I had no intention to involve you in all this, Claire had said when they were parked in the desert. *Not for something random like the guy in the trailer, and not for the rest of this, either. I never meant to drag you into it at all.*

Then why did you?

I didn't, actually.

Dryden tapped the last recording. The audio app opened, and the clip began to play.

Light static, already receding. A man speaking in the steady cadence of a newscaster:

'*. . . just getting this now, CHP has released the name of the victim in that homicide from earlier this morning. The incident, a shooting, taking place outside a residence just after 7.30 a.m. Neighbors heard gunfire and afterward saw a black sedan and a white SUV leave the scene, though police have said nobody reported a license number. The victim is a resident of El Sedero, a thirty-eight-year-old male named Samuel Dryden.*'

PART TWO

Saturday, 5.30 a.m.–12.00 p.m.

Chapter Eleven

Dryden listened to it three more times. He found himself parsing the details, breaking it down logically, and finally just letting the thing hit him in full.

His death, rendered in a sound bite that people would skip past on their drives to the mall.

His whole future, everything he ever wanted to do, and to be – all of it gone, two hours from now.

His death.

He let it sink in just that deep and then forced himself back into logic.

His death was not going to happen. Claire had contacted him to prevent it. She had heard that clip when she was already en route to handle the trailer situation by herself.

Dryden closed the audio player and the file listing. He switched off the tablet and closed the case and sat staring out the windshield for a full minute.

He believed what Claire had said: that she hadn't meant to involve him in any of this, and yet –

What were the chances that his death two hours from now was unrelated to her problems?

Questions, rising and falling in his thoughts.

Possible answers, way out at the edge of his contemplation.

He looked at the dashboard clock. 5.34. He could be in El Sedero by 7.15 if he risked a speeding ticket.

Traffic was light on the freeway. He set cruise control to ten over the limit and focused again on the previous hour.

Certain logistics came to mind: Was it safe to be driving his own vehicle right now? It would only be a matter of time before Claire's enemies started looking for him. They would realize something had gone wrong – that the men bringing the machine back to them weren't responding to phone calls, that the prisoner they had been transporting was now unaccounted for, and must have the machine in his possession.

They would want to find him, just as badly as they had wanted to find Claire.

One difference: They didn't know who he was.

They had not learned his name by way of the events in the Mojave. Of the four attackers, only one had seen Dryden's identity: the man who had taken his wallet. That man had not spoken the name aloud to the others, nor had he called the information in to anyone. Now that man was dead, and the wallet was safely back in Dryden's pocket.

Neither was there any official record for Claire's enemies to search. The doomed patrol car had never been close enough to see Dryden's plate number, and no other cruiser had come within a mile of him as he'd left the area. There was no way the cops could tie him to anything.

Therefore Claire's enemies couldn't know his name, if

they hadn't somehow known it *before* the events in the desert. Which didn't seem to be the case. The four attackers sure as hell hadn't known who he was.

There were other ways, of course, that these people could try to get a fix on him – to guess who Claire might have turned to for help, in a jam. They would look for personal and professional contacts of hers, going back years. Dryden's name would appear in both categories. There would be old military files showing them serving together, and Claire's phone records would show calls made to Dryden's house and cell over the years since.

Except none of those documents would be easy to get to. Maybe impossible.

The military unit Dryden and Claire had served in had been about as secret as anything in the United States government, in part because much of what they'd done had been illegal. There might be records on paper somewhere, in a safe room underground in DC – or more likely in Langley, Virginia. There was close to zero chance any information on that unit existed in a computer database with a physical link to the outside world. Someone who golfed with the president might be able to figure it out. Anyone else would be out of luck.

Claire's phone records would be even harder to find, if they existed at all. In her work in the private sector these past eight years, she had made enemies of a number of tech-savvy people with the means to do harm. As a result, she'd had every reason to make her digital footprints hard to follow. Dryden had seen for himself, on a few occasions, the lengths she went to: the specialized e-mail and phone services she used, the records encrypted or outright purged on a regular basis.

The people now holding Claire would do everything they could to find the unknown man she had been with in the Mojave. They might even see the news about a man and woman saving four girls in a trailer, an hour earlier, and connect the dots. The coverage would probably dwell on the near-impossible nature of the rescue, which would be a hell of a giveaway to Claire's enemies.

But it wouldn't tell them anything they didn't already know about him: unidentified male, white, average height and build.

For the time being, driving his Explorer seemed safe enough. If that changed, he would react accordingly.

He rolled into El Sedero at twelve past seven. The streets were mostly empty, the diners and coffee shops along the waterfront just waking up. The ocean was slate gray with stark white breakers coming in, its horizon blurred out to nothing by a marine fog that hadn't yet burned off.

His house was right up against the beach, a one-story saltbox with cedar siding worn gray over the years. He had been born and raised in Los Angeles, his childhood divided between a high-rise condo in Century City and a boarding school in Oxnard. He'd become good friends with a girl at that school whose family lived out here in El Sedero, and he'd been taken with the town from the first time he saw it. Years and years later, toward the end of his time in the service, he had lost both of his parents in the same miserable summer. When he finally left the military, he sold the condo in the city and bought this house. He ended up reconnecting with the girl he'd known in high school – ended up marrying her soon after that, and settling into the happiest part of his life. It didn't last very long.

He coasted along a street two blocks in from the shore now, keeping well clear of the house. He nosed into the terraced parking lot of a used-book store, and into a space at the edge of the overlook, maybe two hundred yards up the incline from his front door. He could see the whole house from here, like a stage set viewed from high in the nosebleeds.

7.16.

He pulled the Remington 700 into his lap, took a dime from the console tray, and used it to unscrew the scope mounts. He set the rifle aside and kept the scope, but switched it from thermal vision to its standard optical view.

He braced his elbows on the wheel and put his eye to the scope, and waited.

There was a kind of pressure he'd felt only a handful of times, back in his years on the job. Times when he and his people were actually working against the clock. Maybe someone way up high received credible word from an informant – news of some very big, very bad thing in the offing, the fuse burning down on a scale of hours. When that sort of threat came along, things happened quickly. Agencies talked to each other. Phone calls passed through the back channels. Strings got pulled. There was never anything exhilarating about days like that. No good side to it at all. Just tension and dread, and the near-certainty that your phone would go off anytime: *Turn on CNN, it just happened.*

He felt it now, thinking about Claire.

How much time did he have to find her? How short was the fuse?

He kept thinking of a day probably nine years back, downtime on some airbase, waiting for orders. He and a few of the guys had been playing baseball, and someone had goaded Claire into joining. She looked uncomfortable with it – not the game, just the interaction. Being around that many people, even though she knew them all. Her first time at bat she hit one deep into left, way past the outfielder, and made it to third. The next batter hit a single and Claire made it home, and Dryden, playing catcher, had seen up close the way she reacted to the high fives and cheers of her team.

The image was pretty sharp in his mind, even now. How she'd tried to smile and only partly succeeded, as if the muscles in her face wouldn't cooperate. He remembered what she'd looked like a minute later, sitting alone at the end of the bench, trying not to have a panic attack. Hands in her lap, shoulders hunched, her breathing forced and careful.

She had spent her childhood in foster care; he knew that from her file, and from people she'd worked with before. There were reference tags to old police investigations from back when she was ten years old – abuse of some type, unspecified but long-term. Dryden had thought about all that, watching her that day, this twenty-three-year-old kid who looked like she wanted to crawl under a blanket and hide, all because people had slapped her palm and told her she'd done great. She had spent her life learning to do without those things, and couldn't handle them now that they'd finally come along.

Dryden had never had siblings, but he remembered thinking, in that moment, that this must be what it felt like to have a little sister. Someone you were irrationally protective of. Someone you would kill for, just because. He had felt that way about Claire Dunham ever since.

7.21.

He could go to the authorities. He had a few personal contacts he could talk to. A buddy from his and Claire's old unit was a state cop here in California now, pretty high up in the ranks. But the last Dryden had heard, the guy was mostly in charge of coordinating mass media alerts: missing child notifications and emergency broadcast system reports. Technical work, without much authority to investigate anything.

In any case, the FBI would be the right people to talk to. He could simply bite the bullet and show them the machine. Let them see it in action, and tell them everything Claire had shared with him. They wouldn't believe him, at first. Not for a while. But they would – after ten hours and twenty-four minutes. Then everything would change. Their attention would focus like the seeker head of a guided missile.

Maybe that would be enough.

Maybe sending the federal government after the people who'd killed everyone at Bayliss, and who'd kidnapped

Claire, would save her life. There was no question the government would go after those people, whoever they were. This kind of technology, showing up out of nowhere – the government's first priority would be to clamp down on it, get control, contain the situation. Maybe in the course of doing that they would find Claire Dunham alive and well.

Maybe.

Or maybe the official action against these people would be less than perfectly choreographed. Maybe at the first sign of trouble, whoever was holding Claire would get a panicked call. *Get rid of her, burn everything, get out.*

The higher you stacked a pile of *maybes,* the less likely it was to fall the way you wanted.

7.24.

Of all these considerations, one eclipsed the rest: the fact that Claire herself had chosen not to go to the authorities. For three days she had been in hiding, in possession of the machine, and she hadn't taken it to the FBI or anyone else. She must have had her reasons.

Dryden watched his house, the Zeiss scope ready, and waited for another course of action to present itself.

At 7.27 a blue compact car slowed in front of his house.

Dryden steadied the scope and trained it on the driver. A woman, middle-aged, short blond hair. She took something from her passenger seat and flung it out the window onto his driveway.

A newspaper in an orange plastic sleeve.

She rolled on to the next house and did the same.

Dryden exhaled and lowered the scope. Watched the street as the delivery car made its way along, one house after another.

At 7.29 another vehicle turned onto his street, coming on slow and tentative. A white Chevy Tahoe.

Neighbors heard gunfire and afterward saw a black sedan and a white SUV leave the scene.

Dryden put his eye to the scope again.

The driver was male and young, maybe five years out of college. Short hair, light brown. Glasses. He coasted along, looking at street numbers on mailboxes.

The kid stopped in front of Dryden's house, then pulled in and parked and got out. He was tall and lanky, his body language full of hesitation. For five seconds he just stood there beside his SUV, his hands at his sides. He raised one and rubbed his forehead with it.

He was wearing khaki pants and a gray T-shirt, which was tucked in. There was no weapon stowed in his waistband, or anywhere else Dryden could see.

Dryden lowered the scope and scanned the street.

Halfway down the block, a black Taurus angled into a space at the curb. Even with unaided eyes, Dryden could see the driver pick up a pair of binoculars and aim them at the white Tahoe.

Dryden raised the Zeiss and took a better look.

There were two men in the black Taurus. The passenger he could only see from the jaw down, but the driver's face was in full view. A stocky guy, fortyish, dark hair cropped close to the scalp.

Both of them watching the kid.

Tailing the kid – that much was clear. These men had not been anywhere in the vicinity of Dryden's house until just now, when the kid arrived. Wherever the young man had come from, the guys in the Taurus had followed him from there. They had not been watching the house itself.

Dryden swung the scope back to his house. The kid was still standing there beside his vehicle, unsure of himself. Five seconds passed. Then he crossed to the front door and pressed the button for the doorbell. He stood waiting.

Dryden pictured the way it would have played out if Claire had never called him. He would have been up by 6.45, because he always was. Breakfast, a bowl of cereal, would have been done by 7.00, and he would have been out of the shower and dressed by now, ready to head back up to the cottage and get started for the day. He would have answered the doorbell right away.

The kid on the porch waited fifteen seconds and pushed the button again. He looked fidgety. He paced. He checked his watch and rang the bell a third time.

Dryden aimed the scope at the Taurus again.

The men inside were talking, nodding. The driver cut the wheel to the left, angling the front tires to pull away from the curb. Getting ready to accelerate toward the house, where the kid stood waiting on the porch.

The man in the passenger seat raised a pistol and worked the slide. His free hand went to the door handle and pulled it. He pushed the passenger door open just slightly.

The Taurus eased forward in starts and stops, a few

inches at a time. Prepared to move. Like a big cat, low in the weeds, tensed and ready.

At the front door of the house, the kid rubbed his forehead again, nervous as hell.

It crossed Dryden's mind only briefly to consider that the kid might be working with the men in the Taurus. That he might be willing bait, a harmless-looking figure to make Dryden open his front door and let his guard down. It didn't fly. If the kid was working in concert with the men, the two of them would have been standing right against the siding next to the front door, ready to move against Dryden as soon as he opened it.

They were halfway down the block because they were hiding from the kid, too. It was clear he had no idea they were watching him.

Dryden took in the geometry of the scene. The dynamics waiting to play out – the dynamics that *would have* played out. He imagined himself opening the front door, the kid turning to him, just beginning to speak. Imagined the Taurus angling out from the curb and simply rolling the hundred yards to his driveway – not fast, not revving or screeching, not doing anything unusual at all. It would have escaped his attention like any random car moving down his street, until the moment the passenger door opened and a man with a gun stepped out, thirty feet away.

Neighbors heard gunfire . . .

. . . saw a black sedan and a white SUV leave the scene.

Maybe the gunman would have tried to force both Dryden and the kid into the Tahoe. Maybe the kid would have panicked and done something stupid. Maybe the guy would have just started shooting from the outset. The news report had not mentioned a second murder victim – just Dryden. Maybe the kid would have ended up forced back into his Tahoe at gunpoint.

However it played out, it would have done so in seconds, brutal and unexpected. All Dryden's training would have done nothing for him. You could prepare for some things. Others you couldn't.

Down at the house, the kid tried the doorbell one last time.

The men in the Taurus traded looks, a few words. More nods.

The pistol dropped back out of sight.

The kid turned from the front door and went back to his Tahoe. He got in and reversed out of the driveway and drove off toward downtown.

The black Taurus pulled out and followed.

Dryden set the Zeiss on the passenger seat and started the Explorer.

Chapter Twelve

Apparently the kid was hungry. He parked at a restaurant off the main drag, got a booth by the window and ordered, and when his meal showed up it looked like he'd asked for about a dozen pancakes and half a plate of eggs.

Dryden watched from a Walmart lot a hundred yards away; he was parked in its outer reaches but concealed well enough by a cluster of vehicles there.

The two men in the black Taurus had been less cautious; they were right at the edge of the restaurant's lot. Dryden could see the passenger better now, a blond guy roughly the same age as the driver.

Dryden moved the Zeiss back and forth between the Taurus and the kid in his booth. The kid was mostly done with his meal now. He somehow pulled off looking nervous even while stuffing his face.

In the Taurus, more quick discussion. More nods.

The passenger's gun came back into view.

Then the man shoved open his door and got out and closed it again, tucking the gun into his rear waistband and letting his shirt fall over it.

He crossed the lot to a bank of newspaper boxes just beside the restaurant's entrance, no more than twenty feet from where the kid had parked his Tahoe. He paid for a *USA Today* and leaned his back against the brick wall of the building, two paces from the door where the kid would come out.

In his booth, the kid called the waitress over and asked her something. A tight sequence of words. Maybe *Can I get the check?*

The waitress nodded and moved off.

Dryden lowered the scope and took in the layout of the restaurant's lot. The entrance, the Tahoe, the Taurus, the man with the newspaper.

The geometry of the scene.

The dynamics waiting to play out.

He saw himself standing in his own doorway, entirely unprepared for these men.

About as unprepared as they were for him, right now.

The whole thing had a kind of nasty symmetry he could almost enjoy.

Inside the restaurant, the waitress walked past the kid's booth again. She gave him a little gesture, an extended index finger, like *Wait one, I haven't forgotten.*

There would be a minute at least before the kid stepped out the restaurant's front door.

Time enough for Dryden to roll into the restaurant's lot and get in position. Not revving. Not screeching. He had his hand on the ignition key, about to lower the Zeiss from his eye, when movement in the restaurant caught his attention.

The kid was standing partly from his seat, feeling both his back pockets, then his front ones. Then turning to stare out at his Tahoe in the parking lot, mouthing something that had to be *Shit.*

He'd left his wallet in the vehicle.

'Oh hell,' Dryden said.

The kid caught the waitress's eye and said something fast. She smiled and nodded. *No problem.*

Like that, the kid was heading for the door.

'*Fuck,*' Dryden whispered.

It happened so smoothly, nobody in the restaurant noticed. The kid stepped outside, and the blond man tapped him on the shoulder. One of the guy's hands went to his rear waistband and retrieved the gun, though Dryden never caught sight of it. The blond man kept it low, mostly hidden by the newspaper, though visible to the kid.

The guy said something. It took about three seconds. It ended with *now.*

The kid nodded and continued to the Tahoe. He got in on the driver's side, and the blond man got in on the passenger side.

Just like that.

The Tahoe started and rolled out of the lot, the Taurus pulling out ahead of it and taking the lead.

For the second time, Dryden fell into place behind them.

The two vehicles stayed tight together. They turned inland on a two-lane that led out of town toward the low, parched foothills of the mountains.

Seeking a quiet place to stop and tie the kid up properly, Dryden was sure – or simply kill him. Holding a victim at gunpoint and making him drive was not a good strategy in the long term. It was good for a few minutes, maybe. Not even then, if the victim was clever enough or desperate enough.

If the kid was who Dryden guessed he was – he was far from sure – then the clever part might be covered. Maybe the desperate part, too.

Dryden took the turn and hung back two hundred yards. The traffic wasn't sparse enough yet to give him away, if he kept some distance.

He had no real plan for when it did get sparse. There was nothing to build a plan around. If they spotted him, they would react, one way or another, and he would improvise.

A mile inland from town, the Taurus put on its blinker and turned right onto a gravel lane that led upward into the hill country. An old logging road from a hundred years back, maintained now for hikers and the fire department. The Tahoe followed.

Dryden took the turn and saw the two vehicles ahead of him, passing through the outlying trees of the forest that covered the higher slopes.

Just beyond the first curve among the trees, the Taurus passed a white pine on the right side of the road, as thick as a telephone pole.

The Tahoe didn't.

It jerked to the right and slammed into the tree trunk at 40 miles per hour, taking the impact on the passenger side.

Even from far behind, Dryden could see the windows on that side of the vehicle burst and spray pebbles of glass from buckled frames.

The SUV's back end kicked around to the left, like a toy vehicle struck by a hammer. It swung out into the narrow road, kicking up a dust cloud off the gravel and coming to rest with just enough room to get past its back corner.

Dryden floored the Explorer, pushing it to 60. The wrecked SUV and the dust cloud obscured his view of everything beyond the crash site – but he already knew what he would see there: the Taurus, stopped, the dark-haired man shoving his door open, pistol already in hand.

Dryden steered past the Tahoe's back bumper, burst through the dust cloud, and saw those things exactly.

The dark-haired man was ten feet from the Taurus's open door, gun low at his side, running toward the wreck.

At the sight of the oncoming Explorer, the man froze. His brain was trying to process the new arrival, what it meant, and what he might do about it. He was a quarter second into that endeavor when Dryden hit him, still doing 60. The Explorer's grille caught him low in the chest, punching him backward off his feet. His neck snapped downward and his face hit the vehicle's hood with a heavy *thud*. An instant later the body was airborne, flung out ahead in a long, low arc, like the path of a thrown horseshoe.

He landed deep among the trees beside the road, dead beyond any doubt.

Dryden braked, skidded to a halt, dropped the Explorer into park, and shoved open his door. He sprinted for the crashed Tahoe, drawing one of Claire's Berettas as he ran.

The wreck was spectacular. The passenger side was compressed around the pine trunk as if its hood were made of aluminum foil. The crumple zones in the front three feet of the vehicle had done their job, but all the same, hitting a tree at 40 brought all kinds of unforgiving physics into play.

Dryden reached the driver's-side door. The window there had burst, too, though the door itself was mostly undamaged.

His eyes went to the details of the vehicle's interior, logging them in rapid succession.

The blond gunman was dead. He had worn his seat belt, but the passenger air bag had apparently been switched off. Maybe the kid had known that. Maybe he'd even hit the button to disable it, in the instant before jerking the wheel. Either way, the gunman's head had collided with the metal windshield column, which had bent inward in the crash. The guy's body hung slack, leaning forward over the footwell with his arms and head draped. There was blood coming out of his head at about half the volume of a faucet tap, pattering the floor with a sound like rain spilling from a downspout. Cerebral hemorrhaging. The guy was long gone.

The kid was alive.

His eyes were open and he was staring through the window frame at Dryden.

And holding his stomach, just below his diaphragm. There was blood seeping out between his fingers.

'You're the guy,' the kid said. His tone was flat and matter-of-fact, the way people often talked when they were in shock. 'You're Dryden.'

Dryden was still staring at the bloodstain, expanding through the fabric of the kid's shirt. Then his eyes picked out something on the passenger side floor, gleaming in the darkness there. A single brass shell casing.

'He got me,' the kid said. 'Christ, he got me.'

Beneath the kid's hands, the blood was running in rivulets down the front of his T-shirt. Pooling in the folds of his pants, and on the Tahoe's leather seat cushion. A huge amount of blood.

Dryden knew human anatomy from training and from experience. He knew about the thoracic artery, running down through the abdomen and branching to form the two femoral arteries in the legs. A person stabbed or shot through just one femoral artery could bleed out and die inside of sixty seconds, if nobody was around to apply a tourniquet.

The thoracic artery carried twice that much blood, and no tourniquet could be applied to it.

The kid's face had lost a bit of color even in the ten seconds Dryden had been standing there. He was going fast.

'Are you Curtis?' Dryden asked.

The kid's eyes had begun to drift. Now they fixed on him again. He looked surprised to hear that name spoken, but only a little.

The kid nodded.

'Came to find Claire,' Curtis whispered. 'I thought she might be with you. She told me all about you.'

A shiver went through Curtis's body. The morning air was easily seventy-five degrees, but the kid reacted as if it were forty. To him, it was. He forced himself to keep talking. 'I guess she found you, then.'

Instead of verifying the statement, Dryden leaned in through the empty window frame and spoke carefully.

'Curtis, the people who attacked Bayliss Labs have a place they call the interrogation site. Have you heard of that? Do you know where it is?'

Curtis's eyes narrowed. Then he shook his head.

'Are you sure?' Dryden said. 'Think as clearly as you can.'

Curtis nodded, and when he spoke again, his voice was only a whisper. 'All their language is careful. All their e-mails, the stuff on the server. No locations. No names. I copied all of it, though. Took it with me. Figured a lot of it out . . .'

He was losing strength by the second. Fading.

'Curtis,' Dryden said.

'I've been hiding three days,' the kid said. 'I printed it all, got it organized.' He nodded weakly toward the space behind the front seats. 'It's all in a bag back there, for Claire. I even wrote a letter to go with it. It's everything I know.'

The shivering was getting worse.

'I tried to be careful,' Curtis said. 'I made sure they couldn't find me with their . . . system. Maybe they found me the old-fashioned way. Jesus, I went to my old coffee shop this morning. Maybe they were just watching . . .'

His eyes were wet now. The shock was losing ground to the pain, or else the fear.

Then something changed. Curtis blinked and exhaled

hard and forced himself into a state of alertness. He turned and stared out through the shattered passenger window, then swept his gaze left in a slow arc, eyes darting everywhere.

Looking for some threat out there in the woods.

Like Claire had done in the desert.

Exactly like Claire.

Dryden's scalp prickled. He turned fast and raised the Beretta, studying the surrounding trees.

Nothing there.

He pivoted slowly counterclockwise, his eyes and the pistol tracking around, a few degrees per second.

He ended up facing back the way they'd come from: toward the paved two-lane road, which was just hidden from view by the curve in the gravel lane through the forest.

A hand seized his arm. He spun toward it, reflexively.

Curtis had reached out through the driver's-side window frame and taken hold of him. The kid's eyes were intense, keenly aware.

'Hide our bodies,' Curtis said.

'What?'

'You can't leave any record for anyone to pick up on. The people we're up against . . . if there's anything tying me to this place and time, then . . . they'll send other killers here. They'll have . . . *already* sent them. Hours ago. They'd already be here waiting.'

As crazed as the kid sounded, his words lined up eerily well with what had happened in the desert.

The gunmen there had already been in place. Claire had

begun looking for the threat once it was clear the cop was going to stop and question the two of them.

Once it was clear there would be a record of their presence there.

At that place and time.

Dryden felt the dots trying to connect. In some sense they did, but only partly.

'Hide our bodies,' Curtis said again. 'Me and these two guys. Put us in their car and hide it someplace. It has to stay lost for a long time.'

The kid's burst of alertness was leaving him. The skin of his face was paper white. His voice was back to a whisper.

Dryden said, 'But this Tahoe –'

Curtis shook his head. 'Can't be traced to me. I was already careful about that. Stolen plates. Filed off the VIN. Just burn it.'

He took a deep breath. It looked like it hurt.

'Do it,' Curtis sighed. Then a strange little smile crossed his face. 'I already know you'll manage it. 'Cause they're not here right now killing you.'

The odd smile stayed on his face as his eyes went still. Gone.

Chapter Thirteen

When Aubrey Deene pulled into the carport in front of her apartment, one of the maintenance guys was mowing the lawn. Her eyes fixed on the mower: an old Husqvarna, like the kind her father had beaten to hell every summer of her childhood back in South Bend. Sometimes a fouled spark plug would set him off, and he'd burn up a day's worth of anger in five minutes of wrench throwing in the garage. Other times the mower would only get him warmed up, and then Aubrey and her sister and her mother would have a long night in store for them. Rod Deene had been dead for five years now – heart attack a month before Aubrey finished undergrad at Iowa State – but the damnedest things could shove him right back into her head.

The engine of her ancient Miata coughed and threatened to die. She killed the ignition and pocketed the key, then turned and rummaged through the textbooks and folders on the passenger seat. Any day now, the car was going to give up the ghost and leave her hitchhiking. Which would be fitting, in its own way. Her life had taken on a distinctly hitchhiker kind of feeling lately. Like her future was no more plotted than that of a paper cup in the wind.

Not so far off the mark, you know.

That internal voice had an irritating, teen-angst edge to it. If there was anyone less welcome in Aubrey's head than her father, it was her own younger self, two months out of high school, pulling out of her parents' driveway in her rusted-to-shit VW Beetle. Leaving South Bend and heading for the world. Iowa State, then MIT, then whatever Ph.D. program looked right. The girl with all the answers, all the dominoes lined up and ready to fall.

They had fallen. For a while. Iowa State had gone swimmingly, and MIT had played out like a well-rehearsed dance number, exhilarating and challenging, leaving her winded but with her feet right on the intended marks. She'd had her choice of doctoral programs, and she'd picked Cornell, and for a time, things there had followed the game plan, too. She could remember feeling like it was all still clicking along. There were beautiful afternoons on the plaza, maybe her favorite place in the whole world. Sometimes she would take her textbooks and sit inside Sage Chapel, though she had never been religious and never would be. Most of the time the chapel was empty except for a few tourists, moving in little groups, whispering, taking pictures of the beautiful architecture. Aubrey had sat in the shadowy pews, way back from the lit-up altar, and let the silence of the place envelop her like water.

She supposed the doubts had started creeping in around that time. Little uncertainties that gave her pause now and then, like static lines flickering in the movie of her life. There were social issues, for one. She was twenty-four and had never had a boyfriend – nothing that'd lasted beyond a few weeks, anyway. She knew she was pretty, and it wasn't hard getting the attention of boys. Yet the few times she'd let someone in – nice guys from her classes who didn't push for things to get physical right away – had ended horribly. Three or four dates along, she would make the first move. Things would happen, enjoyable things if a little clumsy and brief, and then she'd find herself lying awake all night next to a sleeping body, her mind trying like hell to avoid the unwelcome truth: that she felt nothing for this person; that she wished she was back at her place, alone with her books and her lab notes; that she had no idea what to say in the morning.

Then, two months into her time at Cornell, a different kind of boy had come along. His name was Daryl, and he didn't wait for her to make the first move, and when things happened they were neither clumsy nor brief, and they were way the hell past enjoyable. Sometimes Aubrey had still lain awake all night next to him, but only to worry that she might do something wrong and lose him. That fear had been there from the moment she'd met him, the sense that she had never quite won him over, though she couldn't define it more clearly than that.

She found her interest in the books and lab notes waning just a bit in the months after meeting Daryl, though her academic work didn't suffer much for it. Instead, her time with Daryl came at the cost of time with her friends, a fact Daryl seemed just fine with. He didn't like her friends all that much. He certainly didn't like her spending time with them. In hindsight, that should've been a red flag, but it hadn't been. She had not been looking for any flaws on his side of the equation; all her focus was on worrying about her own flaws.

Other flags should have been more obvious. Like when he would pick her phone up off the table and check whom she'd called that day, right in front of her, as casually as if he were reading the newspaper.

You talked to Laney? he would say. *What was that about?*

Some little spark inside of her wanted to reply, *She's my best friend, and it's none of your fucking business what it was about.*

Then another part of her would think, *Don't lose him, don't lose him, don't lose him,* and when she opened her mouth all that came out was the answer to his question, in detail, and somehow in the tone of an apology.

They'd been together six months when he suggested she drop out of the program. She wouldn't need an income, he said; his own would be mid-six by the time he was thirty. They had never talked about getting married, but the possibility of it had been there for months already, in the subtext of their conversations.

It was in the days after that talk – days she spent giving the idea real consideration – that younger Aubrey started piping up in her head. Younger Aubrey with that old Beetle packed full of clothes and books, rolling out of South Bend on a summer morning. She began to call that version of herself Proust Girl, because among those books in the Volkswagen had been a boxed set of all Proust's published work. Proust Girl had not read a word of the man's writing yet, back then, but fully intended to. She had meant to have it deeply absorbed by Christmas break of freshman year, not just so she could whip out quotes and look brilliant, but for the light it would shine on her understanding of human nature. Proust Girl couldn't have known that she would get fifty pages into the first book and throw the whole goddamned set in the trash. She couldn't have known the writing would feel like ham-fisted overacting on the page, any more than she could have known that nice boys would never be able to get her off – would never even be able to make her smile. Proust Girl was none too happy at the idea of dropping out of Cornell, but what the hell did she know? Proust Girl could never've seen Daryl coming.

When it finally happened, it did so in the most mundane of places: the kitchenware aisle of a Target, just off campus. She and Daryl had been out to dinner and had stopped for groceries afterward. Aubrey saw a vegetable steamer she'd looked at two or three times before; it was on sale now, a hundred dollars instead of one fifty. She set it in the cart, and Daryl took one look at it and told her to put it back on the shelf.

Don't worry, she said. *I'm paying for it.*

No you're not. You can't afford it. Put it back.

No joke in his tone, and nothing in his eyes but sternness, and the expectation of obedience.

That look from him wasn't quite unprecedented, but it caught her off guard this time.

Daryl, it's my money, I'm buying it.

Never taking that locked gaze off of her, Daryl took the steamer from the cart and set it back onto the shelf.

When Aubrey reached to pick it up again, his hand clamped around her forearm hard enough to dig into the muscles. Hurting her. On purpose. And still there was that gaze drilling into her. In that moment she realized she'd seen it before she ever met him. Long before.

And no, Proust Girl really would not have seen Daryl coming, she thought. Not if he'd been standing in a garage with an old Husqvarna, beating it with a wrench.

It ended right there in that aisle full of pots and pans, with Aubrey screaming at him to let go of her, screaming even after he complied, her hands coming up and covering her head, the brink of a nervous breakdown right there in front of a dozen shoppers.

That had been four years ago. She had finished up at Cornell and taken a postdoc appointment at Texas A&M. A year later she'd found herself here, at Arizona State, where she was now contemplating starting over and getting a law degree.

A paper cup in the wind.

She gathered the books she wanted from the passenger seat, stuffed them into her backpack, and got out of the car. On the front walk she nodded hello to the guy with the lawn mower, put her key in the lock, and stepped into her unit.

Her unit – no one else's. There had been no more Daryls, though there had been a few more sleepless, guilt-heavy nights lying awake beside nice guys, in the endless hope that one of them would somehow light up enough of her buttons.

The thing was, she didn't crave her academic work on those nights anymore. She didn't crave much of anything, really, on any night. Which was unnerving as hell, at twenty-eight. Where had all the old rocket fuel gone? Where had Proust Girl gone? She existed only as a nagging thought now and again, all criticism and no advice.

Maybe the law degree would be a way to hit reset. A friend in DC had told her she should come out east and get into policy work. Advocate for something. Find a cause. Maybe. Or maybe there was something else she could do in DC Something she wasn't even thinking of yet.

Aubrey set her bookbag on the carpet, stepped out of her shoes and –

Flinched, her breath coming out in a sharp little convulsion.

There was someone in her apartment.

Right there in the kitchen doorway.

Holding something.

These thoughts, in the tiniest sliver of a second.

In the next sliver her eyes locked on to the object: a handgun with a silencer on the barrel.

The first three shots felt like fingertips jabbing her chest, hard enough to shove her backward – and little balloons of ice water popping inside her, deep behind her ribs.

She didn't feel the fourth shot. It broke the center band of her glasses and punched through the bridge of her nose.

*

The man with the gun watched her fall in a heap of limbs. Watched the carpet become soaked around her head, as if someone had tipped over a pitcher of cherry Kool-Aid.

Her face was just visible in profile, where she lay. She was pretty. Her chin was tiny, and she had a little button nose. It crossed his mind to wonder what she'd done to deserve this, but only for a second. It wasn't his job to wonder about things.

Chapter Fourteen

Dryden felt strange doing what the kid had asked. He would have felt stranger not doing it.

He had the dead men's Taurus backed up close to the wrecked Tahoe, the trunk lid open. The bodies of the two attackers were already stuffed inside, along with their wallets and phones. The phones were identical to those he'd found on the earlier pair of gunmen, and had the same redaction software blotting out the numbers in the call logs. As before, neither man had made a call or sent a text in the past hour – which was good. It meant they had not phoned their superiors and passed along Dryden's address after tailing Curtis there. It meant Claire's enemies still had no idea who Dryden was.

Also as before, the gunmen carried cash and no IDs. Dryden took the money and wiped down the wallets and left them with the corpses.

Crossing back to the Taurus for Curtis's body, Dryden could see the glint of traffic on the nearby two-lane – tiny reflections off chrome and glass, stabbing through the concealing trees.

But no vehicle turned off that road to approach along the gravel route. No random tourist or Forest Service vehicle, the arrival of which would lead to a 9-1-1 call and a police presence within minutes.

He had the strangest sense of assurance that it wouldn't happen. He kept thinking of the kid's last words.

I already know you'll manage it. 'Cause they're not here right now killing you.

Dryden opened the driver's-side door – it groaned at first, lightly jammed by the warping of the vehicle's structure – and pulled Curtis's body out onto the ground. He dragged it to the Taurus's crowded trunk, lifted, and forced it inside, then went through the kid's pockets and found nothing. No phone and no wallet.

The wallet was in the Tahoe, where Curtis had left it when he went into the restaurant.

There was no ID in the wallet, and no credit card or registration either. Nothing with Curtis's name on it. Just cash – ninety-six dollars. Dryden took it, feeling only marginally like a thief. No point leaving it.

He opened the Tahoe's back door on the driver's side. On the floor sat a black messenger bag, stuffed full of something bulky and square-edged. Dryden opened it and saw five white plastic binders, the kind that held three-hole-punched paper. You could buy them at any office store. At a glance he saw that each binder held a thick stack of pages, maybe a couple hundred each.

The information Curtis had stolen from the people who'd attacked Bayliss. The stuff from the secure server, which he'd printed and organized in the past three days while lying low.

In addition to the five binders, there was a slim stack of pages by itself, fifteen or twenty sheets stapled at the top corner.

I even wrote a letter to go with it. It's everything I know.

Staring into the bag, Dryden pictured a kind of thread connecting himself to Claire, wherever she was. A delicate strand drawn wire-taut, its tiny fibers straining and snapping, but the line itself still holding.

Whatever chance he had to find her lay in those pages.

Another kind of assurance suddenly came to him – far less comforting than the belief that no stray vehicle would come barreling down the gravel road.

The second assurance was that Claire's captors would not kill her anytime soon.

If they had no other way to find out who he was – the unknown man who had the machine they wanted – then interrogating Claire would be their only recourse. As long as she didn't tell them anything, they would keep her alive and under questioning. If anything, they would have her on suicide watch.

The notion brought him no relief; it brought only the hope that he could still get to her. That the fuse had length yet to burn.

He closed the messenger bag and took it to his Explorer. He set it on the passenger-side floor, beside the hard plastic case with the machine inside it.

Then he opened the Explorer's back end and grabbed the emergency kit he kept there. Among the items inside were three road flares and a towing rope.

It took only a minute to secure the rope from the Explorer's hitch to the Taurus's frame, at the front end.

He spent another minute giving the entire scene one

last look. He had already kicked dirt and dust over the blood drops the bodies had left when he'd dragged them, and scuffed the ground further to erase the drag marks themselves. Not a perfect solution, but good enough.

There would sure as hell be no useful forensic evidence found in the wrecked Tahoe. For good measure he wiped his fingerprints from the door handles, and held the road flares without the pads of his fingers touching them. He popped off the igniter caps and struck the flares alight one after another. He lobbed two of them into the vehicle – one up front, one into the rear seats – and set the third against the front tire on the driver's side, its white-hot flame directly against the rubber.

By the time he'd sprinted to the Explorer, climbed in, and put it in drive, there were already black tendrils of smoke coming through the Tahoe's open windows, where the upholstery had begun to burn.

Ten minutes later and two thousand feet higher in the hills, he stopped. He was no longer on a gravel road, but a mostly overgrown two-track that punched like a ragged tunnel through the evergreens. On the left side of the path, the land pitched upward at forty-five degrees. On the other side it dropped away just as steeply, toward a brush-choked pond thirty feet below. During summers when he was a teenager, Dryden had been up here lots of times with friends, usually at night. The pond was more than sixty feet deep in the middle, its sides like a funnel angling down into the murk. He'd heard rumors that there were old logging trucks down at the bottom, but he'd never heard of anyone going in with scuba gear to find out for sure.

He unhooked the tow rope and stowed it and pointed the Taurus at the edge of the dropoff. He put the car in neutral and shoved it over the lip. It bounced and jostled its way down the slope, crashed through the shrubs lining the pond, and hit the water with an explosion of mud and foam. Giant ripples rolled outward, crisscrossed, settled. For thirty seconds the car looked like it wanted to float. It bobbed with its front end pulled under by the engine's weight, and drifted out away from the shore. Then physics asserted itself. The passenger compartment flooded and the car pitched farther forward, its back end tilting up, and within another minute the whole thing had gone under. Dryden studied the gap in the brush at the water's edge, where the car had punched through. Most of the plants had simply bent and were springing back now. The scrub-covered earth showed no tire tracks. Someone standing here five minutes from now wouldn't suspect a thing.

From far away through the trees, in the direction of town, came the sound of sirens. Police and fire units responding to the burning Tahoe, the origin of which would forever be a mystery to them.

Dryden got back in the Explorer and pulled away.

He returned to the paved two-lane by a different route than he'd taken to the pond, avoiding the Tahoe.

He drove back into El Sedero and pulled into the broad parking lot of a strip mall three blocks in from the shore. He took a spot at the periphery, far from the packed rows closer in.

He hauled the messenger bag up onto the passenger seat and opened it, and took out the five binders and the stapled letter. *Everything I know.*

It was 8.45 in the morning.

Chapter Fifteen

At 8.46, Marnie Calvert stood at one of the floor-to-ceiling windows of the computer lab in the Wilshire Federal Building. From twenty-three stories up, the window faced south over the 405 freeway. Marnie leaned lightly on the glass with the knuckles of one hand. Far below, a bright red sports car merged onto the freeway from Wilshire. She watched it slip away into the morning haze toward Marina del Rey.

Twenty minutes earlier she'd been in her office, pacing, her mind doing 60. Then her computer had dinged with an incoming e-mail, a positive match on the fingerprint search she'd sent in hours before.

The mystery man who'd saved the girls at the trailer had exactly one blemish on his record: an arrest for assault when he was eighteen years old, the charge dropped almost immediately on grounds of self-defense. He'd flown pretty straight since then: army service immediately following high school, including time with the Rangers and then 1st SFOD-Delta. Then, apparently, he'd vanished into another dimension for six years, because his military record simply went blank for that stretch of time. Not even redacted. Just nonexistent. From age twenty-four to thirty, there was no Sam Dryden.

The paperwork picked up again with his honorable

discharge at thirty. Within the next year there was a marriage license and a birth certificate – in that order, but just barely. Then came two death certificates, the wife and the daughter, and reference tags pointing to police reports about the traffic accident that had taken their lives.

After which Sam Dryden's document trail went almost blank again, though not by way of secrecy this time. Rather, his life seemed to dial itself down to the lowest burner setting. He worked, but only a little: private security stuff here and there, putting his background to use. He didn't generate much income, but then again he didn't need to. He had inherited a significant chunk of money from his parents, back during his time in the service. But for those years after he lost his wife and child, he didn't spend much of the money. His credit card records showed him paying his bills and his property taxes and buying groceries. He didn't do much else. For the better part of five years, there was no sign that he'd traveled or purchased much more than basic essentials. To the extent that paper records could show a man's world shrinking down to a solitary confinement cell, Sam Dryden's seemed to do so.

Then something had changed – not quite two years ago, toward the end of 2013. There was no indication of what had triggered it, but all at once Sam Dryden seemed to begin living his life again. There were airline tickets – flights to places like Honolulu and Vail and Grand Cayman. There were weeklong hotel stays at those places, and boat rentals, and payments for all the things people did on vacations just for the hell of it. The plane tickets were always for two, and the other ticket was always for a woman: someone named Riley Walker for the first seven or eight months, then a few others in succession. Dating. Living. Taking in the world. Something or someone had come along and jolted Sam Dryden out of his exile.

He was working again, too. Buying and fixing and then selling houses, from the look of his financials. Pretty damn nice houses, if the prices and locations were any sign.

And apparently, maybe just for kicks, he had now taken up the hobby of preventing horrifying tragedies no human could have predicted.

'How the hell did you know to be there?' Marnie whispered.

She watched a light business jet take off out of Santa Monica Municipal Airport, a few miles to the south and west. Watched it climb and bank out over the Pacific, a white speck and then nothing.

'You wanted to see me?'

Marnie turned. Don Sumner stood in the doorway of his office, where he'd been on the phone for the past three minutes.

Marnie nodded and crossed to the door. Sumner stepped back and let her through.

Sumner was fifty and going gray at the temples. One wall of his office was lined with deep shelves, on which were arrayed detailed models of mid-twentieth-century automobiles. There was a '64 Mustang, a '51 Bel Air, a '42 Packard Super Eight. Even some kind of Studebaker from the '30s. Sumner had built the models from kits, then airbrushed them and done all kinds of intricate detail work; some of the cars were actually made to look weathered and worn. Marnie had studied the collection up close before, and had concluded that Sumner could have been a special effects guy for one of the movie studios, back before CGI had become the norm.

'Have a seat,' he said, dropping into his own chair. 'What do you need?'

'Help on this Mojave thing.'

There was no need to specify which Mojave thing she was talking about. The story was already in heavy circulation locally, and was beginning to get traction on CNN and Fox. It had all the right ingredients: a miracle rescue, a very nasty, very dead bad guy, and two mysterious saviors who had appeared out of thin air and vanished back into it. The networks would feed on it for days – maybe longer if the two rescuers remained unknown.

'What do you have?' Sumner asked. He nodded at the printout in Marnie's hand: Dryden's info.

She unfolded the thin stack of pages and slid them across the desk. 'This is a match from a set of prints I found at the scene. When I ran the search, I didn't tell anyone where the prints came from. As of now, this guy has no official connection to the case. Outside of you and me, there's nobody who can leak his name. I'd like to keep it that way until I know more.'

Marnie ran through the details of how she'd found the prints while Sumner's eyes tracked down over the material, his eyebrows edging up once or twice.

'Prints on a washing machine,' he said. 'Maybe he

owned the thing. Maybe it broke down and he decided to dump it out in the desert.'

'Two hours' drive from his address?'

'Maybe he was that pissed off at it. Wanted to make sure it didn't find its way home like in that movie *The Incredible Journey*.'

'I think it was two dogs and a cat in the movie. Anyway, the scuff marks I found with the prints were new. Dryden was there last night.'

Sumner exhaled and slid the printout back across his desk. 'So what is he? A vigilante?'

'Even if he is,' Marnie said, 'how did he know enough to show up at that exact moment? Those girls snagged a cell phone off the coffee table and called 9-1-1. That was the trigger for the whole thing. How could Dryden or anyone else have known that would happen?'

'Got a theory?'

Marnie pinched the bridge of her nose. Rubbed her eyes with her thumb and forefinger. 'Not even a stab at one. After hours of banging my head against it.'

'Want to tell me why you're keeping his name off the books?'

Marnie opened her eyes. 'Because there's an easy leap people will make. And I think it's bullshit. I think it doesn't fit the facts of his background, but people will consider it anyway.'

'The idea that Dryden might have known the guy?' Sumner asked.

Marnie nodded.

'Might have been old pals with the guy who kept four

127

little girls in a cage,' Sumner said. 'Knew all about it, and finally got around to doing something.'

'You know how things get covered. What passes for journalism now. *Send us your tweets, America, tell us what you think happened.*'

'He did manage to show up there,' Sumner said. 'There's *something* behind that.'

'Something, yeah. But none of the girls had ever seen this guy before – or the woman. Who I've still got nothing on. I want to know more about this before I open the doors and let the circus in.'

'What are you asking me?'

'I want to set up surveillance on Dryden. Without anyone knowing.'

'By *anyone,* you mean the judge that would have to sign the warrant.'

'Yes,' Marnie said. 'Judges have staffers and assistants. Staffers and assistants have cell phones. Things get out.'

Sumner leaned back in his chair. Swiveled it ten degrees clockwise and then back. He looked very tired.

'All I need from you are a few pieces of information,' Marnie said. 'A couple of access strings you can look up from right here. I'll do the surveillance myself, no assets, no support. If I get busted, there's no proof you set it up.'

Sumner rocked his chair forward again and put his elbows on his desk.

He said, 'This kind of intrusion into someone's life –'

'I'm doing it to prevent an intrusion into his life. Unless it turns out he deserves one.'

Sumner stared into the woodgrain of his desk. In the silence, Marnie heard the wall clock ticking. Five seconds. Ten.

'Christ,' Sumner whispered. Then: 'What kind of surveillance?'

'Phone and vehicle, for now. He drives a 2013 Explorer, base model judging by the price, except it has satellite navigation. Which means we can ping it and track him.'

Sumner thought about it for another long moment. Then he nodded and swiveled to face his computer.

Chapter Sixteen

Still parked in the strip-mall lot, Dryden turned his ignition key partway and cracked open the Explorer's windows. The smells of sea salt and fast food and hot blacktop tar streamed through.

Curtis's five binders were mostly indecipherable. Much of the content inside them was simply computer code, hundreds of pages of it, printed out and arranged in some kind of logical order. Dryden had a passing knowledge of programming, enough to recognize which language this code was written in, but could make no real sense of it. Even the programmers' comments – plain English lines peppered throughout the code as useful labels and reminders – were little help.

This part waits for the sort algorithm to return any value of 5 or higher.

This boolean returns true if both CroA1 and CroA2 are true.

Hundreds of those, scattered like confetti throughout the pages. They must have made sense to the people who'd written this stuff. Maybe they'd made sense to Curtis, too, after hours of paging through the material, jotting down the names of variables and strings and classes, drawing connections Dryden couldn't see on any given page.

He flipped through the first four binders in a couple of minutes and set them aside.

The fifth didn't contain computer code. It was full of printed e-mails instead, but they weren't much easier to make sense of.

All their language is careful, Curtis had said.

Every e-mail address in the message headings was a meaningless string of numbers and letters. Maybe the accounts had been created and discarded on a daily basis, out of paranoid caution. The digital equivalent of throw-away cell phones.

The messages themselves were a little better; they were at least made of words and sentences. But the language was carefully couched and allusive, an extra layer of security by the people who'd written and sent these e-mails.

Still, thumbing through the first of maybe two hundred pages in that binder, Dryden got the impression that there was real information to be gleaned from it. It would require reading the entire thing repeatedly, and scrutinizing key parts more carefully still, but there were probably loose ends to pick at, somewhere in the tangle.

He closed it for the moment, set it with the other four, and picked up the thin, stapled stack of pages. Curtis's letter to Claire.

It was neatly typed, composed on whatever computer Curtis had used when he'd printed the stuff in the binders. Dryden pictured the kid sitting with a laptop in a cheap motel room, bags from an office store all over the bed. The binders, a few reams of paper, maybe an eighty-dollar inkjet plugged in on the nightstand.

The letter began:

Claire,

I hope I'm right about how to get this letter to you. I hope you're alive to receive it.

I know Dale called you, right before everything went to hell. I know he told you some of this, but I don't know how much of it he got through. So I'll start at zero. Sorry in advance if the tone is a little bit Romper Room. Clarity is key. Here goes.

First, I know almost nothing about the people who took out Bayliss Labs. They might be a rival company. They might just be a circle of people with money and connections. Even on their secure server, they were very careful to not make themselves identifiable. In the messages, they refer to themselves as the Group – capitalized like that.

Maybe they were monitoring Bayliss before we even developed the machine, or maybe someone on the inside talked to them. Whatever happened, it's clear the Group was involved from damn near day one, after we got the first machine working. They had their own version of it up and running within probably days, and they got very busy figuring out how to do big things with this technology, things we never even brainstormed at Bayliss.

You already know these machines hear radio signals from 10 hours and 24 minutes in the future. You also know there's no way to tune the things, and they're limited to frequency-modulated (FM) signals between 89.1 MHz and 106.5 MHz, not quite the full range used for FM radio broadcasting in the United States.

A person might wonder whether these things are really all that dangerous in the wrong hands. How much damage could someone really do? They could cheat at the Lotto, I guess. I suppose they could even mess with Wall Street . . . but only if they happened to hear something on the radio about a certain stock going up or down.

That's the trick — there's a limit to what you could ever learn using these things. You're stuck with whatever happens to be on the radio ten and a half hours from now, and even worse, you're limited to what little scraps of those broadcasts the machine picks up.

Pretty serious hindrances, right? But the Group found a way around them.

How to explain this? Let's say you want to make money betting on a football game. Let's make it easy: It's the Super Bowl. I think a person could use one of these machines as normal for that. All you'd have to do is listen to the machine for three or four hours before the game. You'd be hearing radio traffic from a few hours after the game was over — you're definitely going to catch a few seconds of some DJ talking about how it turned out.

Now let's make it harder. What if you want to bet on a college lacrosse game? Duke against Baylor. Not even a championship game or anything — just some regular matchup in the season. Think you're going to catch that score on the radio?

So what can you do?

Well, what if you've got a buddy who's a DJ at a local radio station? You say to him, do me a favor — 10 hours and 24 minutes from now, go online and look up the score for the Duke-Baylor lacrosse game, and just as a joke, keep saying the score on the air, over and over again. Do it after every song and commercial break.

Better yet, you bribe every DJ, at every nearby radio station, to do the same thing.

Now you're going to hear that score. Or the closing price of IBM stock, if that's what you asked them to look up and keep repeating on the radio. Or literally any piece of information a person could look up, 10 hours and 24 minutes in the future. Anything.

That would really work, but it's not exactly subtle.

There's a subtle way to do the same thing, though. That's the system the Group has created. It's a combination of powerful hardware and software that basically does what those DJs would do, but it does it without anybody noticing.

First, it's a pretty simple search program. It can use Google or any number of Web sites where you can look things up (stock exchange sites, news sites, anything). The way the program works, you tell it to run a search, and it simply waits 10 hours and 24 minutes before it executes it.

Then what does it do? It turns the search result into a simple string of text, then translates it into a kind of Morse code the Group invented. The system then hacks into the computers that oversee radio broadcasts, at multiple stations, and hides this coded information within the audio that they're putting out on the airwaves. The code plays at a pitch range human ears can't pick up. (In fact, most people's speakers probably don't even render the sound.) Even if some technician did hear it, it would sound like harmless interference, if anything at all.

The Group's system can hear it, though, and decode it.

In this way, they have removed all the randomness and limitation from using these machines. They don't just hear whatever happens to be on the radio ten and a half hours from now. They hear specific answers to nearly any question they can think of . . . even if all they're picking up is a rock song or a used car commercial. The coded information is hidden in the broadcast no matter what.

Dryden raised his eyes from the letter and stared away over the parking lot, through the heat ripples coming up off the rows of cars.

Curtis's description of the system seemed to break open in front of him, like an egg sac full of a thousand little spiders. Implications scurrying away to all corners, too many to follow.

He kept reading:

In the right hands, this system would be an amazing and good thing. Well-meaning authorities would set it up to tell them about a whole range of potential bad events. There could be a special database in which mass shootings, plane crashes, and a hundred other types of tragedies were always reported, and those in charge would then see those things coming far ahead of time. The authorities would become perfect goalies when it came to the really bad stuff.

It goes without saying that the Group doesn't seem to be interested in that.

What they're using the technology for at this moment (among other things) is to hunt down the loose ends that got away from them when they made their move against Bayliss Labs. That would be you and me, Claire. (And Dale Whitcomb, but I'll come to that in a minute.)

I hope to hell you already know most of the above. I hope Dale was able to explain that much to you, when he called you and told you to run. I hope he made it clear how dangerous your situation is. This system the Group is using, it can do a lot more than run Google searches or look up stock quotes. For example, it's fucking child's play to access the servers on which police departments record

their activity. Any routine traffic stop automatically logs the target
vehicle's plate number, the driver's ID, the time of the stop, and
even the GPS coordinates of the cruiser.

The Group will hunt us using that information. You need to
appreciate how dangerous that is. If you were pulled over, even just
for speeding, and even if you got off with a warning . . . there
would be a police database record of that traffic stop, containing
your name and the exact time and place where it happened.

This system the Group created . . . it could be programmed to
constantly search police servers for a record like that. If it found
one, it would embed that info in the airwaves, and the Group
would learn about it 10 hours and 24 minutes earlier.

Do you understand? If you get pulled over, the Group will
know about it hours and hours before it even happens.

Which gives them all the time in the world to position men to
attack you at that exact location and time.

The dots Dryden had felt trying to connect earlier now
fused together as if arc-welded.

Claire in the Mojave, terrified at the sight of the
approaching cop.

Staring in all directions, searching inexplicably for some
threat in the darkness around them.

'Jesus Christ,' Dryden whispered.

He tried to get his mind around it: what it meant to be
up against an enemy who knew your mistakes before you
even made them.

Then he kept reading the letter, and saw that the problem was a lot bigger than that.

Chapter Seventeen

I don't believe you know the rest of this, Claire. I'm not sure Dale understood it well himself at the time he called you. It was more important to warn you quickly and tell you the immediate stuff.

The rest is scarier, though. Maybe a lot scarier, and on the scale of big things. I think we have real trouble here.

The system I've described is powerful, obviously. When you think about it, it's basically sending information to itself, back in time. Ten and a half hours back.

But the information it sends back doesn't have to just come from the Internet or police records. The information the system sends back can come from any source. Including the system itself.

The system can listen to its own information coming back from ten and a half hours ahead in time . . . then turn around and send that information to itself ten and a half hours in the past. Like a daisy chain. And there's no real limit to how far the chain can stretch.

Did you ever plug a video camera into a TV, then point the camera at the screen? You get that tunnel of screens reaching away into infinity. This is like that, but the tunnel reaches through time instead.

It works, Claire. They really did this. The setup for it is there in their programming code, and their e-mails reference it over and over, behind all the careful language.

I know about at least two early trial runs. The first one was simple. They used the system to learn the closing value of the Dow Jones five days in the future. They ended up being dead-on.

The second trial had a longer reach: just shy of ten years. They told the system to give them the high temperature in Des Moines, Iowa, for July 1, 2025. Eighty-nine degrees, it said. I guess we'll find out someday.

Far away across the parking lot, in the direction of the beach and the boardwalk, kids' voices shouted and laughed. Something about a Frisbee. Dryden brushed his hair off his forehead. He felt his hand just perceptibly shake.

The trial runs ended almost three weeks ago. Since then, they've already begun using this long-term function for real. They have something planned, Claire. I don't know what it is, but it has to be large-scale. It's on a timeline of years. You'll get a sense of it in their e-mails, if you read enough of them. These people, the Group . . . they have some kind of agenda, some ideology driving them. There are no specifics about it in their messages, but the general tone is hard to miss. They want something, and they're going to use this technology to get it.

The parts of it that they've set in motion so far are small components, I think. Like they're still testing the waters. But even with these little steps, they've demonstrated what an advantage their system gives them.

The way it works is, they can set a chain of events in motion (maybe paying certain people to do things, maybe writing up detailed strategies and committing resources to them), and then they search the future for news stories to see how it will turn out. And if it doesn't turn out the way they want . . . they just change their plan in the present. Then they check the future again to see how that version would work. They can change it over and over, until they see a future they're satisfied with. It's like correcting artillery fire onto a target, based on watching where the shells are hitting . . . except their spotters are looking across years, not miles.

I know for a fact they've had people killed. (On top of killing everyone at Bayliss, and trying to kill us.) What I mean is they're seeing future news reports about politicians or journalists who get in their way, even years from now . . . and they're killing those people in the present time. We're talking about people who don't even necessarily work in those fields yet, or even realize that they someday will. They're being murdered now over things they would have eventually done. This is really happening, Claire.

Movement at the edge of Dryden's vision. He glanced up. A couple in their twenties walked to a minivan, five cars over. He stared at them without quite seeing them. His mind was far away, trying to grasp the scale of the situation Curtis had described.

After a few seconds he dropped his eyes to the letter again.

There was more to it. A lot more.

He turned the page and kept reading.

Chapter Eighteen

Marnie was on the freeway, passing Thousand Oaks, thirty minutes yet from El Sedero.

She had her phone in its dash mount, switched on. The map application was open, showing not her own location but that of Sam Dryden – the location of his Explorer, anyway: a little red thumbtack symbol currently positioned in what looked like a strip-mall parking lot.

Dryden had been there since Marnie had left the federal building.

She had the radio on. She flipped through the stations, one every second or two. She caught the tail end of a U2 song that gave way to a news report: the latest on the Miracle in the Mojave. The whole mediasphere had begun calling it that about two hours ago. Now as Marnie listened, she heard a sound bite that had become the go-to clip for all the networks. It was Leah Swain's mother, being interviewed at the hospital where she'd just been reunited with her daughter. Through tears that cracked her voice almost beyond discernibility, she had a message for the man and woman who had rescued her little girl.

Thank you. Whoever you are.

Then someone – maybe a reporter, but more likely a random onlooker – yelled, *Do you think they were angels?*

There was no answer to that, because by then – as Marnie had seen in the televised version of this clip – Leah's mother had turned to go back into the hospital.

'Let's just go see,' Marnie said.

She pushed the Crown Vic to 90 and changed lanes.

She was five minutes from El Sedero when the little red thumbtack on the map started moving. She watched the phone's display in glances as she drove: Dryden left the strip-mall parking lot and headed east on a surface street, away from the oceanfront. He crossed under the 101 freeway, then turned onto the northbound on-ramp, accelerating and merging in. The map screen automatically scaled out to a wider zoom as Dryden sped along, moving up the coast toward Santa Barbara.

A data tag popped up next to the thumbtack, showing Dryden's speed: just above the posted limit. Marnie still had the Crown Vic doing 90. Watching the map, she did the rough math in her head: She would overtake him within five or ten minutes. Well, she'd catch up, anyway. She had no desire to overtake him. Better to hang back half a mile, just in visual range.

Dryden had his windows all the way down, the ocean air rushing through the Explorer's cab. As he drove, the last portion of Curtis's letter cycled through his thoughts, key passages standing out from the rest:

Dale Whitcomb is alive, Claire. He and I were in touch for a few hours, that last day, when everything went to hell – the day he left the machine in a safe place for you to find. I know he also left a phone number for you, along with the machine, but I'm guessing you got no answer when you tried to call him. When the Group's people attacked Bayliss Labs that day, Whitcomb got away, but he had to leave behind everything, including the phone you could have reached him on. He just wasn't expecting so aggressive a move, so quickly.

He did manage to contact me after that, just for a few minutes. Even that was a risk (to both him and me, I'm sure), but he had to talk to me.

Whitcomb said he knows who these people are, Claire. Who the Group really are. He said there are things he never shared with us, that he didn't think mattered. He wants to tell us everything now.

He says there may be a way to go after these guys, off the record. A way to shut them all down in one shot, and possibly even erase this technology in the process. Everyone who's known about it would be dead, at that point, except the handful of us – and we could take it to our graves.

Whitcomb asked me to meet him three days after that last call – meaning today, Saturday. He would spend the time in between trying to contact people on that list he was making – the powerful people he meant to show the machine to in the first place. He says some of them have the means to help us make a move against the Group.

The meeting is at 3.00 this afternoon, in a little town called Avenal, just off I-5 up in Central Valley. There's an old scrap-yard outside town. That's the place. Whitcomb picked it at random as we spoke.

My job for the three days was to find you, Claire. We need the machine you have, or else the people Whitcomb wants to recruit *will never believe any of this. They need to see it for themselves, just like we did.*

I hope I'll be telling you all this in person, but if all I can do is get this information to you indirectly, then I hope it's enough. Please get to that meeting, and bring the machine. Good luck, Claire.

Curtis

It was 10.30 in the morning now. Four and a half hours until the meeting in the scrapyard. Dryden could reach Avenal by then without any trouble.

He watched the freeway rolling by, the white line segments coming at him like distinct thoughts.

Whitcomb.

The Group.

He says there may be a way to go after these guys, off the record. A way to shut them all down in one shot.

Dryden saw the delicate thread again. The one connecting himself to Claire. Wire-taut under a world of strain.

But holding.

He felt the edge of weariness creeping in on him as he drove. He did the math: thirty-some hours now without sleep, and probably twelve without food. Five miles farther on, an off-ramp sign advertised a McDonald's. He took the exit and hit the drive-through, then parked in an Albertson's lot next door, with a double order of sausage biscuits and hash brown patties and a large coffee.

He reached to turn on the Explorer's radio out of habit,

then stopped himself. He leaned over and grabbed the hard plastic case instead, lifted it onto the passenger seat, and opened it.

He turned on the tablet computer and pulled up the program that controlled the machine. The machine itself was off, silent except for the low cyclic hum from deep inside it.

Dryden tapped the ON button on the tablet screen. He heard the machine's hum speed up and change pitch, as it had done when Claire had switched it on before. A second later the computer's speakers began playing the familiar static. Dryden heard something trying to break through it right away: some '80s song he couldn't quite put a name to. A few seconds later it was gone, lost in the hiss.

Somehow, it felt right to have the thing turned on.

No – that wasn't quite true. Dryden thought about it a few seconds longer, then understood the feeling better: It wasn't that it felt right having the thing on, it was that it felt wrong having it off.

His mind kept going back to the four girls in the trailer. If Claire hadn't been listening to this thing last night –

All at once he pictured her, sitting at the wheel of her Land Rover, dark hollows under her eyes after three days of hardly any sleep.

Maybe this machine was like a drug, once it got in your head. Something you couldn't let go of. You would never know when you might hear about a car accident that killed a mother and two little kids – three people still alive and well, somewhere out there in the here and now.

Maybe Claire had saved other lives before the trailer

last night. There were all kinds of bad things reported on the radio, around the clock.

Three days without sleep.

Had she just been unable to turn away from the damn thing?

Knowing what she might miss by five minutes?

Dryden listened to the steady hissing from the speakers and thought of metal bars and tiny hands gripping them, and lighter fluid and blue flame and smoke and screams.

He pushed the images away – but left the machine on.

Marnie saw the Explorer from two hundred yards away. She pulled into the parking lot of a Pizza Hut that bordered the much larger Albertson's lot, and parked the Crown Vic. She took a pair of binoculars from her center console compartment and fixed them on Dryden's vehicle.

He was sitting at the wheel, eating a little breakfast sandwich – probably fast food from the McDonald's right next door. His gaze stayed trained mostly through the windshield, out past the edge of the parking lot, to the sharp blue water of the Pacific below. The morning haze had nearly gone, leaving a choppy surface that glittered in the early light.

Marnie's phone rang in its dash mount. She lowered the binoculars and answered the call on speaker.

Don Sumner's voice came through. 'I've got something you want to hear. Might be about your guy.'

'Let's have it.'

*

Dryden felt the coffee taking the edge off the weariness. If that was a placebo effect, he didn't care.

Way out on the ocean, maybe five miles offshore, a giant container ship crept by. It was moving south, gradual as the minute hand of a clock at this range, maybe heading for the Port of Long Beach.

'I'm looking at a story about a dead cop in the Mojave,' Sumner said. 'About an hour's drive from the trailer where the little girls were being held.'

'That's a long way,' Marnie said. 'Who says there's a connection?'

'No one, but the cop's dash cam says the cruiser was approaching two parked vehicles off the roadside. One of which looks like a Ford Explorer, recent model.'

'Do we have a plate number?'

'The cop didn't get close enough for that before he was killed.'

Marnie was silent, still watching Dryden.

'What I'm saying,' Sumner said, 'is there's probably enough here to bring Dryden in for questioning, if you want to.'

'I've got prints on a junked washing machine at one scene,' Marnie said, 'and a vehicle that kind of looks like his at another. That's pretty thin.'

'We don't need enough to charge him with a crime. I've seen someone detained as a person of interest on less than this.'

Marnie lowered the binoculars. Even without them, she could see Dryden pretty well.

'I can have the assistant US attorney on the phone in

thirty seconds,' Sumner said. 'He can fax me the signed warrant in another minute or two. You'd be free to arrest Dryden yourself at that point.'

'I'm not ready to drag him in over the trailer thing,' Marnie said. 'Not on the record.'

'Then drag him in over the cop in the desert. It's only for questioning. What's the downside?'

A dark green Ford Fusion rolled past Marnie and coasted into the lot Dryden was parked in. It pulled into a space thirty yards behind him, two men up front, the back windows tinted.

Marnie took note of the car absently, her mind working through the decision in front of her.

'Why don't I go ahead and set up the warrant,' Sumner said. 'And instead of you making the arrest, I'll give Dryden's current location to police dispatch and let them take him down. That's a better approach, given his background – he's potentially dangerous. He'd still be yours to question, either way.'

Marnie thought about it, still idly staring at the Fusion. The men inside were just sitting there, talking about something.

Marnie returned her gaze to Dryden, who was still staring off at the ocean.

'It's your call, Marnie,' Sumner said.

Dryden heard a commercial flit through the static. Something about a pizza place where kids' meals were half off on Fridays. The signal cleared for five or six seconds, then washed out.

He finished the last hash brown patty and stuffed the wrapper into the bag everything had come in. He rolled the bag down into a compact shape and set it on the floor in front of the passenger seat. He was reaching for his coffee again when another signal began to fade in. For a second he thought it was a weather report, or maybe a station identification – it was a man's voice, still too choppy to make out.

Then the static cleared entirely.

'... *death toll is confirmed at twelve, but with nine critically injured, it's likely to go higher, Katelyn.*'

Dryden turned toward the machine.

'Yes or no,' Sumner said. 'It's not a hard question.'

Marnie barely heard him. Her attention had suddenly locked on to Dryden.

There was something going on.

Dryden had turned his head and was now focused intently on something on his passenger seat.

Dryden studied the tablet computer's screen, filled by the application that ran the machine. He hadn't tried recording with it yet, but there was no question about how to do it. The four buttons could not have been simpler: ON, OFF, RECORD, and STOP.

He pressed RECORD as the news report continued.

'*With an incident like this,*' the male reporter said, '*we know we're going to hear lots of questions in hindsight. Was the construction site as safe as it could have been? Any time you've got heavy equipment, with people milling around, folks are going to be asking whether all the guidelines were followed –'*

'Are there guidelines that could have prevented this type of accident?' a woman, presumably Katelyn, asked. *'Has there been any statement from the construction firm managing the site?'*

'There's been no statement all day, and nothing from the developer except the press release earlier, offering thoughts and prayers.'

Watching Dryden, Marnie was only dimly aware of the men in the dark green car getting out. The driver opened the back door on his side and leaned in, reaching for something out of view in the rear seats.

'Let's give his information to the cops, Marnie,' Sumner said. 'You want to question him, so let's just do it.'

She chewed her lip, thinking. Felt herself leaning in Sumner's direction.

'It's possible the developer is worried about the legal risks of saying anything public right now,' the male reporter said. *'Certainly the equipment failed, but of course there were extenuating circumstances, so –'*

'Right,' Katelyn said, *'and the project itself was considered controversial even before today. Mission Tower has gotten a lot of pushback from Santa Maria residents just for its size. It's really not the type of building you expect in a town like that –'*

'That's absolutely right –'

Static began to edge back in, distorting the man's words.

'– but obviously on a day like this, all we're hearing from the community is consolation for those killed and their –'

The signal dropped away into the hiss.

Dryden stared at the tablet's screen a second longer.

Santa Maria. An hour's drive north of here, he thought – he had been there before but couldn't remember the exact directions to reach it. It was definitely not along the route he'd planned to take to Avenal, but it couldn't be far off of it, either.

There was some amount of time to spare – not a hell of a lot, but probably enough, depending on what had happened in Santa Maria. What *would* happen.

Death toll is confirmed at twelve.

Likely to go higher.

Dryden swore under his breath and reached for the glove box, where he kept a small road atlas.

Even with naked eyes, Marnie saw Dryden lean over in the telltale movement of someone opening a glove compartment. A second later he had a booklet in his hands, flipping through its pages rapidly.

Thirty yards behind him, the driver of the dark Fusion was still leaning into his backseat. The passenger was just standing there on his own side of the car, staring forward in Dryden's direction.

'I need an answer, Marnie,' Sumner said. 'Let's set up the warrant. Let's bring him in.'

She opened her mouth to say yes –

Then stopped herself.

Dryden had the booklet braced on his steering wheel, tracing a hand over one of its pages, like someone following a route on a –

'He's going somewhere,' she said.

'What?'

'He's got an atlas out. He's about to go somewhere.'

'He was on the freeway. He was already going somewhere.'

'Something just changed, though,' Marnie said. 'He looks amped up for some reason.'

'And?'

'And I want to know why,' Marnie said. 'I'm going to see where he's going. So no warrant, okay? Not yet.'

Over the speakerphone, Sumner exhaled. 'Fine.'

Thirty yards behind Dryden, the man leaning into the Fusion drew back and straightened up. He had a toddler in his arms. A baby girl in a pink outfit. He bounced her gently in the crook of his elbow, which made her laugh. He shut the door, and he and the passenger headed toward the Albertson's.

By then Dryden had set the atlas aside. A second later he started the Explorer. He pulled out of his space and accelerated across the lot to the nearest exit.

Marnie put the Crown Vic back in drive and followed.

Chapter Nineteen

The atlas had confirmed what Dryden had already guessed: The 101 was the fastest route. Along the coast through Santa Barbara, then inland through the mountains. Total drive time would be just over an hour, at the speed limit. A bit less, if he pushed it.

The lack of a timeline was maddening. For all the details he'd heard in the broadcast, there had been nothing to say when the accident would happen.

Well, there had been a hint.

Has there been any statement from the construction firm managing the site?

There's been no statement all day . . .

All day.

Dryden had heard the broadcast around 10.40 in the morning. That put the actual time of the broadcast around 9.04 tonight.

No statement all day, as of 9.04 tonight.

Whatever was going to happen at Mission Tower, whatever was going to kill twelve people and injure nine more, it would happen early in the day. Anytime now.

Could he just call somebody? Walk into a gas station right now and ask to use their phone for an emergency? It would take only a few phone calls, starting with 4-1-1, to track down whoever was building Mission Tower in Santa

Maria, but when he got through to someone, what exactly could he tell them?

Something to make them clear the construction site?

Would that fix the problem?

Maybe. If the accident was going to be caused by some one-off human error, like someone dropping an air-nailer and rupturing a fuel line, or pulling the wrong lever of an earth mover, then simply shuffling the deck might change everything. If it were that simple, then the solution might be as easy as calling in a bomb threat. Shake up the whole day, shut down the site for hours while cops scoured the place. By the time the crew got back to work, the fluke accident would probably never happen.

If it was a fluke.

And if it wasn't? If the danger was some loose bolt in a machine – say, the pulley of a construction elevator? Something sure to go wrong, given a few more hours of use?

Then a bomb threat would only delay the tragedy – and make it that much harder to address the real problem. How would Dryden call in later and urge someone to inspect all the site hardware, if they'd just gotten a crank bomb threat the same day?

How would he even know whether to make that call? How would he know if the bomb scare had solved the problem or not?

He had the Explorer doing 90, the Saturday morning traffic sparse enough to permit it.

Fifty minutes, give or take, and he could be there to look around for himself.

On the passenger seat, the machine was still on. Maybe he would get lucky and catch another update. Twelve people dead was a big story. Lots of coverage.

He passed a semi and veered back into the right lane.

Marnie stayed half a mile behind him. No need to get close enough to risk him spotting her. On her phone's display, the little red thumbtack traveled neatly along the 101.

Chapter Twenty

Mangouste had five cell phones on the desk in his den. One was a smartphone he'd had for a year. The other four were burners – throwaway units he replaced daily, whether he ended up using them or not. Every morning at 6.00 he dumped the previous day's collection into an industrial blender in the basement, grinding them to plastic crumbs, and at 6.15 his courier would arrive with four new ones. Each phone had a white sticker on the back, with a list of names – well, alphanumeric codes that stood for names – of the people who could reach him via that unit.

Caution was like money: More was more.

The third of the four burners rang at 10.55 in the morning. Mangouste got to it on the second ring.

The caller said, 'We're getting some headway on the trailer in the desert. Not sure if any of it's going to pan out, but we're trying.'

In the background, over the line, Mangouste could hear a keyboard clicking – his people hard at work, using the system. His jaw tightened at the notion of it: all that numinous power, sidetracked for three days now to play cat-and-mouse. The hunt for Claire Dunham and Dale Whitcomb and Curtis Wynn. Like using an aircraft carrier to dredge for clams.

Until today there had been no leads at all, and then in a

span of hours, in the middle of the night, there had been two: A stakeout team had pegged Curtis at a coffee shop, and the system had found Claire in the Mojave – had picked up a police report describing a run-in between her and a patrol unit out there, several hours before the event took place.

That police report, describing the original version of the incident – with no intervention by Mangouste's people – made it obvious that Claire knew about the system. She knew the danger of having her name and location officially logged by the police.

She had very nearly avoided that outcome.

According to the report, a San Bernardino County sheriff's deputy, doing a routine patrol, had spotted two vehicles parked in the darkness, far off of a remote highway in the Mojave. The deputy had stopped to investigate, at which point one of the two vehicles left the scene before the cruiser's dash cam could resolve its plate number. The other vehicle, a Land Rover, U-turned and rammed head-on into the deputy's patrol car to disable it.

This crash also crippled the Land Rover, whose female occupant then fired several shots from a handgun toward the deputy's car, forcing him to take cover behind it. The woman fled the scene on foot and was picked up by the unidentified second vehicle several hundred yards away.

The crashed Land Rover turned out to have stolen license plates on it, and its VIN had been physically removed. Only a fluke had allowed authorities to identify its owner at all: The oil filter had a unit-specific identifier stamped into it, traceable to a point-of-sale record at a service garage in San Jose, where the Land Rover's owner, Claire Dunham, had gotten an oil change six months before.

All of which had been enough for Mangouste's purposes. The police report included a time stamp and GPS data for the incident, from the patrol car's dash computer. It gave Mangouste enough information to send a team to that spot, in advance. Which he had done, immediately.

The report also tantalized him, though. It offered no further information about the person who had been with Claire in the desert – the driver of that second vehicle. The police had not yet identified that suspect at the time the report was filed.

Might it be Dale Whitcomb? Was that too much to hope for?

It couldn't have been Curtis. He was already accounted for at that moment, being tailed by the stakeout team that had spotted him, hundreds of miles away.

It made good sense, of course, that Claire would be with Whitcomb, and for a while there, when that possibility seemed solid, Mangouste had let himself believe he had all the loose ends in reach. All three strands, right there in front of him, ready to be tied off forever. Curtis, Claire, Whitcomb. Easy as that.

It would have been nice to know for sure, in the moments after first seeing that police report. It would have been helpful to run further searches with the system, and find later reports detailing the police manhunt for Claire Dunham and her unknown friend, in that original version of the future. Maybe some document would eventually name Whitcomb as the second suspect.

Except there was no chance of finding any later reports like that.

No chance at all.

Here was one bona fide weakness the system had, and would always have: Once it showed you a useful piece of the future – some bit of knowledge you were sure to act on – then the future itself changed accordingly. How could it not? From the moment you saw that information – in this case, the time and place at which to attack Claire – then the old future no longer existed. You could run all the searches you wanted, but all you'd find would be information from the *new* future.

Mangouste had searched anyway. And had seen what he expected: a police report about a San Bernardino County sheriff's deputy stopping in the desert to investigate two vehicles, only to be killed seconds later by rifle fire from unseen assailants. By the time police reinforcements descended on the remote site, more than twenty minutes later, there were no other people in the vicinity. Just a wrecked Land Rover, eventually traceable to Claire Dunham by way of the same trick with the oil filter. No identity for any second person at the scene. No other info at all.

Mangouste hadn't minded seeing that report. It told him enough. It told him the attack would work: that his men would capture Claire and her friend and escape the scene. Good news, all around.

And the attack *had* worked. His men followed protocol and kept their phones switched off while they were in the desert, so that the authorities couldn't later check the cell network and see that multiple unknown parties had been out there. Burner phones were untraceable, in theory, but why give the cops anything more than you had to?

Mangouste had watched the clock, starting from the point when his men would carry out the attack. He guessed it would be another half hour after that before they would reach the crowded safety of a freeway, switch on their phones, and report in.

Two of them had. They had Claire and were en route to the interrogation site. They said the other team was bringing the stray machine home, along with Claire's companion – a man in his thirties, by their description, which told Mangouste it was most certainly not Dale Whitcomb. Who the hell was he, then?

Mangouste waited for the second team to report in and tell him the rest of the story. They never did. Neither did they respond to calls made to their cells, even long after they should have reached the interstate.

There was no pleasant way to interpret that set of facts. No way to fill in the blanks without assuming the two men were dead and the stranger was loose out there some-where. With the machine.

Mangouste had set his people to work using the sys-tem, scouring the future for news reports of unidentified bodies. Assuming the worst – that the stranger had left the dead men someplace remote – it might be weeks before they were found. By that point their fingertips would be too decomposed to identify them, and they had no official ID on their bodies.

The system had found a result right away – and then

about three dozen more. As it turned out, Southern California produced a fair number of unidentified corpses in a given month or two. Even when you narrowed by age range and race, it was information overload. It occurred to Mangouste that it wouldn't help much anyway to find where the mystery man had left the bodies. That moment must have already come and gone.

Even as that search had begun to prove pointless, other news reports started filtering in – ordinary news on TV, in the present time. Reports about the miraculous rescue of four little girls at a trailer in the Mojave, by a man and woman who had shown up just in time to prevent a tragedy. Authorities seemed baffled as to how the two, who had quickly fled the scene, had known to show up there at all.

Into the phone, Mangouste said, 'Tell me what you've got on the trailer. Tell me the cops eventually have a name for this guy.'

'In a way, they do,' the caller said. 'Two days from now, a man named Clay Reynolds comes forward claiming he and his girlfriend were the ones who saved those kids.'

Mangouste's eyes narrowed. 'He identifies *himself*?'

'Proudly, according to the articles we've seen. But later the same day, a second couple speaks to reporters and says Reynolds is lying – claiming *they* saved the kids, not him. By the next afternoon there are two other couples taking credit.'

Mangouste pressed a hand to his forehead, shutting his eyes hard. 'You've got to be kidding me.'

'It ends up being a real sideshow for the next month or

more. Something like fifty different people swear they were the ones – anyone who even loosely matches police sketches the girls provide. It's like that time all the Z-list celebrities ran for governor of California. We found a *Newsweek* rundown of Jimmy Fallon and Conan O'Brien's best jokes about it, dated six weeks from now.'

'There have to be real leads the police end up following. There must be something.'

'We're still working on it. It's just . . . kind of a busy haystack to sift through.'

Mangouste didn't reply. He stood there, gripping the phone, thinking it all over.

Hours earlier, everything had seemed to be in the bag. Three targets, three apparent leads. Now two of those had come up empty. There was no sign of Dale Whitcomb, and even Curtis Wynn had slipped away, somehow taking the stakeout team with him. There had been a final check-in from those men, tailing the kid down the Pacific Coast Highway around 6.00 in the morning, but that was the last contact. They had vanished as completely as the guys who'd been transporting the stranger from the Mojave. Even a search using the system had proved fruitless: There was no record of their vehicle being found anywhere, at any point in the foreseeable future.

'What is this?' Mangouste asked softly.

'Sir?' the caller said.

Mangouste opened his eyes. 'Keep working on the trailer,' he said. 'Call me when you have something.'

Chapter Twenty-one

Dryden took the first exit for Santa Maria at 11.35. He could already see the building.

Mission Tower has gotten a lot of pushback from Santa Maria residents just for its size. It's really not the type of building you expect in a town like that.

From the elevated exit ramp, the whole city appeared spread out like a carpet; Mission Tower could not have looked more out of place in the sprawl if it had been a pyramid with a sphinx guarding it. Standing at least twenty stories tall, it was probably the only structure in the city that topped out above forty feet.

Structure seemed like the right word for it – not so much a building as the skeleton of one, a framework of steel uprights and concrete slab floors, like a parking structure without perimeter walls.

Dryden put its distance at just over a mile. He could see a tower crane braced to the north side. The crane's mast, standing three hundred feet tall, looked as delicate as a vertical truss of glued-together toothpicks. The long horizontal jib and counterjib, balanced atop the mast, swung slowly around as the operator lowered some kind of load onto the building's rooftop. Dryden couldn't see the workmen from this distance, but they had to be there.

He turned off the exit ramp onto the surface street.

Marnie managed to stay one light behind him, all the way across town. She watched Dryden turn onto the main drag that ran east-west through the city, at the far end of which stood a huge building under construction. Two minutes and three stoplights later, she saw the Explorer pull to the curb twenty yards from the build site, its boundary protected by orange mesh fencing and NO TRESPASSING signs.

Marnie pulled over half a block behind him. She killed her engine and sank down a little in her seat.

Dryden was out of his vehicle within seconds of stopping. He had something in his hand – a hard plastic case of some kind.

Without so much as looking around, Dryden crossed the distance to the construction zone, shoved down the mesh fence, and stepped over it into the site.

Marnie stared after him, as confused as she had been at any point since arriving in the Mojave at four in the morning.

She got out of her Crown Vic and followed.

Twelve dead. Nine injured.

None of that was going to happen on the ground floor of the tower, Dryden saw. There was nobody at all on the first level. Not inside, anyway. He could hear men shouting to each other outside the structure, way on the other side. Crewmen positioning the heavy loads that remained for the tower crane to pick up.

Dryden could see the crane's reinforced base, midway along the north side of the building. A massive footing of steel and concrete, probably bolted to foundation piles that punched fifty feet down into the earth.

Whatever was going to go wrong, the crane's base was not going to be a part of it. It looked solid enough. It looked like it would stay right there for five hundred years, even if everyone went away and left it to the elements.

Certainly the equipment failed, but of course there were extenuating circumstances . . .

What sort of equipment – and what extenuating circumstances?

And why *of course?*

Something in that phrasing had troubled Dryden since he'd first heard it.

He came to an exposed stairwell – there were no walls yet boxing it in; it was wide open to the surrounding space of each floor. The stair treads were bare steel that would someday hold ceramic tile or padded carpet. He stopped at the bottom and cocked his head. From high above came the sound of voices echoing down through the vertical space. All of them seemed to come from way up in the building, closer to the top than the bottom.

Distracting him from the sound was the static coming from the plastic hardcase in his hand. He had cranked the tablet computer's volume to its highest setting, loud enough that he could hear it even with the case shut.

He started up the stairwell.

*

Marnie waited for him to disappear up the stairs before crossing the orange fencing outside the site. She walked softly on the concrete, her footfalls all but silent.

She started toward the stairwell Dryden had gone into, then saw another, twenty yards to the left. She made her way across to it and climbed to the first landing. She stopped and listened, and found she could hear Dryden easily. He was making no attempt to be quiet as he climbed through the structure.

She kept thinking about the hard plastic case.

What the hell was in it?

Obvious possibilities came to mind. Drugs. Money.

Other scenarios were less likely, but uglier. Like a bomb.

None of those things made any sense at all, but neither did anything else about Sam Dryden.

Marnie started up the next flight, unsnapping the safety harness of the Glock 17 holstered beneath her jacket.

For the first fifteen stories, Dryden saw nothing that could pose a threat to anyone. Just one empty floor after another, each one a wide-open concrete space running out to its edges. Beyond was blue sky and the spread of Santa Maria planing away to the mountains that encircled it.

Equipment failure.

Extenuating circumstances.

Of course.

No equipment on any of these floors. No people around to be killed by it, even if there had been; the voices were all still above him.

He was turning to start up to the sixteenth level when the static from inside the case guttered. He stopped, knelt down, and cracked the case open an inch.

He heard the Red Hot Chili Peppers singing about a girl named Dani California. He clicked the case back shut and kept climbing.

The first floor that wasn't empty was Level 22, the one directly below the rooftop. On this floor there were still no people, but there were stacks of building materials everywhere: plywood and granite slabs and huge volumes of Sheetrock, which were plastic-wrapped against exposure to moisture.

And here at last was the equipment. Giant air compressors with tanks the size of couches. Table saws of all kinds, only some of which Dryden recognized. These were specialized, heavy-duty tools built for cutting metal and masonry and high-density composites.

None of the equipment looked like it was about to kill anyone. Most of the machines weren't even plugged in – to electrical power or pneumatic lines.

Maybe one of the big air tanks could go off like a bomb. It seemed plausible until Dryden walked among them and eyeballed each pressure gauge. The tanks were empty. They were about as capable of exploding as the stacks of Sheetrock.

He could hear all the workers on the rooftop above him. Their voices, shouting and sometimes laughing, rang clear in the late morning air.

Atop one of the stacks of granite slabs, a dozen men

had left their jackets. Four had left hard hats, and three had left cell phones.

Dryden turned and stared out past the north edge of the floor, into empty space. The crane's mast was right there, hugging the building, fifty feet from where he stood. At this range it didn't look like it was made of glued-together toothpicks. The steel members of the truss structure were as big around as Dryden's leg, and fused together by welds and bolts that looked unlikely to spontaneously come loose.

He walked to the north edge. Put his feet right to the lip, beyond which a drop of two hundred and fifty feet yawned. He'd never had much of an issue with heights. Respect for them, sure. He braced a hand on the nearest corner of the crane's mast and leaned out over the void, looking up.

A hundred feet above him, the crane's jib arm stuck out almost straight north, away from the building. The jib's cable trolley was positioned about a third of the way out on the arm, bearing the pulley system from which the lifting cables extended down – all the way down to the hook, which was currently lowered to ground level. Dryden couldn't see anyone down there hustling to attach a new load. What he could see were men sitting around, eating from lunch boxes and drinking from Thermoses. Break time. The voices he heard just above him, on the roof, suggested it was break time there, too.

Dryden stepped back from the edge. He turned and looked up, as if he could see right through the concrete above him. Could see the men up there, sitting around on stacks of materials like the ones down on this level. Then he imagined he was looking up beyond the men, a hundred feet higher, to what was hanging directly above the building right now. The crane's counterjib arm. The short arm that balanced out the long one. Balanced it out because it weighed just as much, by way of the counterweight attached to it: a massive concrete block assembled in sections, the whole thing weighing – what? A hundred thousand pounds? More?

He was still looking up when the static crackled and receded again. He looked down at the case, and even before he opened it, he heard a man's voice coming from the tablet computer's speakers.

Not a commercial. A news report. The cadence was a dead giveaway.

Then he cracked the case open, and realized he recognized the man's tone, though the words themselves were still too distorted to make out.

The man speaking was Anderson Cooper.

Dryden had heard local radio stations carry CNN reports at times. Some kind of affiliate deal. Usually it happened during large-scale events. Election-night coverage. Maybe a hurricane.

When the static began to clear a few seconds later, the first words Dryden discerned from Anderson Cooper were *Santa Maria*.

His stomach gave itself a little twist.

What the hell was about to happen in this place?

Equipment failure.

Extenuating circumstances.

Of course.

Anderson Cooper said, *'I mean, you can just see it behind me. The power is still out throughout the entire city, and the only lights we're seeing are the worklamps of the search teams, obviously all of them working at just the one site.'*

Anderson Cooper wasn't just talking about Santa Maria. He was *in* Santa Maria. He was here. *Would be* here. Ten hours and twenty-four minutes from right now.

Worklamps of the search teams.

Just the one site.

'I want to bring in Aaron Spencer again,' Anderson said. *'You've got something new?'*

'Anderson, yeah, I've just gotten the latest revised numbers from USGS. They're mostly dialing it in at this point, but they're now saying the magnitude was 6.1, the depth was very shallow, only about nine miles, and the epicenter was close to the city, striking just minutes before noon today.'

Dryden looked at his watch.

11.54.

'Again,' Anderson said, *'not a massive quake, not a great deal of shaking, but enough to trigger the accident that brought that highrise down.'*

Chapter Twenty-two

He could run.

He could just run for it, right now.

The stairwell was right there, thirty feet away.

Twenty-two flights, two to three seconds each, he could be out of the building in about one minute.

One minute, out of six remaining, at most. A one-in-six chance of surviving. Russian roulette odds, even if he hauled ass immediately.

He clicked the case shut and ran, but not for the stairs. He ran to the stack of granite slabs with the jackets and hard hats and cell phones on it.

He set down the plastic case and grabbed the nearest of the phones. He switched it on and hit the phone icon and punched 9-1-1.

Marnie moved slowly, keeping low among the stacks of Sheetrock and the industrial tools. She stuck her head up and saw that she was just twenty feet from Dryden. He was facing the other way, holding a phone to his ear.

A moment earlier she'd heard him listening to what sounded like a radio with bad reception. She hadn't caught any of the transmission — some kind of news clip, she thought, but she'd been too far away then to tell.

Over the short distance to where Dryden now stood, Marnie heard the phone call connect. Heard the other party answer: a rapid little burst of syllables through the earpiece, rehearsed and automatic.

Into the phone Dryden said, 'I just parked a panel truck full of high explosives at the corner of Second and Palm.' He spoke clearly but kept his voice low, inaudible to the men talking and laughing on the rooftop above. 'Second and Palm,' Dryden said again. 'Right by that big tower they're building.'

On the last word he hung up and tossed the phone onto some guy's jacket, and in the same movement he scooped up a yellow hard hat and ran for the stairs, putting the hat on as he went.

Dryden hit the first tread and vaulted upward, taking the steps three at a time, running, forcing himself to hyperventilate, making it look and sound like he'd just sprinted up the full height of the stairwell.

He burst into sunlight atop the structure and started yelling even as he took in the men sitting there.

'Everyone listen!' he shouted. 'I have an evacuation order from the police!'

Marnie crossed to the stack of granite slabs where Dryden had left the hard plastic case. There was static coming from inside it – the radio with the bad reception.

One level up, she could hear him yelling at the work crew, talking about a bomb threat, telling them to vacate the site. He made it sound like the real deal. Marnie heard one of the men start to ask a question, but the guy cut himself off after the first word.

The reason was obvious.

From far away over the city, a police siren had begun wailing. An instant later a second one started up, and then a third. Coming in from all over, converging toward the building. From the rooftop, it had to be a damn convincing visual.

In the next second Marnie heard the scraping and thudding of men on the roof getting to their feet and running.

Dryden stood atop the stairs and waved them down ahead of him, his eyes automatically doing a head count as they passed.

Twelve men exactly, one of who had to be the crane operator; the cab atop the mast was empty now.

The report had described twelve dead, nine injured. The nine must have been bystanders in the street.

As the last of the men went by, Dryden swept his gaze over the roof for any possible straggler.

No one there.

He threw aside the hard hat and ran full-out down the steps, one flight behind the workers. He reached the twenty-second floor, turned toward the granite slabs where he'd left the machine in its case –

And stopped.

A woman had just stepped out from behind a stack of plywood, ten feet away.

She had the plastic case in one hand, and a pistol in the other – leveled at his chest. She looked shaken but held the weapon steady enough.

'Keep your hands out,' she said.

Chapter Twenty-three

Marnie thought of her training at Quantico, with regard to holding a subject at gunpoint by yourself. You stayed out of the subject's reach – that much was obvious. You allowed no ambiguity into your voice or your physical presence. Above all –

When Dryden moved, maybe a second after she'd spoken to him, it was like nothing she had ever seen before. It was sure as hell nothing she'd trained for.

A friend of hers in college had tried to give her a few boxing tips once. Had shown her how a jab was supposed to be launched, the leading shoulder pointed at the target, the back foot pushing off, the jab coming up directly inward along the opponent's sightline, because the human brain was slower to react to inward movement than side-to-side movement.

Dryden didn't throw a jab at her, but he sure as hell moved in along her sightline. Beyond that, she didn't know what he did. What she knew was that in one instant she had him at gunpoint, and in the next she was being slammed bodily backward into the plywood stack she'd stepped out from behind.

He had one hand around her neck, his fingertips applying just a bit of pressure to her carotid arteries. His other hand was holding her Glock 17 – when exactly had he taken it? – with the barrel touching her cheekbone.

Just like that, he had every advantage on her.

Yet he looked scared.

He looked rattled all to hell, for some reason.

His eyes narrowed. He looked like a man trying to work something out in bare seconds. Like some huge piece of bad news had just been dropped in his lap, and he was trying to grasp its implications.

The moment lasted maybe two seconds, and then he seemed to shove all the confusion away and refocus on her.

'When I let go,' he said, 'you're going to run down the stairwell as fast as your body can move. Or else you're going to die.'

No ambiguity in his voice. Or his physical presence.

'And hang on to the case,' he said.

Marnie found herself nodding, the movement difficult with his hand tight under her jaw.

Then he let go of her, grabbed her by one shoulder, and shoved her toward the stairs leading down.

She got her balance under her and kept moving, taking the steps three and four at a stride.

Dryden didn't count the flights as they descended. There was no reason to. They would make it or they wouldn't.

He had the woman's Glock stuffed in his rear waistband now, his hands free to grab for her if she lost her footing.

From a few flights below, he could hear the thunder of the workers' boots, the metal of the stairwell transmitting the vibration upward in strange harmonics and shudders.

Preview of the coming attraction, Dryden thought.

Coming soon.

Maybe thirty seconds had passed since he and the woman had started down. Hard to tell. He didn't look at his watch. No reason to do that either.

Flight after flight, they ran. A controlled plummet, palms shoving off against steel uprights as they rounded each landing. Down and down. Every second feeling borrowed.

All at once the boots-on-metal thudding from below them ended, replaced by the flat, dampened slapping sound of sprinting footfalls on concrete. The workers had reached the bottom.

Ahead of Dryden, the woman rounded the final landing and took the last flight in three falling strides, catching up to her center of gravity at the bottom and sprinting across the ground floor. Dryden closed distance and then stayed one pace behind her.

The orange mesh fence loomed just past the edge of the foundation slab. They vaulted it together, and then Dryden grabbed her by the upper arm, steering and propelling her farther.

'The Explorer, up ahead,' he said. 'Get in.'

'What are you —'

'Just do it!'

She nodded. She wasn't even looking back at him. Maybe she assumed he was still pointing the gun.

They covered the distance to the SUV in another five seconds, the woman still holding the hard plastic case. Dryden, still gripping her arm, pushed her toward the driver's-side door, and she fumbled it open and climbed in. He got in right after her, the two of them briefly tangled up in the space behind the wheel; then she clambered over the center console and dropped herself into the passenger seat.

Dryden shoved the key into the ignition and started the vehicle, then spared half a second to lean forward and crane his neck up at the tower's bulk. With its base just twenty yards away, the thing loomed over them like a man over an insect.

Dryden threw the Explorer into reverse, turned in his seat, and floored it. In his peripheral vision he saw the woman thrown forward at the dashboard, just getting her hands up in time to keep from banging her head.

'*Goddammit,*' she said.

Dryden ignored her. He watched out the back window as he reversed, doing 25, veering left and right as cars braked and steered out of his way.

'*What are you doing?*' the woman yelled.

'We need distance,' Dryden said.

'I already know the bomb is bullshit. I heard you call it in.'

They'd covered a block and a half now, a greater distance than the building's height. Safe enough. Dryden came to a stop with the vehicle centered in the one-way road, blocking traffic from approaching the building. He put the selector in park and hit his hazard lights.

The woman in the passenger seat was staring at him, any initial fear now replaced by anger and confusion.

'It's fake,' she said. 'I know it's fake. I heard the call.'

Dryden nodded. He wasn't looking at her. He leaned forward over the steering wheel and stared at the tower.

From this distance he could see the whole structure, including the crane – and its counterweight. It was exactly as Dryden had pictured it: The giant weight hung dead-centered over the building, a hundred feet above the roof. The sword of Damocles.

Behind him, someone honked a horn. The traffic leading toward the building had clotted six or seven cars deep.

Far ahead, around the building's base, men from the site were yelling at bystanders to get back, waving off cars, and getting the hell away themselves.

At the edge of his vision, Dryden saw the woman staring at him, her eyes narrowed. She opened her mouth to say something, but didn't get the chance.

The first shock wave of the tremor felt like an impact against the underside of the Explorer. Like the vehicle was on a lift, and someone had come along and hit it with a battering ram from below. The SUV rose up on its shocks and slammed back down. The woman grabbed the armrests for support.

A second and third jolt followed immediately, and before Dryden could process them, the lateral shaking started – the signature movement of a big quake. The whole world was suddenly shuddering, sliding violently left and right. A city on a card table, with a giant gripping its edges and wrenching it forward and backward, again and again and again.

The Explorer rocked side to side on its suspension. Dryden could see every other car on the street doing the same. He saw people on sidewalks throw themselves down on the grass. Saw the stoplights over every intersection jerk and twist and swing.

And Mission Tower.

Twenty-two stories. Concrete and steel. Swaying and pitching and reeling – but handling it.

It actually looked like it was doing fine. There were ripples racing up and down its height, the whole structure just visibly moving in a kind of belly-dance sway; Dryden had the distinct impression that it was designed to do this. Engineered to move in precisely this way, to dissipate the shock waves. To bend so it wouldn't break.

The tower crane was a different story.

There were ripples racing up and down its height, too. It did not look like it was handling it.

As Dryden watched, he could see a kind of cumulative effect building up, each oscillation of the crane's mast just a little more pronounced than the one before it. Like a child on a swing going a bit higher with each pass.

And then it failed.

Midway up the mast's freestanding portion – the part above the building, anchored to nothing – something gave way. Some bolt or weld, marginally weaker than the rest, let go, and in an instant the failure cascaded up and down through the mast, turning rigid steel into something that looked more like cable.

The giant horizontal arm that formed the top of the crane – the jib and counterjib – simply dropped. Like a two-by-four held out flat and then released.

The counterweight punched through the tower's roof

without stopping. A massive block of dumb, dead weight, probably twenty mixer trucks' worth of concrete, it obeyed the primeval physics of gravity and acceleration and momentum. It didn't even slow down; it crashed through floor after floor, as if the building weren't there at all. It tore a ragged tunnel straight downward, and left a dust-choked wake above itself, and even as Dryden watched it smash into the ground beneath the tower, his eyes were drawn back up to the building's top.

Where the floors were failing. The highest one first. It sagged at its center like a collapsing pie crust, settling its weight onto the floor beneath it. After only a few seconds, both floors gave way; they crumbled and pancaked downward and took the whole building with them, compressing it into its own footprint with brutal speed and efficiency. The collapse kicked out a cloud of concrete dust. It surged outward, channeled through the spaces between buildings, as ugly a déjà vu as Dryden had ever experienced. In a matter of seconds the dust cloud had reached the Explorer and engulfed it, plunging the inside into a murky twilight.

In the light that remained, Dryden turned to the woman in the passenger seat.

She was staring at him.

Her mouth hung slack.

Her lower eyelids ticked upward once, and then again, as if she were thinking of something to say. But she said nothing. She just stared.

PART THREE
Saturday, 12.00 p.m.–9.10 p.m.

Chapter Twenty-four

Ghosts emerged out of the dust from the collapsed building. The shapes of people, dark gray against the light gray. They materialized from the gloom three feet from the Explorer's hood, drifted past, vanished behind its back bumper.

Wind scoured the vehicle. It moaned in the wheel wells and the complex spaces of the underside. It scurried little snakes of soot across the windshield.

Dryden felt the adrenaline leaving him. Felt the live-wire thrum in his limbs settling out, calming. He forced his breathing back to normal – and felt his attention go back to where it had been earlier, in the moment after he'd disarmed the woman.

Who was she?

A cop of some kind.

The implications of that came at him from every angle. Made him want to look around outside for some sign of a threat, in spite of the dust choking off the visibility.

If the authorities knew enough to be looking for him, what else did they know? If they had his name tied to Claire's in any official way, then surely the Group would have already learned about him.

Dryden turned to the woman. 'Tell me who you are. Tell me how you found me.'

For a second it didn't seem like she'd heard him. She was staring forward into the haze, as if still trying to take it all in. The quake and the collapse. The fact that she'd been inside the building twenty seconds before that. She kept looking up at where the tower had stood.

She was thirty, give or take. Brown eyes, and brown hair to her shoulders.

Dryden grabbed her arm. *'Hey.'*

She turned to face him. Her eyes widened a little.

'Are the police looking for me?' Dryden asked. 'Is there an investigation with my name on record?'

The question seemed to go right past her. She blinked, and when she spoke, she still sounded half-dazed. 'How are you doing this? How are you showing up in these places before things . . . happen?'

Places. Plural.

How much did she know?

Dryden gripped her arm tighter, and found his voice getting louder of its own accord. *'Are the police looking for me? How did you find me?'*

She drew back from him, scared again.

'Tell me,' Dryden said.

She blinked. 'The trailer in the desert. You left finger-prints. In the arroyo.'

Dryden opened his mouth to tell her that wasn't pos-sible. There had been nothing in the arroyo except strewn trash and –

The washing machine.

Christ.

'I was there,' the woman said. 'I'm an FBI agent.'

Dryden felt his mind working rapid-fire, like he was mapping a minefield while driving through it at freeway speed.

He let go of the woman's arm and willed himself to speak evenly, but he locked his eyes onto hers and didn't blink.

'I need to know how much you know about me,' he said. 'You need to tell me everything, right now. This is life and death, maybe for both of us.'

She stared. 'I don't understand –'

'Everything,' Dryden said.

She looked into the eddying dust again, toward the unseen rubble of Mission Tower. 'But how are you –'

'Look at me.'

She turned back to him. Met his eyes.

'If someone could access police computers,' Dryden said, 'and FBI computers, what would they see about me right now? What is my name attached to, in the past twelve hours?'

The woman shook her head, thrown by the question.

'What would they see?' Dryden asked.

'Nothing. Well . . . no, nothing.'

'What were you going to say?'

The woman hesitated.

'*Tell me.*'

'There was almost a warrant.'

'Almost?'

'We wanted to question you. We were going to name you a person of interest –'

'For the trailer?'

185

The woman started to answer, but checked herself.

'*For the trailer?*' Dryden asked again.

The woman shook her head. 'A cop that got killed, out in the Mojave.'

Icy little needles seemed to pierce Dryden's skin. Down to his bones, where the chill spread deep and wide.

The Group knew all about the dead cop in the desert. Obviously. If Dryden's name was linked to that on any police computer –

'We held back on it,' the woman said. 'There's no warrant. There's nothing official at all.'

'Who's we?'

'Me and one other person. There's no official –'

'What other person?'

The woman shook her head. 'I don't understand what's going on –'

'Someone you work with?'

'Yes.' The woman looked baffled as to why he was asking.

Dryden stared at her. His mind was still flooring it across the minefield, jostling and bouncing.

'Call them,' he said. 'Whoever this person is. Call and make sure they don't still go through with creating the warrant. You don't understand how much this matters.'

For a long moment she just stared at him. She was calming a bit, but still entirely lost. 'What is this? What the hell is any of this?'

He held her gaze for a beat. Then he turned and stared away over the hood, thinking.

There was only so much he could push her to do. Or not do. He couldn't hold her against her will.

He exhaled deeply. Rested his arms across the wheel. Lowered his forehead to them. He was tired. Maybe not as tired as Claire had been, but getting there.

'You want to understand all this?' he asked.

From the corner of his eye he saw the woman nod. 'It's why I followed you.'

From the passenger footwell, Dryden could hear the machine hissing in its case. He drew upright again, reached into his rear waistband, and took out the woman's Glock 17. He held it out to her, grip first.

'Make the phone call,' he said, 'and I'll show you.'

Chapter Twenty-five

She called. She put her phone on speaker and talked to a guy named Sumner. She told him she was looking into something, and told him to hold off on doing anything with the name Sam Dryden until he heard from her again. She made him promise.

When she hung up, Dryden said, 'I need you to put your phone in airplane mode, so no one can ping it to track your location. Call it paranoia if you want, you'll see the point in a few minutes.'

She didn't argue. She switched the phone's setting, then pointed to the Explorer's dashboard, and the satellite navigation screen built into it.

'If you're paranoid,' she said, 'you should disable the GPS for that.'

For a second or two, Dryden only stared at it. The idea that the vehicle's navigation system might be a liability had never crossed his mind. He rarely used the thing, and today it hadn't once struck him as a means for tracking him. Staying unidentified in the first place had taken up all his attention.

'Jesus,' he said.

He knew how to cut the GPS unit's power. There was a dedicated fuse for it in the panel below the glove box. He leaned over and looked up under the dash, found the fuse, and pulled it out. Then he pressed the nav system's power button to be sure. The screen stayed dormant, dead.

When he turned to the woman again, she was staring at him. Waiting.

'My name's Marnie Calvert,' she said.

'Sam Dryden.'

'I know.'

She continued to hold his gaze. Still waiting.

Dryden pointed to her feet. 'Hand me the case.'

It took half an hour to show her, and to tell her everything he knew. By ten minutes in – around the time she seemed to get past her denial over the machine itself – the dust was clear enough that Dryden could see to drive. He retraced his route back to the 101 and took it north again. The freeway would lead to US 46 at Paso Robles, which would take them east toward I-5 and then to the town of Avenal. They would be there comfortably ahead of the meeting at 3.00 p.m.

When Dryden finished speaking, Marnie sat for over a minute saying nothing at all. She had Curtis's letter in her lap, and her eyes kept going from its pages to the machine, back and forth. Outside, the landscape slid by: low hills dotted with scrub vegetation.

At last she said, 'All the men on top of that building would have been dead.' She wasn't asking. Just firming up her grip on it.

Dryden nodded anyway.

For another long beat Marnie was quiet. Then: 'I would have died, too.'

'Yes and no,' Dryden said.

'What do you mean?'

'The way it would have originally happened, you wouldn't have been there at all. You were only there because I was trying to stop it.'

She shut her eyes. 'Right. Christ . . .'

'You don't have to be part of this,' Dryden said. 'I understand why you wanted answers, but now you have them. If you want to walk away, you can.'

It took her a long time to respond. Most of her attention was still on the machine, her mind trying to come to terms with it. Dryden imagined he had looked the same way when Claire had first shown him the thing.

'I can stop in the next town and let you out,' Dryden said. 'You can forget you ever heard of all this.'

'I wouldn't.'

'You know what I mean.'

Marnie nodded. She turned to him. 'I know what you mean. I don't want out.'

Dryden glanced at her. 'You understand what's going to happen, right? What this guy Whitcomb is talking about doing? There's not going to be any due process. We're going to track these people down and kill them. There's no other way it would work.'

Marnie nodded again. Her eyes dropped to Curtis's letter, in her lap. Her fingertips brushed over a paragraph in the middle of the page. Dryden saw what it was: the passage about the murders. Victims who had been killed for things they hadn't done yet.

'I know,' Marnie said. 'And I don't want out.'

Chapter Twenty-six

The third burner phone on Mangouste's desk rang again. He grabbed it.

'Tell me you have something.'

'It's not about the trailer,' the caller said.

'What, then?'

'One of the trip wires caught something.'

Mangouste was silent a moment, taking in the news. The so-called trip wires were a series of routine searches to be carried out using the system, once an hour by default. Mangouste had come up with the idea not long after getting the system up and running, weeks before. These routine searches were defensive in nature – a quick digital survey of his own bank accounts, and certain accounts belonging to the Group at large, to see if any outside party had tried to gain access.

To see if someone was snooping around – and getting close.

Banks and other companies had used such technology for years: flagged files and the like. What made the system's trip wires special was obvious, of course: If somebody tripped one of them, you could learn about it in advance.

'Tell me,' Mangouste said.

'Tomorrow morning, just before ten o'clock, someone

at a private security firm in Las Vegas tries to access one of our offshore holdings.'

Mangouste sat down. He took a notepad and pen from the tray drawer and set them in front of himself. He said, 'Do we have a name? An IP address?'

'Not yet, but we're narrowing it. We're hoping to get something actionable on a tighter timeline – something we can move on today instead of tomorrow.'

'Tell me everything,' Mangouste said.

He picked up the pen and began writing notes as the caller spoke.

Chapter Twenty-seven

Dryden exited I-5 at Avenal ten minutes before two o'clock. The small town hugged the transition between the mountains to the west and the vast plain of Central Valley to the east, a flat checkerboard of farmland, green and gold, extending to the horizon.

They could already see the scrapyard; it had been visible even before Avenal itself. It lay south of town, overlooking the freeway, a series of ascending shelves cut into the side of a foothill ridge. It looked like an Incan terrace farm that somehow grew rusted-out vehicles and piles of sheet metal.

There was a single road leading south from Avenal toward the yard, winding with the curve of the foothill slope. A quarter mile short of the yard's front gate, Dryden stopped the Explorer on a rise. He pulled to the shoulder, reached down, and took the Zeiss scope from the floor near Marnie's feet. He rested his elbows on the steering wheel and studied what he could of the site.

It didn't appear to be in operation. Not today, at least, and probably not any day in recent years. Just inside the gate — a metal fence section on rollers, closed at the moment — Dryden could see a double-wide trailer that must have once served as a kind of management office. Its windows were broken out, and waist-high weeds had grown up all around it, blocking the one visible entry door.

Beyond the trailer lay the expanse of the scrapyard itself, row upon row of stacked wreckage: crushed cars, appliances, torn and twisted structural metals that might have come from demolished buildings. Dryden pictured dump trucks loaded with scrap, rolling in from torn-down shopping malls and office mid-rises all over central California. Material just valuable enough to escape the landfill, but not urgently needed by anyone right now. There was probably a few decades' worth of it here.

The yard formed three terraces, like broad, shallow stair treads cut into the hillside, the whole thing stretching maybe half a mile down the face of the slope. Wide empty lanes ran between the stacked piles of junk, big enough to admit the heavy machinery that must have piled it all up, long ago.

There was no sign of Dale Whitcomb, but that was what Dryden had expected – and not just because they were early. If Whitcomb was here, he had probably been here for hours. He would almost certainly be watching the approach road right now, from some concealed place in the ruins.

'This is going to be tricky,' Marnie said. 'He's not expecting us. How do we convince him we're on his side?'

'If he's smart, it won't be a problem.'

'What do you mean?'

'We have the machine with us. That should demonstrate well enough that we're the good guys.'

'Why do you say that?'

'Because if the bad guys had the machine, they wouldn't bring it here and risk losing track of it again. And they wouldn't need to, anyway. If they were to recover this thing, I don't think they'd worry about loose ends like Whitcomb anymore. What damage could he do, if he didn't have the machine himself? Who could he convince to help him, if all he had were stories? He'd sound like a nutcase in a tinfoil hat.'

'So if Whitcomb is smart,' Marnie said, 'we don't have to worry about him shooting us.'

'Something like that.'

'What if he's not smart?'

'If he's made it this far, I'm not worried.'

Dryden set the scope aside, put the Explorer back in gear, and accelerated forward.

Where the rolling gate met the scrapyard's perimeter fence – an eight-foot-high chain-link affair, no barbed wire at the top – the latch mechanism was secured with what looked like a bicycle lock. Which wasn't locked. Dryden slipped the thing out of the way and rolled the gate aside. It creaked and whined on bearings that hadn't been oiled in a very long time.

There was no way to tell whether anyone had driven through the entrance recently. The dry, hardpan ground might as well have been concrete. Dryden walked back to the Explorer and rolled through the opening.

They drove a single loop of the scrapyard, just inside the fence. At each place where one terrace met another, there were shallow gravel ramps to allow passage. The rows of piled scrap were enormous, standing three stories high in places. It was like a scaled-up version of a supermarket, with the stock shelves rearing high above twenty-foot-wide aisles.

Passing the end of each open lane, they slowed and stared down its length as far as they could see. Most lanes ended in blind turns, suggesting a random maze of unseen passages beyond.

There was no sign of Whitcomb, or anyone else – until they came to the lot's southeast corner.

Dryden stopped. He was looking to his left, out the driver's-side window. He heard Marnie lean forward to look past him. He buzzed the window down and stared.

Twenty feet in past the mouth of an open lane was a makeshift fire pit: an old steel tractor rim that had been rolled into the middle of the channel and laid flat.

Thin tendrils of smoke snaked up from inside it.

'Let's take a look,' Dryden said.

He killed the engine and got out, taking one of the Berettas in one hand and the plastic hardcase in the other. Leaving the machine unguarded for even a minute felt like a very bad idea.

He shut the driver's door behind him as Marnie came around the hood. She had her Glock held ready.

There was no sign of anybody near the fire pit. Beyond it, the open lane between the stacks of scrap metal stretched away for nearly a hundred feet, to where it bent ninety degrees to the right, out of view. Between the fire pit and the distant corner, there were no openings leading away on either side.

Dryden crossed to the tire rim and crouched next to it. There was a bed of mostly cooled embers at the bottom, the carbonized remnants of what might have been ply-wood scraps – whatever firewood had been available amid the heaps of junk in this place.

There was an improvised grill suspended across the rim, some kind of grate that might have covered an air return duct in a building, years or decades ago. On the stony ground beside the rim, two metal cans stood open and empty. Their labels were gone, either torn off or burned off. It was clear the cans themselves had been used as makeshift pans to cook whatever had been inside them.

'Looks like he spent some time here,' Dryden said.

'We don't know this was Whitcomb. Maybe high school kids come out here to party. Seems like the kind of place for that.'

'I don't see any beer cans or cigarette butts,' Dryden said.

Marnie shrugged. 'Litter-conscious high school kids.'

'Funny.'

Dryden turned in a slow circle, studying the rows of scrap metal on both sides. They seemed to form unbroken walls running from one end of the lane to the other. Except –

'Look at this,' Dryden said.

He went to the north-side wall, twenty feet farther in from the fire pit. There was a sheet of corrugated metal, the kind people used for pole barn roofs, leaning against the wall of scrap. The sheet stood upright, easily four feet by eight. Dryden took hold of one edge and pulled it sideways.

Behind it was a framed doorway leading into the scrap pile itself.

'What the hell?' Marnie said.

She came up beside Dryden. They stood and stared.

It was clear within seconds what they were seeing. Embedded in the base of the huge scrap pile was a standard-sized shipping container – the kind of modular unit that could serve as a train car, a semitrailer, or a massive cargo crate aboard a ship.

This one had been set down at a rough angle at the bottom of the stack of wreckage, and then mostly covered by it over time; only one corner of the container was visible, exposed like a portion of a fossil jutting from a shale outcropping.

The framed metal doorway was wide open; its door appeared to have been torched off and discarded ages ago. Where the hinges had been cut through, the exposed metal was long since rusted and pitted.

The space beyond the threshold loomed black like the depth of a cave. Dryden could smell the air inside – lots of smells, and none of them good.

'Got a flashlight?' he asked.

He glanced at Marnie and saw that she was already holding a pocket Maglite. She clicked it on and aimed its beam into the darkness. Dryden ducked and stepped through the opening, and Marnie followed.

The inside of the container was more claustrophobia-inducing than Dryden had guessed. In a normal one of these units, an adult could stand upright with headroom to spare. Not this one. It had been compressed by the tons of weight piled atop it. The metal roof sagged in bulges, reducing the ceiling height to maybe five feet. The walls bowed outward to compensate. Here and there, where the sides met the top, the welded seams had torn like foil under the stress; scrap metal crowded inward through the ripped openings.

The floor of the unit was pooled with rainwater in places, all of it rusty brown. Half submerged in the farthest of these, just visible in the light beam, lay the remains of some animal, probably a raccoon. Dryden could see a rib cage and a few tufts of fur.

Much closer, only a few feet from the doorway, someone had made a crude bed out of a bench seat from a pickup truck. There were ratty old movers' blankets hanging off one end, as if kicked there after a night's sleep.

Dryden put a hand on Marnie's arm and guided the light to a point beside the bed.

Where the floor was spotted with blood.

'Shit,' Marnie whispered.

'Hand me the light.'

Marnie pressed it into Dryden's hand; he crossed to the bench seat and knelt beside it. The blood was mostly dried on the metal floor, in little dime-sized spatters. But a small amount had filled an indentation in the surface, some kind of stamped rivet hole about as deep as a tablespoon. The blood that filled it wasn't exactly liquid, but it wasn't dry either. In the harsh glare of the Maglite beam, it looked tacky.

Marnie crouched next to him, her eyes fixed on the same indentation.

'I've seen plenty of blood,' Dryden said, 'but I never had to guess how long it'd been there. This is more like your line of work.'

Marnie leaned closer, narrowing her eyes. 'Maybe twelve hours. Maybe longer.' She pointed to the sides of the indentation, discolored by a kind of high-water mark of dried blood. The tacky portion was lower down in the dimple. 'It's had time to settle. Time for some of the water content to evaporate off. I never know for sure until I hear from forensics, but after a while you get pretty good at guessing what they're going to say.'

At the edge of the light beam, beneath the makeshift bed, something caught Dryden's eye. He reached under and drew the object out into the light: a leather wallet. He flipped it open.

Most of its contents appeared to have been taken. There were only empty slots where credit cards would have been. Only a bare plastic sleeve in place of a driver's license. No cash, of course.

All that remained was a ticket stub from a movie theater: AMC CUPERTINO SQUARE 16.

'Cupertino is a few miles from San Jose,' Marnie said.

Dryden nodded. 'Where Dale Whitcomb lived. Where he worked, anyway.'

He stared at the stub, then at the dried and congealing blood.

'If the Group figured out that Whitcomb was coming here,' Marnie said, 'then they could have known about the meeting, too. Including the time it was supposed to take place. They could be hidden somewhere outside right now.'

'If it's the Group that got him. If it wasn't just some transient that lived in this container, and attacked him out in the scrapyard and dragged him back here. Granted, that doesn't sound all that damned plausible, when you look at the odds. I mean, if someone killed him, I guess the smart money should be on the people hell-bent on killing him. Except . . .'

He trailed off, his attention suddenly fixing on the wallet. The empty sleeve where the driver's license would have been. And the ticket stub.

'Interesting,' Dryden said.

'What is?'

Before Dryden could answer, the space around them darkened. On impulse, they both looked at the flashlight, but its beam still shone as bright as before.

Then, from behind them, came a man's voice. 'Weapons down. Slowly.'

Chapter Twenty-eight

Dryden felt his hand tense around the Beretta. Felt Marnie's entire body go rigid beside him, the sensation transmitting through the point of contact between their shoulders.

'Do it,' the man in the doorway said.

Marnie turned her head halfway toward Dryden, her breath coming in fast, shallow bursts.

Dryden pictured the sequence of moves it would take to open fire on the newcomer. Four things to do: spin in place from his kneeling position, raise the Beretta, center it on the target, pull the trigger.

The man in the doorway only had to do one thing – assuming he had his weapon leveled already. Or two things. Two shots in rapid succession. Dryden and Marnie, right there in the guy's field of fire, at can't-miss distance. Damn near punching distance.

No contest.

'We're putting them down,' Dryden said. 'Stay calm.'

Marnie's head turned the rest of the way, her eyes locking onto his. *Are you sure?*

'It's okay,' Dryden said. He lowered his shoulder and eased the Beretta onto the metal floor, and let it go. Marnie hesitated, her breathing still fast, then did the same.

'Stand up and turn toward me,' the newcomer said.

Dryden got his feet beneath him and stood. He turned and saw a man maybe sixty years old, dark hair going gray, hard features, sharp eyes. The guy was just outside the doorframe, lit by the indirect sunlight in the channel between the scrap piles.

A second man stood behind the first, ten years younger, blond hair going thin on top.

Both men held pistols. The man in the doorway had his leveled on Dryden, but the guy's gaze was pointed elsewhere. It was focused on the plastic case Dryden still held in his other hand.

'You know what this is, don't you,' Dryden said.

The man nodded just visibly. 'Open it.'

Dryden unlatched the case. He eased the lid open with his free hand, so neither the machine nor the tablet computer would come loose.

The man stared into the red glow shining through the machine's slats. For a moment he seemed almost entranced by it. Then he raised his eyes and looked back and forth between Dryden and Marnie. 'Who are you people?'

Dryden said, 'We're on your side – Dale. But you're a smart guy, right? So you must already know that.'

The man seemed to consider these words, holding Dryden's gaze. Then he exhaled softly and nodded, and lowered his gun.

'Where are Curtis and Claire?' Dale Whitcomb asked.

'Curtis is dead,' Dryden said. He watched the news hit Whitcomb like an elbow to the chest. Watched him brace for whatever was next.

'Claire's been abducted,' Dryden said. 'I believe she's alive. I believe we can get her back.'

Whitcomb stood there in the metal doorway, trying to process it all. At last he stepped back to let the two of them exit.

'Let's talk,' Whitcomb said.

The four of them sat on the hard ground around the improvised fire pit. The wind coming down out of the mountains was chilly, coursing through the shadowy channels of the scrapyard. Dryden found a few short lengths of two-by-four lumber in the back of the Explorer, and set them on the bed of embers. Within a minute they began to blaze.

He also brought the bag with Curtis's binders in it.

Whitcomb addressed Dryden and Marnie. 'You know my name. I'd like to know yours – and how you've ended up here.'

Dryden took stock of the man. Dale Whitcomb looked exhausted, though not the same way Claire had. Whitcomb was stressed, not tired. Instead of sleep, he needed half an hour with a punching bag, pounding it until his knuckles were cracked and bleeding. Beyond the frayed nerves, he looked like a decent enough guy. Claire had trusted him; that counted for a lot.

'Fair enough,' Dryden said.

He introduced himself and Marnie, then spoke for ten minutes, covering the basics of what had happened since midnight. Claire's phone call, the race to the trailer in the Mojave, Claire's abduction, Curtis's death. Then Santa Maria, the tower, Marnie.

When Dryden finished, Whitcomb introduced the blond man. His name was Cal Brennan, and he and Whitcomb had known each other for more than thirty years.

'We served together, way back,' Whitcomb said. 'Our careers took different paths, but we kept in touch. Brennan's here because I trust him, and because he can put together the kinds of resources we need, to go after the people we're up against. I've brought him up to speed on everything I know. He hasn't seen one of these machines in action yet, but . . . he's aware of the kind of work I do. We'll turn this one on and demonstrate it, as soon as we're done talking.'

Brennan's gaze kept going to the plastic case that held the machine. It was sitting on the ground between Dryden and Marnie, along with the bag full of binders.

Brennan, fifty years old, give or take, looked like a guy who rarely smiled. There were no laugh lines around his eyes. He looked like a hardass. He was also tanned in a way that suggested he had recently come from someplace even sunnier than California. He had a pair of Oakleys hanging from his shirt collar, their plastic bands scratched to hell as if someone had taken steel wool to them. Dryden had seen that effect before, in places where windblown sand was a constant feature of life. He would have put serious money on Cal Brennan having some connection to the world of private security contractors. He had the look.

Whitcomb turned to Dryden and Marnie. He seemed about to speak but then stopped himself, struck by something. He glanced at the nearby shipping container, its empty doorframe still exposed, and then looked back at Dryden.

'When you first saw me from inside there,' Whitcomb said, 'you knew who I was. Had you seen a picture of me somewhere?'

Dryden shook his head.

'Then how did you know?' Whitcomb said.

'Because of the wallet,' Dryden said. 'It was missing everything that could identify you in any official way, but it had a movie ticket stub from Cupertino in it. That was strategic, on your part. You knew the Group might get to Curtis, and learn about this meeting. And if they showed up here, you wanted them to find something that made it look like you were dead. Something they'd have to wonder about, at least. Blood on the ground, a wallet with a ticket stub from where you live – the Group would have picked up on that. They know where you live. But if the Group didn't find this place . . . if some random person came along instead, and saw the blood and the wallet, and called the cops . . . you'd never want *them* to tie your name to this location, on some official record. That really would bring the Group straight here. They might have shown up at this place days ago, if the cops found your wallet here today. Right? So that's why there was a ticket stub and nothing else. Something the Group would associate with you . . . but the police wouldn't. Best of both worlds.'

Whitcomb nodded, studying Dryden.

'You're already looking at this game the way I do,' Whitcomb said. 'Chess in four dimensions.'

Something in the way the man said it chilled Dryden,

though he tried not to show it. He only nodded, and waited for him to start talking.

'The way Claire understood it,' Whitcomb said, 'and the way she explained it to you, this technology was discovered by a fluke. Bayliss Labs stumbled onto it without any idea what they were looking for. Right?'

Dryden nodded.

Whitcomb leaned over the improvised fire pit, holding his hands out to the heat. 'It wasn't a fluke,' he said. 'It wasn't *just* a fluke. My people at Bayliss may have stumbled onto the design, but they were being pushed toward it. They were looking for it without knowing it.'

Dryden traded a glance with Marnie, then looked at Whitcomb again and waited for him to go on.

'I need to start a little further back,' the man said. 'Actually a lot further back, but it won't take long. Please bear with me.'

Far away to the west, in the wooded foothills rising above the scrapyard, a crow screamed and took to the air. Dryden turned and saw it, a tiny speck of black against the early afternoon sky.

'My father served in World War II,' Whitcomb said, 'in North Africa and Europe. He landed in Morocco under Patton, November 1942. My dad was infantry, but a few weeks into the invasion he was transferred to a group under the Office of Strategic Services, OSS, which was military intelligence. He had a background they liked: radio engineering, pretty advanced work at Stanford before the war. OSS had a job for him right away. Scout planes had seen something out in the desert in northern Algeria, some small German installation, all by itself in the middle of nowhere. Someone up the chain wanted to know what the hell it was, so my dad and his guys went in with a commando unit. The Germans defending that site must have thought it was pretty important, because they fought to the last man. When my father and his team finally got in to look at the place, they found most of it demolished. But not all of it. From what they could see, it had been some type of research station. There was one machine in particular that seemed to be the main event. A great big thing, the size of a pool table, with cables running out to speakers beside it. A radio of some kind, they thought. Its power supply had been cut, and someone had put a few bullets through its casing, but nothing vital had been hit. They got it powered up and switched it on, but at first all they heard was static. Then, every so often, they'd hear radio traffic coming through. Mostly it was music, sung in local languages, like what they'd heard on the streets in Moroccan towns. It was strange as hell to hear that stuff being broadcast on the radio, though, in German-occupied North Africa.'

A knot in one of the two-by-fours popped in the fire pit, sending an ember arcing out onto the dirt beside Whitcomb. He hardly seemed to notice.

'My father and his people only had control of that site for a day before word came that heavier German forces were en route. Other teams from OSS had arrived by then. They boxed up all the paperwork they could salvage and carted it off, but the equipment itself was too heavy to move on short notice. The commando unit rigged everything with high explosives, including the big machine with the speakers. They blew it all to scraps, and then everyone got out of there. In those hours that my father had been able to listen to the machine, and the static, he only heard one thing he could actually make sense of. One thing in English: the chorus of a song apparently titled "She Loves You." He heard those three words and then the word *yeah* repeating a few times before he lost the signal.'

Dryden had been staring down into the flames. His gaze snapped up now, meeting Whitcomb's. Beside him, Marnie did the same.

Whitcomb nodded. 'He heard that in the desert in North Africa, in 1942. At the time, he had no reason to think it was anything strange. Just some song he wasn't familiar with. How it was being broadcast in Algeria, he couldn't imagine. Maybe someone was transmitting English music out of occupied France. Maybe the machine could pull in signals from that far out, all the way across the Mediterranean. Or farther. Maybe Britain.'

Whitcomb took hold of a two-by-four sticking out of the tire rim on his side. He used it like a poker, prodding at the bed of coals below.

'I saw for myself the moment it hit him,' he said. 'I remember the date. February 9, 1964. I was ten years old. I guess just about anyone my age remembers the Beatles on *The Ed Sullivan Show*, but it's not the show itself I remember now. What I remember is my dad getting up off the couch, his expression like I'd never seen it before. I remember him going into the kitchen and splashing water on his face, and my mom asking him what was wrong, and I remember that he couldn't answer her. He went up in the attic and got out some old boxes of his stuff from the war. Journals he'd kept at the time. In 1964, he was still in the military. Still working in intelligence. I remember him putting his coat on, after he came back downstairs, and saying he had to go to work. And then he left, and I didn't see him again for weeks.'

Whitcomb set aside the two-by-four and went on. 'I learned the whole story years later, when I was in military intel myself, and working with him. In the days after that television broadcast, my father tracked down some of the former OSS men who'd been with him in North Africa. Men who'd gone to that site. Together they got clearance to dig into the old paperwork that had been found there, and even to lead an expedition out to that spot in the Sahara where the site had been. They didn't find much there. They had better luck with the boxes of papers, which were lab notes by the Germans who'd built that machine, in 1942. But the notes were incomplete. Most of them had been burned before the American commandos secured the site. What was left was . . . frustrating. Like a treasure map missing half the route, including the X to mark the spot.'

'The US military wanted to build their own version of that machine?' Dryden asked. 'If they could figure it out?'

Whitcomb nodded. 'But there was more to it than that. Think of all the questions they had to consider. Had those few Germans out in the desert really been the only ones who knew about this technology, or did others know? If there were others, what happened to them? When the US and Russia divided up Nazi scientists after the war, like battle spoils, could the Russians have gotten someone who knew how to build one of those machines? In 1964, when my father and his colleagues started digging into this, the Cold War was pretty close to its worst days. It was like the whole government ran on paranoia. There were serious incentives to look into this matter. But . . . there was also no proof any of it was true. Just my father's say-so, versus all common sense. The one bit of evidence he had was his journal from the North Africa campaign; he'd actually written that Beatles line in it. In '64, the military went as far as running chemical analysis on the ink he'd used to write it, and they determined it was a hell of a lot older than the song "She Loves You." I think that test bought my father and his friends more credibility than anything else, but only to a point. Try looking at it from the military's perspective, back then. What's the more likely explanation? That an intel officer really heard a message from the future, back in 1942, or that he found a way to make ink that could fuck with the chemical tests? What would you believe?'

Marnie said, 'So what happened?'

'A half measure,' Whitcomb said. 'The military ana-lyzed the paperwork from that site and pulled from it everything they could make sense of. Everything that offered a hint of how the machine might have worked. They weren't willing to spend money on trying to build another one; there had to be a million ways to interpret those technical notes. A million different machines you could build, on the off chance one would be the right one. If there *was* a right one. If the whole thing wasn't a fantasy.'

'So what was the half measure?' Dryden said.

'Sitting back and watching. Watching the world, and watching new communication technologies emerge naturally, over the decades. Scrutinizing the details, seeing if some new field of work started to look oddly familiar – along the lines of those old German tech notes. I've always thought it was a smart approach. Whether the Germans back then just made a shot in the dark, or even if they had some equivalent of a Nikola Tesla, way ahead of his time, it stood to reason someone else would eventually discover the same technology again. We figured by watching closely enough we might actually see it coming. Some project at a place like MIT or Caltech might be stumbling in the right direction and not even realize it . . . but we would. For that matter, we could give them a little push now and then, this way or that way, based on the notes from 1942. Like that kids' game, warmer or colder, only they wouldn't know they were playing it. That's how I ended up at Bayliss Labs. Their work with neutrinos, starting a few years back . . . the devices they were building . . . it was uncanny how well they matched those old notes. They were on the right track without knowing it. Once I became head of the company, I was able to give them a few nudges. Educated guesses that were more educated than I let on. Like I said, the end result wasn't a fluke. Not just a fluke, anyway.'

'So the military knows what Bayliss created,' Marnie said. 'If they sent you to oversee it –'

Whitcomb shook his head. 'They sent me to try. I never told them I succeeded. When the damn thing finally worked, my reaction was genuine. It scared the hell out of me. I could see then how dangerous it could be, and what people would do to get control of it. The approach Claire told you about – my putting together a list of powerful people I trusted – that was all I could think of. At the time, I wasn't seeing it in terms of destroying the thing, disinventing it. I just wanted to get it into safe hands. I thought that was possible, then. I don't anymore. This technology needs to disappear. If we're lucky, it'll be another half a century before someone else invents it. Maybe the world will be readier for it by then.'

He said the last part like he didn't put much stock in it. He started to say more, but Dryden cut him off.

'Wait a second. The machine your father found, in 1942 . . . how did it hear something more than twenty years in the future? Are you saying the Germans had a system like the Group has today? How could they? It takes computers, search engines –'

Whitcomb shook his head again. 'If you want to *control* what you hear in the future, then you need search engines. But to just *hear* the distant future, a pretty crude feedback loop between two of these machines could be rigged up. That's what the Germans had. It would have been primitive, compared to what we're up against now.'

'Let's get to that part,' Marnie said. 'The Group. Curtis said in his letter that you know something about them.'

Whitcomb's eyes went past the fire pit to the machine in its plastic case.

'I've known about them for years,' he said. 'In a way, they're the original owners of this technology.'

Chapter Twenty-nine

'There was another side to the work my father did,' Whitcomb said, 'and that I later did. It wasn't just about trying to re-create these machines. There was all that paranoia I mentioned. The fear that some other government would build one of these things, if it were possible. We wondered if anyone in Germany remembered this research. If they'd shared it with others. We did a lot of snooping to find out – human intel, eavesdropping, anything we could manage. Over the years we picked up a few crumbs. We ended up pretty certain nobody else in the world knew how to build one of these. But we also learned there were people just like us out there: people who knew there had been a working model once and wanted to reinvent it.'

'Were they from the original project?' Dryden said.

'Not really. I don't believe any of the initial researchers survived the war – but some of their knowledge did. As far as we could piece it together, we think there were detailed project files kept somewhere in Berlin, and in the last days before the city fell, somebody who understood the value of those files got them out of there. Out of harm's way and into a hiding place. We think it was a German soldier, probably someone who'd done security for the project along the way. Then at some point in the postwar, he took that information to people who could make use of it. His own idea of *safe hands* to put it in, I suppose.'

'What kind of hands?' Marnie said.

'Rich ones. Old money, aristocratic types. That's what all our sources pointed to. We never had absolute certainty on every last name, but we had very solid hunches. I got the impression they were people who weren't all that happy with how the war turned out.'

Dryden fixed his gaze on Whitcomb. 'You're saying the Group are –'

'I don't think they fit any simple category. I think they're a mix of a lot of things that most of the world has tried to leave behind. My father used to say power has a good memory for bad ideas. The people this German soldier took the project files to . . . it makes sense he would have chosen people whose views he agreed with. These days, the Group is made up of their children and grandchildren; who knows what exactly their goals are. We've seen for ourselves what they'll do to achieve them. That's enough for me.'

To the west, above the hills, the crow screamed again. Dryden could see it circling, catching some kind of updraft coming off the terrain.

'In any case,' Whitcomb said, 'those old files weren't enough to let them actually rebuild one of these machines. Same problem we had. So they settled on the same strategy: watch and wait. I didn't appreciate how good they might be at it. Not until it was too late.'

Marnie put her hands to her face and rubbed her eyes. 'Maybe they just want money. Maybe it's not anything ideological, or political. Just money. Isn't that all that matters to people like that, in the end?'

There was a wishfulness in the way she said it.

In response, Whitcomb pointed at the black bag with Curtis's binders sticking out of the top. 'Did either of you look at that material? I know you read Curtis's letter, but did you get to the printouts?'

Dryden shook his head. 'I glanced at the binders, but that was it. We haven't had time to do more than that.'

'It's interesting reading,' Whitcomb said. 'Curtis e-mailed me copies of those files before we broke contact. I didn't bother with the computer code stuff – I'm not a programmer – but the last batch there, all the Group's internal e-mails . . . there's a hell of a lot to learn from it.'

'The few e-mails I read didn't make much sense,' Dryden said.

Whitcomb nodded. 'Most of them don't. Some do.' He held his hand out toward the open bag. 'Let me show you something.'

Dryden slid the fifth binder out of the bag and handed it to Whitcomb. The man opened it and paged quickly through the bound stack of printed e-mails, zeroing in on some particular passage. Finally he stopped.

'There's a chain of messages here that contain file attachments,' Whitcomb said. 'Text files. Curtis was able to open those attachments and print them. The e-mails themselves are vague and pretty meaningless, but the attachments are clips from newspaper articles. Future articles. Take a look.'

He passed the open binder to Dryden and Marnie.

The first article began at the top of the printed page. The headline read: EVERSMAN WINS 54–46

The first sentences of the article removed any doubt over what the headline was referring to:

At the stroke of 11.00 p.m. Eastern Time, as polls closed in California and Oregon and Washington, Hayden Eversman officially became the next president of the United States. Thirty minutes later, before a jubilant crowd at Boston's Fenway Park, Eversman took to the podium to declare victory.

The snippet of the article ended there. Dryden looked up at Whitcomb, along with Marnie.

'This is the outcome of the next election?' Marnie asked.

'I've never heard of Hayden Eversman,' Dryden said. 'How is he the next president, when the election is a year from this fall? Everyone who's running is already in the race.'

'He's not the next president,' Whitcomb said. 'Look at the dateline.'

Dryden looked down and focused on what he'd skipped over before: the slug of text just below the article's headline.

AP – Wednesday, November 6, 2024.

Chapter Thirty

Keep reading,' Whitcomb said. 'There's more to it.'

Dryden turned the page to the next printed article. This one came from the same year as the first, 2024, but from an earlier point in time: four weeks before the election – October 8. In the simple text format of the attachment, the headline was the same size and font as the rest of the article, though in an actual newspaper, this headline would have screamed from the page in letters three inches tall:

HAYDEN EVERSMAN SHOT TO DEATH IN DES MOINES

'What the hell?' Marnie said.

As with the previous article, only the first several sentences were included, but that was enough to cover the basics. According to the story, Eversman had been speaking at an outdoor venue in Des Moines when he was killed. The bullet had come from some distance away, probably a rifle shot, and as of print time, no suspect had been named. Hayden Eversman, the Democratic candidate, had held a comfortable lead over his Republican opponent, whose name didn't appear in this part of the story.

Marnie looked up at Whitcomb. 'How can both of

these articles exist?' she asked. 'How does this man win the election and also get killed a month earlier?'

'The articles are from different versions of the future,' Whitcomb said. 'Just like there would have been different articles about the death toll from that building collapse in Santa Maria. Different outcomes, different news reports.'

Marnie nodded slowly, getting the idea squared in front of her. 'In one future,' she said, 'Hayden Eversman gets elected president, and in a different version, he gets killed a few weeks before that.'

Whitcomb nodded. 'In the construction site, you two changed something that was a few minutes from happening. These articles show how the Group changed something that was nine years away.' He nodded at the binder. 'In fact, they changed it more than once. Keep going.'

Dryden turned to the next attachment: a third article about Eversman. Another headline that would have been shouted across the printed page in real life:

HAYDEN EVERSMAN'S PLANE CRASHES – NO SURVIVORS

This article was dated September 15, 2024, another few weeks before the previous one. The text told of Eversman's campaign jet going down just minutes after takeoff from Richmond International Airport in Virginia. The crash investigation had not yet begun, but even this article, written within hours of the incident, reported that the wreckage was a debris field more than a mile long – indicating the plane had exploded in midair.

The next article, the fourth one, was dated June 26. The headline and story had Eversman once again being shot and killed, this time while speaking to a crowd in Tampa.

The fifth article was similar: another shooting death, though it took place on June 5 in Chicago.

The sixth article described another midair explosion of Eversman's campaign jet, after takeoff from LAX on May 23 – just two weeks after he'd officially claimed the Democratic nomination.

The seventh and final article was dated Wednesday, May 1, 2024. Both the headline and the text drew allusions to Robert F. Kennedy, for obvious reasons. Hayden Eversman, minutes after making a victory speech upon winning the California primary, was shot and killed. It didn't happen in a hotel kitchen. It happened on the sidewalk five feet from the limousine he was walking toward. No suspect had been detained in the few hours before the article was published.

'What the hell is all this?' Marnie asked. 'They're trying out different ways to kill someone who would have become president nine years from now? And how are they doing that? How are they arranging an assassination almost a decade in the future?'

'It could be done,' Dryden said. 'You could use sealed orders, blind go-betweens. Tell someone, 'Hold this envelope for nine years and then deliver it to so-and-so.' If you pay people enough, you can get them to do anything. Obviously it works. It looks like they did it six times.'

'Which in itself doesn't make sense,' Marnie said. She looked around at the others. 'Why find six different ways to kill him? After it worked once, wouldn't that be enough?'

Whitcomb managed a smile. 'You'd think so.'

'Why do this at all?' Dryden asked. 'I don't mean why kill him, I mean why kill him *then*? In 2024. If the Group wants this guy dead before he becomes president, it would be easier to kill him right now, when he's nobody.'

'Much easier,' Whitcomb said. 'And they've already done that with other people. You read as much in Curtis's letter, and I've seen the e-mails that reference some of those murders.'

'So why is Hayden Eversman different?' Marnie asked.

Whitcomb shook his head. 'I don't know. I've racked my brains over it, and all I've got are half-assed maybes. Like maybe it's not Eversman they care about. Maybe they want his running mate to be president, and killing Eversman right at the end is a way to pull that off. But –'

'But that doesn't work,' Marnie said.

Dryden nodded, flipping back through the preceding articles. 'If they wanted his running mate in office, they'd sit back and let Eversman win like he was supposed to, and *then* kill him.'

'That's right,' Whitcomb said. 'So I have no idea. I only showed you this to make the point that these people *are* thinking in terms of politics. They have big plans, and they're going to achieve them if we don't shut it all down.'

On those words, Whitcomb turned to Cal Brennan. Dryden looked at him, too. Sized him up again. The hard skin, the result of sunburn after sunburn. The sandblasted Oakleys. Dryden pictured the guy on a plane, maybe yesterday or the day before, flying in from Iraq or Syria or one of half a dozen other places.

'What sort of resources do you deal in, Brennan?' Dryden asked.

Brennan's eyes turned toward him. The eyes without laugh lines. 'Human resources.'

'Guys with guns,' Dryden said.

Brennan nodded. 'Among other hardware.'

Whitcomb spoke up. 'There's no clean way to go about this. It comes down to killing these people. All of them, if we can. Do either of you have a problem with that?'

He aimed the question at Dryden and Marnie.

'No,' Dryden said.

Marnie hesitated. Whitcomb and Brennan watched her.

'I'd want to know about collateral damage,' she said. 'Some of these people will have children around –'

'We'd be careful within reason,' Brennan said. He rattled it off like he was used to saying it. Spoken boilerplate.

'You need to find them all first,' Dryden said. 'Every location where they're set up. Wherever they've got their own versions of the machine, wherever their system is.'

Whitcomb was nodding. 'There's an intelligence aspect to it. We can manage it – between the printed e-mails and what I already knew of these people, there's a base of facts to start from. Besides . . . they've made it easy for us, in at least one way.'

Dryden waited for him to go on.

'Though the e-mails don't mention any names, they make

it clear there's one person in charge of the Group's activities in California, maybe the whole western US. A kind of regional head, you could call him. Like a caporegime in the Mafia. All the e-mails come across as if . . . well . . . as if the only people writing them are this man and a few others below him. Not a word from anyone above him.'

'You don't think they told the rest of the Group about the machines,' Dryden said, not asking. 'About the system, or any of it.'

'I'd almost guarantee it,' Whitcomb said. 'Why the hell would this guy hand that kind of power up to his superiors, anyway? *He's* the superior if he's got all this to himself.'

Dryden thought about that. It fit everything he'd ever learned about human nature. It was almost reassuring, in its own ugly way: a scrap of normalcy in the four-dimensional chess game.

'I still plan to take out as much of the Group as I can,' Whitcomb said, 'but as far as shutting down the system, erasing this technology right out of the world . . . I believe we can do all that here in California.' He pointed to the binder full of e-mails. 'I've read that material at least ten times now. I've made notes. I'm convinced they've got their entire system, including every machine they've built, in a single secure location. We find that site and hit it, it's game over. Then we destroy our own machine for good measure.'

'Wherever their machines are,' Dryden said, 'that's not where they took Claire. They were taking *me* to the machine site, before I got free. Claire was going

224

someplace else. We need to know where. We need to hit that site at exactly the same time we hit the other place, if we're going to save her.'

Whitcomb nodded. 'We will. We'll do this right.'

Dryden looked back and forth between Whitcomb and Brennan. 'So what's the first move? Whatever it is, we start right now.'

Brennan shook his head. 'No. We start ten and a half hours from now, at the soonest.'

The man was looking at the machine in its case as he finished saying it.

Dryden stared at him. Saw what he meant. Felt his pulse accelerate as his adrenaline spiked.

'You're not serious,' Dryden said.

'I am,' Brennan said. He turned his gaze on Whitcomb. 'I've listened without rejecting this, because I *do* know the kinds of projects you work on, and because in thirty years I've never heard you lie about anything. But you can't expect me to commit my people until I've seen for myself that this is real.'

Dryden took a step toward him, past the edge of the fire pit. 'My friend is locked in a room somewhere, being interrogated. I'm not burning ten and a half hours for nothing.'

Brennan shrugged. 'Have at it. I'll help as soon as I've seen proof.'

Dryden turned to Whitcomb. 'We start now. If your friend wants to wait –'

Whitcomb was already shaking his head. 'We can't do this piecemeal. We get one shot at it –'

'If Claire dies because we wasted half a fucking day –'

'If you were him,' Whitcomb said, nodding at Brennan, 'would you believe the rest of us? Think about it.'

Dryden started to answer, but stopped. He saw himself in Claire's Land Rover, in the darkness of the Mojave, right after she'd shown him the machine. He'd already seen the proof by then – the trailer and all that had happened there – but the fact was, he still hadn't believed her. Not right away.

Dryden ran a hand through his hair. 'Goddammit . . .'

He turned in place, saw Marnie looking at him, her own frustration palpable.

Then Dryden's eyes narrowed. A thought had come to him. Another memory from those few minutes in Claire's SUV.

'What is it?' Marnie asked.

Dryden shook his head. 'I need to think for a second.'

He stepped away from the fire, pacing, his gaze going everywhere and nowhere. He shut his eyes and let the memory come all the way through.

Then he opened them again and looked at his watch.

2.37 p.m.

'It was going to be two fifty-one,' he said. 'Two fifty-one this afternoon.'

'What's at two fifty-one?' Whitcomb asked.

Dryden ignored him. He turned and looked at Brennan again. 'You need proof? Fine. But we're not waiting for it. Fifteen minutes is all it'll take.'

'What do you mean?' the man asked.

Dryden said, 'You follow baseball?'

Chapter Thirty-one

Dryden leaned into his Explorer, put the key in the ignition, and turned on the radio. He stood there at the driver's-side door, using the seek button to cycle through the stations.

Marnie came up beside him, Whitcomb and Brennan close behind.

'What are you looking for?' Marnie asked.

'The Padres are playing right now,' Dryden said. 'Or they're about to be. At two fifty-one they'll be in the top of the second inning. I heard part of it on the machine ten and a half hours ago.'

He gave up on the seek button and used the knob, clicking one step at a time through the frequencies. Here and there, barely audible songs filtered through the distortion. He'd almost made it back around the dial when he heard a man's voice coming through the static, deep and measured, unmistakably familiar.

The game itself hadn't started yet. The announcer was talking about a sponsor, some insurance company in San Diego.

Dryden sat behind the wheel and opened the glove box; he found a pencil, then tore out the last page of his road atlas for something to write on. He pressed the page to the flat top of the center console, then stopped. He shut his eyes and put himself back in Claire's vehicle again, listening to the game.

'Almodovar,' he said. 'It was two balls, two strikes when I first heard it.'

He opened his eyes and began writing in the margin as the details came back.

'There was a curve ball – outside. That made it three-two. After that he hit the pop-up – two fifty-one, Claire said. It was foul, to the left. Count was still three-two, and then . . .'

He went quiet again, thinking. What had happened after the pop-up?

At the edge of his vision he saw the others watching him, waiting.

'Ball four,' Dryden said. 'The pitch right after the pop-up was ball four. Almodovar walked.'

He jotted it down, dropped the pencil in the cup holder, and got out of the vehicle. He held the page out to Brennan.

'That's more than a person could guess at,' Dryden said. 'Keep listening to the game. In a few minutes you'll be up to speed with the rest of us.'

Brennan took the page. From the Explorer's speakers the announcer kept talking, static-laden but easily discernible. Dryden's watch showed 2.40.

They waited. They stood near the vehicle as the game began and the minutes passed.

At 2.45, Marnie looked up and met Dryden's eyes, then Whitcomb's. Something had occurred to her – whatever it was, it made her breath catch.

'What?' Dryden said.

'These people,' Marnie said, 'the Group . . . their system lets them get information from the future – even years away. Police records, articles, anything. They learn about the future so they can change it, right?'

'Right,' Dryden said.

'So why don't they use it to change the past? Why don't they send a message to themselves one week ago, before things went wrong for them? Before Whitcomb and Claire and Curtis got away? Any kind of warning to themselves would fix everything, and that would be easy to do, the way the system works.'

Dryden thought about it. The idea hadn't occurred to him, in all the clamor of the day's thoughts, but Marnie was right. There was no reason the Group couldn't do that, given the system Curtis had described in his letter.

For a second he wondered if the Group could send a message even further back in time – months or years – but then he caught himself. That wasn't possible. The earliest point they could send a message back to would be the day they first had the system working. Before that, there would be no machinery to receive such a message. They could send something back a few weeks, no further.

But Marnie had nailed it: Even one week would change everything.

So why hadn't the Group done that already?

Whitcomb was shaking his head. 'I worried about it, too, until I read their e-mails. There's a long exchange where they go over this very point. They could do what you're describing . . . but they never will.'

Dryden and Marnie both stared at him, waiting for more.

'There's something you have to appreciate here that's not so obvious. It wasn't obvious to me. The people we're dealing with . . . they've been obsessed with the idea of this technology for their entire lives. They grew up with the secret of it, and the talk of it, like it was a religion: this impossible thing that existed once, and might return someday – like a savior. It was different for my father, and later myself. For us it was a technical goal, like stealth planes or cruise missiles. Something we wanted for the military – for the country. It was never going to be just ours. But the Group *did* want it for themselves. It was a personal obsession, and they've had seventy years to dwell on it. To dream up the things they would do with it – and the things they wouldn't.'

'Why *wouldn't* they send information back in time to themselves?' Marnie asked. 'That would be the most powerful way to use this stuff. By far.'

'Because they're terrified of trying it,' Whitcomb said. 'I'll show you the e-mails later. You'll see what I mean. It's the one thing they absolutely will not do.'

'But why?' Dryden asked. 'Why does that scare them?'

'Picture yourself doing it,' Whitcomb said. 'Imagine you type a text message to send to yourself one week in the past – a warning about something. Maybe you're in Florida on vacation, and the weather's sucked all week, so you're going to tell your past self to go to Colorado instead.'

'Okay.'

'You've got the message ready to go. All you have to do is tap SEND. Now think about it. What exactly is going to happen when you hit that button? From your point of view, standing there in Florida ... what's going to happen? Are you going to disappear from there, and reappear in Colorado? *Something* is going to happen. But what?'

Dryden stared. He thought about it. He traded a look with Marnie and saw her wrestling with it, too.

At last he said, 'I don't know what would happen to me.'

'Neither do they,' Whitcomb said. 'Seventy years trying to get their heads around it, and they don't have a clue. The only way to find out would be to try it, and nobody wants to do that. It scares them like nothing else in the world.'

'But you wouldn't always be a thousand miles from where you would have been,' Marnie said. 'It wouldn't have to be that extreme.'

Whitcomb shrugged. 'What if it's a foot? The problem is the same. There would always be some difference in the present, if you changed your past. The instant switchover to that difference ... what it would feel like to you ... that's the unknown. I wouldn't try it myself for a million dollars.'

A few feet away, the name *Almodovar* came over the Explorer's speakers. Next up to bat.

Brennan, leaning beside the open driver's door, glanced down at the page in his hand.

It was 2.49 by Dryden's watch.

'I think it's important to know their weaknesses,' Whit-comb said. 'Again, like a chess game. Their fear of screwing with the past is a big one.'

'Do they have any other weaknesses?' Marnie said.

Whitcomb smiled. 'Oh, yes.'

'Like what?'

Before Whitcomb could answer, Dryden said, 'Radio waves.'

He had voiced the thought even as it crossed his mind. The others turned to him.

'What do you mean?' Marnie asked. 'Radio is how it all works in the first place. How would it be a weakness –'

She cut herself off, catching at least part of what he meant.

'Exactly,' Dryden said. 'It *is* how it all works. So it's a weakness. The Group uses radio station broadcasts to grab information from the future. Could we use that against them somehow? Jam the signals, set up some kind of interference?'

'It might have worked in the beginning,' Whitcomb said. 'Not anymore.'

'Why not?' Dryden asked.

Over the speakers, Almodovar came to the plate.

'Because they knew that was a vulnerability,' Whitcomb said. 'Using radio stations. It was a weak link. Sooner or later, some stations would have noticed the software hacks. Or routine upgrades would erase them. Or a hun-dred other problems. Too much room for error, especially in the long run – like using the system to get news articles from ten years in the future.'

Almodovar swung and missed. Strike one.

'But how could they avoid using radio stations?' Marnie asked.

'They built one for themselves,' Whitcomb said. 'Sort of. This system of theirs . . . it's a boxed-in setup: their own little antenna sending out FM signals, with their machines right there to receive them. All of it together in a package about the size of a refrigerator, buried underground. According to the e-mails, it has a geothermal generator to power it, zero maintenance. They wanted it to be . . . future-proof. That way, in any version of the future, their system will still be there, underground, doing its job. *That's* why they can look ten years ahead in time.'

Fastball, low inside. Ball one.

'They said this thing would keep working,' Whitcomb said, 'even if the rest of the secure site burned down and took everyone there with it. Even the system's Internet connection, which it obviously needs, would survive. It's a pirated access, separate from the service for the rest of the buildings, and basically untraceable. They thought of everything.'

Another swing and a miss. One ball, two strikes.

'Pretty clever,' Dryden said.

Whitcomb nodded. Then: 'It's also very, very stupid. It creates their biggest weakness of all. It's how we're going to beat them.'

'What are you talking about?' Marnie asked.

Breaking ball, high over the plate. Ball two.

'This is it,' Brennan said.

Dryden looked at his watch. 2.51.

For a moment he returned his gaze to Whitcomb and thought of continuing the conversation.

Then Whitcomb waved it off. 'Tell you in a minute,' he said, and turned his attention to the game broadcast.

'Two and two on Almodovar, who has a four-game hitting streak coming into this one,' the announcer said. *'Curve ball outside, that'll make it three balls, two strikes. We've got one out and one runner on, top of the second, score is one-nothing San Diego.'*

Every word, every stressed syllable, matched what Dryden had heard in the Mojave ten hours and twenty-four minutes earlier. It was as though he'd been looking down a tunnel then, and was seeing down it from the other end now. The feeling was surreal in a way he had not expected.

Marnie turned to him. 'You okay?'

Dryden nodded. He blinked and took a hard breath to clear his head.

'Fastball, Almodovar gets a piece of it, pop-up foul left, still three and two.'

Brennan was staring at the page of jotted notes in his hand. The paper shook, just visibly, picking up a tremor in his arm.

'What do you say, Cal?' Whitcomb asked.

Brennan didn't answer. Didn't seem to have even heard him. He stared at the page as the crackling audio washed over him.

'Low and inside, and that'll do it. Ball four. Runners on first and second, Watkins comes to the plate.'

Brennan kept his eyes on the sheet of paper for another five seconds, though there was nothing more on it.

'Is that enough?' Whitcomb asked.

No reply.

A second later Brennan dropped the page on the Explorer's driver's seat, then turned and crossed to the fire pit twenty feet away. The binder full of e-mails was lying on the ground beside the closed plastic case with the machine inside it. Brennan stooped, picked up both the binder and the case, and tucked them under his left arm.

Then with his right hand he drew a pistol from his rear waistband and leveled it at the three of them.

'You're not destroying this thing,' Brennan said.

Chapter Thirty-two

For a long moment no one said a thing. The static-choked baseball game continued to wash from the Explorer's speakers.

Then Whitcomb spoke. 'What are you doing, Cal? What is this?'

'You're not destroying it,' Brennan said again.

His voice had none of its previous reserve. He was breathing quickly, and his cheeks had reddened even behind the rough surface of his tan.

Whitcomb spoke as if talking to a jumper on a ledge. 'Why don't you put the gun away? We're all rational here.'

'I'm rational,' Brennan said. 'You three are out of your minds.' He nodded to the case under his arm. 'It works. Christ, it *works*. Everything you said was true. Why would you want to throw this thing away?'

'Because it's dangerous,' Whitcomb said, 'and we'll never get another chance to put the genie back in the bottle. We can do that right now, if we destroy all of these things. The world will never know it existed.'

Whitcomb took a step forward. Brennan took a step back. He pressed his left arm tightly toward himself, holding the machine and the binder of e-mails securely.

'There's too much that can go wrong with this stuff,' Whitcomb said. 'You know that.'

Brennan shook his head. 'Too much goes wrong *without* it.' His eyes went from Whitcomb to Dryden and Marnie, back and forth. 'Listen to your own stories, for God's sake. Those four little girls out in the desert. The guys on the roof of that build site. All those people would be dead if it wasn't for this thing. And that's just one day's worth of using it.'

'The downside is still bigger,' Whitcomb said. 'What happens when governments get ahold of this technology? What about corporations? Political groups. We've already got people being murdered for things they haven't even done yet. You want a hundred different special interests using this stuff?'

'It doesn't have to come to that,' Brennan said. 'I can keep this one working copy, and never tell anyone. Why shouldn't I?'

'And leave the Group out there running around?'

Brennan shook his head. 'I'll do what we already planned. That was going to come down to me anyway. My firm, my manpower. I don't need your help for that.'

'You do,' Whitcomb said. 'You need my intel to do it the right way. If you get it wrong, you have no idea what's going to come down on you.'

Brennan tapped the binder of e-mails with his free hand. 'Everything you know came from this.'

Whitcomb shook his head. 'I know a lot more than what's in that binder. Don't do this, Cal. You're going to make a mistake, and then —'

'My firm has its own intelligence assets. Our Vegas office alone does counterintel work for three of the top twenty companies in the US We know what we're doing.'

He took another step backward, moving away from the three of them while keeping the gun leveled. It was clear he meant to back up some farther distance and then turn and run down the long channel between the scrap piles, to where it angled blindly to the right, a hundred feet away. His car was probably parked somewhere deep in the maze. If he made that corner, there would probably be no catching him. Getting in the Explorer and racing to block the exit road would be useless; Brennan could crash through the chain-link fence anywhere and drive away down the broad slope of the hillside. The freeway was right there at its base, a few hundred yards down.

Brennan took another step back. And another.

Dryden had one of Claire's Berettas in his own rear waistband, but going for it was pointless while Brennan had them all covered. When he turned to run, shooting at him would be easy. Accidentally hitting the machine would also be easy.

The man took another step back. He was ten feet beyond the fire pit now, thirty feet from where the three of them stood.

Whitcomb said, 'If you slip up at some point, next month or next week or tomorrow, these people will learn about it today. You don't understand what you're up against.'

'I'm a quick study,' Brennan said.

On the last word, Dryden saw a pinprick of light flash behind the man, high in the wooded hills west of the scrapyard. Half a second later, Brennan's head blew apart above his eyes.

Chapter Thirty-three

Dryden was moving even before the shot hit Brennan. He got a hand on Marnie's shoulder and shoved her sideways. The two of them, and Whitcomb, were standing at the mouth of the long channel between the scrap rows. To their left and right, the ends of the rows would provide cover from the shooter on the hillside.

Marnie staggered, caught her balance, and threw herself the rest of the way past the end of the row. Dryden caught a glimpse of Whitcomb going in the other direction, dropping flat, scrabbling fast for cover on the other side of the channel.

Adrenaline-rush math flashed through Dryden's thoughts in a tiny fragment of a second. How many shooters up there in the woods? Logic said it was just one, because two shooters would have synchronized their first shots – an easy opportunity to drop two targets before all the rest scattered.

There had only been one first shot, though.

Therefore, one shooter.

How much time would there be between shots?

Two seconds, maybe, if the shooter was skilled. Which seemed to be the case. Brennan could vouch for it.

Dryden threw himself after Marnie, behind the cover of the scrap metal stack. In the same quarter second that he cleared it, he heard the insectile whine of a rifle bullet passing close by, cutting through the space his head had just occupied.

He turned and looked back. He saw Whitcomb standing behind cover on the far side of the open lane, looking across at him and Marnie.

Between their two positions, in the wide space of the channel's mouth, the Explorer sat parked like an offered sacrifice. Its driver's-side door still hung open. The baseball game was still playing over the sound system.

Dryden stared at the vehicle. He expected a shot to punch through its front quarterpanel into the engine block. Or the fuel tank. Or the tires. Or all of the above.

Five seconds passed. Nothing happened.

Dryden understood. From the shooter's point of view, it was temporarily better to leave the vehicle drivable. To leave it as bait.

Across the lane, Whitcomb edged up to the corner of the stack he was hiding behind. He lowered his eye to a narrow horizontal gap between a pair of crushed car bodies, and looked through into the empty space of the channel. Toward the fire pit. Toward where Brennan had fallen.

'Brennan drove here in a rental,' Whitcomb called out. 'Parked it somewhere in these stacks. Probably has GPS on board. Whatever slipup he was going to make, looking for these people – next week, whenever – they probably saw it hours ago now. They would have narrowed down his name after that, and then where his car would be. Chess in four dimensions.'

Twenty seconds had passed since the last shot.

'If we get away,' Marnie said, 'would they have learned *that* a few hours ago? Would that make them send extra people to compensate?'

'They'll have seen police records and news articles showing someone died out here,' Whitcomb said. 'If those documents don't say anything about us . . . then no, the Group won't have known about us until right now.'

Whitcomb dropped his eye to the narrow gap again. Stared once more into the open channel.

'We can't leave without the machine,' he said. 'If they get it, the whole game's lost.'

He took a deep breath, then another. His body language made it clear what he intended to do.

'Don't be stupid,' Dryden said.

Whitcomb's eyes stayed locked on the plastic case. 'It's only thirty feet. Sixty there and back.'

'You won't make it fifteen.'

'I might. He's sighting on the vehicle right now, waiting for someone to run for it.'

'Takes about a second for a sniper to retarget,' Dryden said. 'Maybe less.'

'I'll be moving the whole time.'

'Yeah, straight toward him and then straight away. That's an easy lead.'

'We need the machine. There's no choice.'

'Whitcomb –'

'After the first shot, you should go for the vehicle. Move it to cover while he's distracted with me.' Whitcomb managed a smile. 'Or maybe he'll shoot you, and I'll survive. It's all good.'

241

The man turned and met Dryden's gaze across the space between them. He took another deep breath.

'Now or never,' Whitcomb said.

And ran.

Dryden watched the moment unfold in awful clarity. Saw it in a kind of precision that wasn't quite slow motion but might as well have been. Whitcomb was ten feet from cover when the zip of another bullet passed through the channel. Dryden saw the man flinch and draw to his right – which meant the sound must have passed just to his left – without breaking stride as he sprinted.

Then Dryden forgot about him and turned his focus on the Explorer, and broke from cover himself.

Behind him, Marnie was suddenly screaming.

He couldn't process the sound.

The world had scaled down to the strip of space between himself and the open door of the vehicle, fifteen feet away. His thinking had scaled down to the sequence of moves he needed to make. Simple actions in linear order. Planting each foot, pistoning with his legs, tilting his upper body forward, hurling himself at the Explorer.

The window in the open door burst right in front of him, close enough to shower his face with crumbs of tempered glass.

He rounded the door, didn't bother shutting it, crammed his body behind the wheel, ducked and turned the ignition the rest of the way forward. Heard the base-ball game momentarily cut out. Heard the engine rev and catch and roar. Heard the passenger-side window explode.

Felt another shower of glass bits. He reached up and worked the selector, already jamming his foot on the gas. Beneath him, the vehicle lurched forward like a living thing. Its momentum slammed the door shut beside him, and a second later the shadow of the tall scrap pile slid over everything.

Dryden braked.

Sat upright.

The Explorer was behind cover and running smoothly. No damage to anything except the two windows.

He looked down at himself. No injury. Nothing.

He sat there for five seconds, letting his pulse stabilize, letting his thoughts become words again. He took a breath and released it. It came out sounding like a laugh. Maybe it was. He had drawn the fire off Whitcomb after all. He'd have to give the guy some shit for that.

He opened the door and stood, and saw Marnie sitting ten feet away.

She was holding on to Whitcomb, who'd been shot through the neck.

Dryden ran to them and dropped to a knee.

Whitcomb had the plastic case in his hands – he even had the binder full of e-mails.

His blood was all over both things. It was coming out of the bullet wound in pulses. The carotid artery on the right side of his neck had been ripped open.

'They don't know you,' Whitcomb said. His voice was high and reedy; his windpipe had taken part of the hit.

Marnie had an arm around his shoulder, and one of his hands in her own.

'Don't try to talk,' she said, though she had to know it was pointless; Whitcomb would be gone in another minute. Two at best.

The man shook his head, his eyes hardening. Whatever he was saying, it mattered to him.

'They don't know you,' he said again. 'The Group. Don't know your names. Don't let them find out.'

Dryden nodded, if only to make the guy feel better in these last moments. Whitcomb's words made sense, but they were also obvious. Maybe it was some simple thought Whitcomb's brain had fixed on, as he faded.

The guy looked at Dryden. Seemed to read the patronizing thought in his expression. Whitcomb's eyes narrowed further. He looked angry.

'*License plate,*' he whispered. Then with great effort he jerked his head in the direction of the distant shooter. '*He'll see it when you go. Cover it. Put . . .*'

His breath hissed out. He sucked in another, and then his body was racked with a coughing fit. By the time it passed, he'd lost consciousness. He wasn't going to regain it. His breathing rattled in and out, weakening.

'We need to go,' Dryden said.

Marnie nodded, but her eyes stayed on Whitcomb.

'Do we bring him?' she asked.

Dryden thought about it. Then he thought of the man's last words. Whitcomb was right: The license plate had to be covered before they made their break. But with what? The dirt all around them was dry and sandy. Not so much as a handful of mud or clay to smear on the plate. Dryden scanned the nearest parts of the scrap pile. Nothing useful there.

Cover it.

Dryden looked at Whitcomb's unconscious body, each breath a little shallower.

'Christ . . .' Dryden said.

Marnie looked at him. 'What?'

Dryden only shook his head. Then he took the plastic case and the binder from Whitcomb's hands. He gave them to Marnie.

'Can you take those and buckle up in the passenger seat? We don't have much time.'

She stared. 'What are you going to do?'

'Please just do it,' Dryden said.

She hesitated another second. Maybe she knew what was about to happen – more or less – and maybe she could have stomached seeing it. Dryden had no doubt she'd seen worse things before. In her line of work, she might have seen even worse things than he had.

But he didn't want her to see this. He didn't want anyone to see it.

'Please,' he said.

Marnie stared – then nodded and stood with the case and binder. She took them around the back of the Explorer to the passenger side.

Dryden turned his attention on Whitcomb.

Still breathing, just audibly.

Still unconscious.

Never coming back.

Dryden grabbed a fistful of the man's shirt, below the collar. He dragged him around to the back end of the Explorer, then lifted him so that his back was positioned against the license plate.

Still breathing. Barely.

Dryden drew the Beretta from his waistband, put it to Whitcomb's chest and fired. Four times. The hollow-points made small holes on the way in, and huge ones coming out. They ripped through the back of Whitcomb's shirt, spraying a thick sheet of blood onto the license plate and the metal around it.

Dryden dropped the body and ran for the driver's door.

Twenty seconds later, doing 70, they crashed through the roller gate, fishtailed, and then accelerated north on the access road.

A single, wildly aimed shot hit the vehicle a second later. It skipped like a stone off the front corner of the hood, denting the metal. That was it. In another ten seconds they were beyond any possible range.

They got back on I-5, northbound. No goal at the moment but distance. Wind roared through the vehicle, through the blown-out front windows on each side.

For five minutes neither spoke.

The roadbed caught and scattered the hard sunlight, rendering it painful.

'He would have told you to do it,' Marnie said. 'Almost *did* tell you. There wasn't any other choice.'

Dryden kept his eyes on the road.

Marnie turned to him. 'Focus on what's next. What are we going to do?'

Dryden didn't answer right away. He thought of something Claire had said: that she had arranged security for Whitcomb and his family, a couple years back. In these past few days, when everything had gone bad, he must have hidden his family away somewhere safe. Someplace where, right now, they were waiting for him to come back.

'Hey,' Marnie said.

Dryden blinked. Glanced at her.

She indicated the machine and the binder of e-mails. 'He died to get these back. It can't be for nothing. What's our next move?'

Dryden nodded. He exhaled hard and pushed away every thought that wasn't practical.

'Hayden Eversman,' he said. 'The guy they want to stop from being president in nine years.'

'But who they're not killing in the present.'

Dryden nodded. 'They plan to kill him eventually, but they're afraid to try it now. There has to be a reason for that. I'd love to know what it is.'

'So would I.'

'Then let's find out where he is in 2015.'

Chapter Thirty-four

Where Hayden Eversman was, at that moment, was a hundred and twenty miles north and west of them, watching his four-year-old daughter try to put a pink cape on a shih tzu. The daughter's name was Brooke; Eversman and his wife had chosen it carefully after two weeks of considering every option they could think of. The shih tzu's name was Meatball; Brooke herself had picked that one, after five seconds of considering probably zero alternatives.

So far, Meatball didn't seem to grasp that the cape was supposed to go around his neck. As a result, the spectacle playing out on the living room carpet looked like the least dangerous bullfight in the history of the world.

Above the dog and the girl, the TV on the wall was tuned to C-SPAN. The current broadcast was sedate, even by C-SPAN's standards: live coverage of oral arguments before the Supreme Court. Because cameras weren't allowed in the courtroom, the coverage was simply an audio feed spruced up with still photos. Whenever someone was talking, that person's name and picture filled the screen.

Softly, so that his daughter wouldn't hear, Eversman said, 'These assholes should have bowls of tea leaves on their shelves instead of law books.'

He was leaning back against the kitchen island that bordered the living room, watching the TV.

Nearby, seated on a stool and looking over documents spread on the island's marble countertop, was Eversman's business partner, Neil Chatham.

'They do seem to come in with their minds already made up,' Chatham said.

'Made up for them.' Eversman pushed off from the island and crossed to the sliding doors that overlooked the pool and the grounds.

He was forty-one years old and had been in the venture capital business since his late twenties. He'd had more ups than downs in that time; his net worth at the moment hovered around the three-quarters-of-a-billion mark.

It could have been higher by now – a hell of a lot higher – if he hadn't limited himself to the world of renewable energy, though he didn't regret that decision in the least.

On TV, Justice Scalia interrupted one of the lawyers and started droning on about a case from thirty years back, *Fenley v. Oregon,* which was about – well, what the hell did it matter what it was about? It was another tea leaf. One of tens of thousands of cases that a justice could pluck out of the stockpile to prop up a premade decision.

Eversman wasn't directly tied to today's case – in the sense that he had no stake in any of the parties involved.

Yet the outcome would affect him. No question about that. It would also affect everyone in America who felt like putting solar panels on their roofs, and the effect would not be positive.

It would be plenty positive for other people: enterprises that had tens of billions of dollars tied up in pipelines and tanker ships and refineries. For them, it would be time to pop open bottles of wine that cost more than most people made in a year.

Not that the Court's decision was going to surprise them. Or anyone. It was going to be five to four. In fact, it already was, in every practical sense.

Why even have the arguments?

From the island, without looking up from his array of documents, Chatham said, 'It's Washington, Hayden. What are working stiffs like us going to do about it?'

Eversman didn't answer, but he thought about the question. The fact was, he'd been thinking about it for a very long time.

Chapter Thirty-five

Dryden saw the problem five seconds after they walked into the Coalinga Township Library. It hit him as abruptly as the rush of cold air they encountered when the automatic doors sucked open.

'Dammit,' he whispered.

'What?'

They were still moving, slowing now, crossing the broad entryway that opened up to the central space beyond. Dryden stopped.

The library was essentially one giant room, sixty by sixty feet, with white stucco columns here and there supporting the ceiling. The different sections of the place – reading area, bookshelves, periodical racks, computer terminals – were all visible from anywhere in the room. And the place was packed, 3.10 on a Saturday afternoon.

'What is it?' Marnie asked.

Dryden swept his eyes over the space. There might have been fifty people or more. Two-thirds of them were kids. Of the adults, most seemed to be there with their children, but more than a few of the grown-ups were by themselves. There were men browsing the shelves or the magazine racks, or seated at computers. They wore jeans or shorts, with their shirts untucked and hanging loose. Any one of them might have a gun stuffed into his waistband – Dryden had one of the Berettas in his.

In any case, potential threats weren't limited to the crowd. Dryden turned in place and took in the glass front wall of the building, facing onto the parking lot. Dozens of vehicles out there. Many with tinted windows. Anyone could be in one of them, watching the interior of the library.

'Hayden Eversman's not a very common name,' Dryden said.

'No, it's not. That's good. If the guy in the articles was named Robert Smith, we'd never figure out who he is in 2015.'

'It's bad, too, though,' Dryden said. 'It makes it easy for someone to monitor Web traffic to watch for text searches of that name.'

Marnie seemed to consider it.

'We should assume the Group has the resources to do that,' Dryden said. 'They were smart enough to catch Brennan, whatever kind of snooping he would have done. He was going to trip some kind of alarm, at some point in the future.'

'And the Group found out about it today,' Marnie said.

'Yes.'

Marnie shut her eyes for a second, exhaled slowly. 'Okay. So he dug into some account of theirs, and a flag went up, and they found out. Sorry, he *would have* dug into some account. But personal accounts are one thing – you really think these people could have flags for Google searches?'

'For certain keywords, maybe,' Dryden said. 'You're an FBI agent, you must know about monitoring ISPs for suspicious activity. People looking up how to make nerve gas, that kind of thing.'

Marnie nodded. 'We have software for it. I guess the Group could, too. But why would they flag that name?'

'Because they know Curtis stole their e-mails. And they should assume anyone he met with has read through them, and seen those articles about Eversman. Googling him would be an obvious move, on our part. And a predictable one.'

Marnie thought it over. Her eyes went past him, tracking slowly along the row of computers nearby.

Dryden said, 'We might be easy for their system to spot, if we Google that name. There might be nobody else running searches for it these days. Eversman doesn't get elected for another nine years. How many people were looking up Barack Obama in 1999?'

'If they really are monitoring it,' Marnie said, 'and we sit down and do a search . . .'

'Then they would have known about it hours ago. Whoever they sent to kill us would already be here right now. They'd probably know the exact time of the search, and which computer would be used, based on its ISP address. Someone in here, or in the parking lot, would be watching that computer and waiting to see who comes along and sits down at it.'

Dryden stood staring at the computers, thinking it all through. Would the Group have sent people to both the scrapyard and this library, two locations within a few miles of each other, in the span of an hour or less? Why not? Multiple leads, multiple responses.

He rubbed his eyes.

'What do you think?' Marnie asked.

'I think Claire's going to die if I don't find her, and I think if the tables were turned, she'd take this risk for me.' He looked at Marnie. 'But that doesn't mean you should have to risk it, too. I'll take a shot at it myself. I'll try to play it safe – just Eversman's last name and whatever keywords seem worth a try. Wait near an exit. If it goes bad, just get out. Get the machine and get away, okay?'

He took his keys from his pocket and pressed them into her hand.

For a second she made no move to take them. Then she simply nodded.

Dryden browsed a table of old books on sale for a quarter apiece while Marnie made her way to the shelves off to the left side of the room. There was a fire exit over there. Dryden waited another minute and then turned to the computers, twenty feet away.

It crossed his mind to wonder if choosing one at random would make any difference, in terms of faking out whoever might be watching, but the idea fell apart almost at once. There was no way to pull a feint here: Whichever computer he chose, that would be the one the Group learned about, hours before. Cause and effect, presented by M. C. Escher.

He thought about it another five seconds and then gave

it up and walked straight to the nearest computer. He pulled the chair out and –

A girl in the reading area screamed, and someone shoved a table hard, scraping its legs on the floor.

Dryden spun fast, his eyes locking like gun sights on the commotion, even as his hand shot for the Beretta hidden under his shirt –

It was just kids screwing around.

A ten-year-old boy had scared a teenaged girl with a picture in a science book: a full-page blowup of an insect's face.

Her cheeks flushed, the girl straightened her chair and table back out, then swatted the kid on top of his head.

Dryden turned and spotted Marnie among the shelves. She was staring at him, her face tense, her own hand just dropping back from under her coat, where her Glock was holstered.

She held his stare for another second – and then she walked out from the shelves into the open space of the library. She cleared her throat and spoke loudly enough for the entire room to hear:

'Excuse me, everyone?'

Chair legs scraped. Fifty-plus heads turned toward her.

'Sorry to bother you,' Marnie said, 'but can anyone here tell me who Hayden Eversman is? I've got it stuck in my head and I can't remember where I heard it.'

Most of the crowd just looked annoyed. An older woman who looked like she might be the librarian stood up, maybe meaning to give Marnie a scolding, but a male voice spoke up first.

'He's a green energy guy.'

Dryden and Marnie both turned. The speaker was a college kid with long hair tied back in a ponytail, standing among the shelves Marnie had just come from. He had answered her without looking up from the book he was paging through. He looked supremely calm.

'Are you sure the name is Hayden Eversman?' Marnie asked.

The guy nodded, eyes still on his book. 'I read about him in *Wired*.'

'Thanks,' Marnie said.

The guy offered a nod and said nothing more.

Marnie crossed to Dryden, smiling a little. 'Low-tech approach,' she said. 'Let's see them monitor that.'

'Don't tempt them,' Dryden said.

In ten minutes of manual searching in the periodical section, they found four different articles about Hayden Eversman. One was the *Wired* write-up the college guy must have seen. The other three were in *Forbes, Scientific American,* and *Business Week*.

Dryden and Marnie split the articles between them to scan through them more quickly. Dryden started with the *Forbes* article, which was actually a long interview. He found what he was looking for almost immediately: The interviewer described arriving at Eversman's fifteen-million-dollar home in Carmel, California. There was even a photo of the place, a sprawling ten-acre estate surrounded by wooded highlands above the seaside town. The grounds were fenced in by a brick property wall, and centered in the space was a colonial brick house that looked more suited to New Hampshire than California. One feature in particular seemed to explain why this photo accompanied the article: The house's roof was covered entirely by solar panels.

'We got it,' Dryden said.

They spared another three minutes photocopying all four articles, then got back on the road. Carmel was two hours away if they pushed it. Dryden drove while Marnie read the copied articles aloud.

Hayden Eversman was forty-one years old. He had a wife and a young daughter. He had spent most of his adult life funding green energy start-ups, and clearly had made good at it. He was a scratch golfer and a private pilot, though by his own admission it was hard to make time for flying. He was notoriously protective of his privacy, especially with regard to his family.

There was no mention of an interest in politics.

There was nothing that hinted at a conflict with anyone powerful – beyond the obvious understanding that big oil companies were no fans of his.

That was it.

Marnie folded the articles and stuffed them into the center console compartment.

They rode in silence for a minute, and then she opened the plastic case and turned the machine on. Static, soft and inexorable as the flow of a stream. As the flow of time.

'Feels weird not to have it on,' Marnie said. 'Like we might . . . miss something. Doesn't it?'

257

Dryden thought of the hollows under Claire's eyes again. He leaned and glanced at himself in the rearview mirror, and saw the faint beginnings of his own dark circles.

'It does,' he said.

Chapter Thirty-six

'I keep coming back to the news report about the trailer,' Marnie said.

They were an hour from Carmel, rolling north along a valley that snaked among baked-brown hills.

'The news report that ended up not being true,' Marnie said. 'About how the girls were dead. Burned in that cage.'

She was quiet for a while, then said, 'In some way, it really must have happened, right? That original version. It happened, and it got reported, and because of that . . . it *didn't* happen – you stopped it that time.'

'I guess you could think of it that way.'

'Some version of me really showed up at that scene,' Marnie said.

Dryden imagined she was picturing it, whether she wanted to or not: the nightmare she would have rolled up to if things had gone differently. The trailer, probably burned away to nothing but a few blackened supports. The cage intact within the charred ruin. The bodies. The smell.

Marnie stared forward at the road and the valley, the folds of the terrain revealing themselves one by one, like secrets.

'What Whitcomb said about the Group,' she said, 'that they're afraid to change the past . . . would you ever try it?

259

I mean, if you had to? If something bad happened . . . something you couldn't live with . . . would you change the past to fix it? Even if you had no idea what would happen to you in the present?'

Dryden thought about it. Whitcomb's description of the idea – and Whitcomb's own fear of it – had made perfect sense. What *would* it feel like, to do a thing like that?

'I don't know if I would,' Dryden said. It was the only honest answer he had.

'I can think of times I would have been tempted to do it,' Marnie said.

The static from the machine ebbed. Some kind of gospel station came through. Dryden caught the words *shepherd* and *praise* before it faded back out.

'I've worked on kidnapping cases for six years,' Marnie said. 'I had one that made me come close to giving it all up, finding some other job. It started with a home invasion at a house in the Central Valley, middle of nowhere, broad daylight. A woman and her daughter, ten years old, lived there. The mom called 9-1-1 and screamed for about a second and then the call cut out. The first black-and-whites got there twelve minutes later and found the house empty. There was a bathroom off the little girl's bedroom that had been locked from inside, and broken in around the latch. Like the girl tried to hide in there, and the intruder kicked it in. But while she was in there, in those seconds or whatever time she had, she tried to write something on the vanity mirror for the police to find.'

Dryden glanced at Marnie. She had her hands balled

tightly in her lap, but he saw them shaking, just noticeably.

'It was the letters *COI*,' Marnie said, 'written with her fingertip. She must have been smart enough to not breathe on the mirror first, so her attacker wouldn't see it.'

'*COI*. Did she get cut off in the middle of writing a name?'

'I might have thought so,' Marnie said, 'but she wrote it big, right across the mirror. There wouldn't have been room for a fourth letter, so ... *COI* seemed to be the whole message. We thought it might be someone's initials, strange as that would be for a ten-year-old to write. We made a list of everyone the girl and her mother might know, and started working through it. I was on-site about an hour after the first responders. I took over the case, and the list. I thought about the girl's teachers, her friends' parents and relatives, anyone and everyone. But we didn't find one person with those initials.'

She unballed her hands and pressed them flat to her pantlegs. The shaking was still visible.

'We tried license plates, even though it didn't make a hell of a lot of sense. The girl couldn't have seen the driveway from that bathroom, and anyway, not many license plates use the letters *O* or *I*; witnesses mix them up with 1 and 0 too often. That approach came up empty right away. Then, about two hours in, we thought we had a lead. We found out the mom had been dating her boss and keeping it secret from her co-workers. A week earlier, she and the boss had been out at dinner with the little girl, and there had been some kind of fight between the couple – bad enough that the restaurant called the cops. An officer showed up and talked to them, took down their names but didn't arrest anyone. It made the boss at least a hell of a *maybe* in my book, even though his initials didn't match the three letters. And then we found out he'd been at a conference two hundred miles away when the break-in happened. He had about a hundred people to vouch for him.'

Out ahead, the hills flanking the road drew aside. Dryden could see broad, flat expanses of farmland planing away to the north.

'COI,' Marnie said. 'I sat in that woman's living room all that afternoon and evening, while the crime scene techs came and went, and I tried to figure it out. I kept going into that little bathroom and picturing the girl in there, scared out of her mind, listening to her mom being attacked down the hall. I asked myself what could be so damned obvious and simple that even a little kid, under that kind of stress, would think to write it on the mirror. And then, about six hours in, it just hit me.'

She was about to go on, when the static broke again. Dryden heard a man speaking slowly, his tone flat and calm. It reminded him of the baseball game. Almodovar at the bat. Then the last of the static fell away and the man's words came through. It wasn't a play-by-play.

'. . . *minutes from now, so that you'll hear it at present. We look forward to meeting you and reaching a fair agreement. Message begins here: Whoever has the machine, we hope you're listening to it. We will trade your friend for the machine. At nine this evening, bring it to the place where you last saw her. We are programming our system to compromise multiple broadcast stations and play this message ten hours and twenty-four minutes from now, so that you'll hear it at present. We look forward to meeting you and reaching a fair agreement. Message begins here: Whoever has the machine, we hope you're listening to it. We will trade your friend for the machine. At nine this evening . . .'*

Dryden listened as static slid back over the transmission, washing it away.

Chapter Thirty-seven

Neither of them said anything for thirty seconds. There was no sound but the rushing static. An exit came up on the right. Dryden took it and pulled to the shoulder at the end of the off-ramp.

Even as he coasted to a stop, he heard the static falter again. What came through was the same message, no doubt from some other radio station. The same man's voice, speaking the same words clearly and slowly. The message looped back to the beginning, and then it cut out; an automated recording announced that the station was experiencing technical difficulties. A moment later it all faded into the hiss.

Dryden was already doing the math in his head. It was just past 4.00 in the afternoon. That allowed five hours to reach the place in the Mojave where he and Claire had been attacked. He could get there with time to spare – if he turned around and headed south right now.

'You know you can't just do it,' Marnie said. 'You can't just show up out there, like they want. And obviously not with the machine.'

'I know that.'

Dryden shut his eyes and rubbed them. He considered the problem, and all the jagged edges of it that he could feel.

'What are you thinking?' Marnie asked.

'That it's still a lead. That I can't ignore it.'

For a third time, the hiss from the speakers withdrew; Dryden heard another transmission of the message. He felt a grudging admiration for the Group's thoroughness.

'Going up against these people blind is suicide,' Marnie said. 'We're an hour from talking to Hayden Eversman. What if that ends up telling us something that changes everything? There's *some* reason they're afraid to make a move on the guy.'

'There's no time to meet with Eversman and still reach the Mojave before the deadline,' Dryden said.

'Not by road there isn't, but I have some discretion to use FBI assets, including choppers. I'd have a bit of explaining to do later on, but I can make it happen.' Marnie turned in her seat and leaned closer. 'If we come up empty with Eversman, you can still reach the meeting site in time to do . . . something. If you can think of something.'

Dryden stared forward. Way out on the flat farmland ahead of them, a combine harvester made a turn at the end of a field. Its metal edges and panels winked in the sun.

Dryden hardly saw it; all his focus had suddenly gone back to the message from the Group, the audio replaying in his mind. One line stood out from all the rest, revealing maybe a bit more than the Group had intended. Dryden almost smiled, but didn't.

'What is it?' Marnie said.

Dryden turned to her. 'I don't have to think of

anything. I know exactly what I'm going to do in the Mojave, no matter how things go with Eversman.'

He put the Explorer in gear and rolled across the two-lane to the on-ramp, accelerating north, back onto the highway.

'Turn your phone back on and make the call about the chopper,' he said. 'Arrange a pickup in Carmel, two hours from now.'

Chapter Thirty-eight

Three times, during the rest of the drive, they switched off the machine and listened to the Explorer's radio for news reports. Coverage of the quake was everywhere, and already the central story was the stranger who'd shown up yelling about a bomb threat just before Mission Tower came down in the tremor. So far, the word *miracle* hadn't been appended to the story; most newscasters were treating it with skepticism, though the fact that a bomb threat had also been phoned in to 9-1-1 lent some credibility to it.

They reached Carmel just before five o'clock. Dryden already knew where to go. After arranging the helicopter, Marnie had used her phone's map application – set to satellite imagery – to find Eversman's house. There were only so many neighborhoods with fifteen-million-dollar homes, and only so many fifteen-million-dollar homes with solar panels covering their roofs; in fact, there was just one. Marnie had found it in less than five minutes' worth of dragging the map around, without ever risking a text search.

They rolled up to the gate, a heavy wood-and-iron structure hung on massive hinges. To its left and right, the brick property wall blocked all view of the estate beyond.

There was an intercom mounted on a post beside the entry drive, with a small camera atop it. Marnie traded places with Dryden at the wheel, then held her badge out for the camera and pushed the talk button. She identified herself by name to the voice that answered.

After that, nothing happened for a long time. Minutes passed. Dryden pictured someone inside calling the FBI field office in Santa Monica and verifying her information. He thought of the digital paper trail generated by those kinds of calls. Database entries. Computer records.

There was no obvious reason to think the Group could connect any of these dots. Up to now, they knew nothing of either him or Marnie.

All the same, Dryden turned and swept his gaze up and down the street. He saw other property walls lining the road, making a narrow canyon of its winding route. He saw rooftops beyond the walls, and other gates with their own intercoms and cameras. He saw nothing moving. No cars creeping along. Nothing at all.

In front of them, Eversman's gate suddenly hummed and came to life. It swung inward, drawn by an unseen mechanism, revealing a driveway of paver bricks leading up to the house Dryden had seen in *Forbes*. Red brick with black shutters, a huge central mass flanked by symmetrical wings leading away to the left and right. The place had to be ten thousand square feet. It had a guesthouse off to the left, thirty yards from the end of that wing, its exterior matching the look of the larger structure. Maybe it served as living quarters for a waitstaff, or security guards.

Marnie put the Explorer in drive and rolled through the gateway toward the main house.

*

Dryden expected an attendant of some kind to meet them in front of the place. Instead, the man who stepped out the front door as they parked the Explorer was the same one they had seen in all four magazine articles.

Hayden Eversman was six foot one, athletically built. He wore jeans and an oxford shirt, untucked. Even at a glance, Dryden saw in him the natural confidence that came from a lifetime of being the smartest person in the room. Eversman crossed to the edge of the porch and stood watching them, waiting.

Dryden and Marnie got out of the vehicle.

'What's this about?' Eversman asked. He directed the question to both of them, his eyes going back and forth. Dryden noted that the voice was the same one that had answered over the gate intercom a moment earlier.

'Have you caught much of the news today?' Dryden asked.

'Some.'

'You heard about the earthquake?'

'Yes. What about it?'

Dryden reached into the vehicle and pulled out the hard plastic case. Marnie had wiped most of Whitcomb's blood off of it during the drive, using a work glove she'd found in the back of the Explorer. The machine was silent, switched off for the moment.

'We need to sit down and talk to you,' Dryden said.

Chapter Thirty-nine

To Claire Dunham, everything in the room where she was tied up seemed to have heat shimmers above it. Like sun-scorched blacktop, though it wasn't especially hot inside this place. No hotter than the forest she could see outside, she guessed.

The shimmers were an illusion. That much was obvious. They were in her head – a side effect of the drug she'd been given.

As it happened, Claire knew all about this drug. She knew about most of the drugs people employed when it came to making other people give up their secrets. For a while, back in the day, she'd been in the interrogation business herself. She'd been tech support for people who did it, anyway.

The shimmers were beautiful. They rose up even from objects that weren't quite objects: a knothole on the wall to her left, the rough-hewn trimwork above the doorway leading out of the room. Sometimes vivid colors swam up into the ripples: reds and purples and greens, like little rainbow patterns on a soap bubble.

The shimmers were one of two classic side effects of this drug; the other was a different story altogether, though still pleasant in its own way.

Claire had encountered this drug and its effects before,

years back, during training with Sam Dryden and his guys. Someone way up in the political ranks at Homeland had decided field operatives like herself should be familiar with interrogation drugs – intimately familiar – just in case they themselves were grabbed off a street corner in Yemen and found the tables turned.

A whole school of thought had grown up around the idea, and terms like *counternarcotics training* and *chemical agent preparedness* had been coined, and people like her and Sam, in carefully controlled settings with doctors present, had been given all sorts of fun intoxicants.

The point wasn't to build up tolerance. That would have taken months of serious use, and would have gone away after you went cold turkey – assuming you could do that, by then, or that you weren't dead.

No, the point was practical knowledge. The point was to know what these drugs felt like, for whatever good it could do in a pinch. To learn what the side effects were, and how to cope with them. To learn if the drug had weaknesses that could be exploited.

With this drug, the primary effect – very different from the two side effects – was a kind of mindless euphoria; it waxed and waned in a cyclic pattern as the nervous system rebelled against it. Five minutes of slightly greater lucidity, five minutes of slightly less, over and over. It was the sort of thing you'd never notice if you weren't trained to spot it.

Claire's training had involved five or six long sessions with this drug. Its full name escaped her now. Thiozene di – no . . . Thiozene per –

Good-Cop-in-a-Vial.

That was what the docs had always called it. Which more or less covered what the drug was meant to do: make a subject relax to the point of making friends with his or her captors. Making friends and sharing stories.

For the captors, the trick to using this drug was simply to be nice. The interrogation manuals Claire had read went so far as to recommend adding the smell of fresh-baked bread or chocolate chip cookies to the room.

For the captive – one that was trained, anyway – the trick was to make the most of those periods of relative lucidity. To do your critical thinking when you could, and to consider your options, if you had any. There had even been close-quarters combat training for each particular drug, since things like balance and depth perception were affected differently by each one. If you were going to slam the blade of your hand into the pressure point below someone's ear, or break their neck, you had to compensate for the distortions in your fine motor control. Claire had rather enjoyed that part of the training.

She was in the middle of one of the lucid spells now. It had rolled in a couple of minutes ago. It would roll back out in a couple more. She used it, as she'd been doing for hours, to take stock of her predicament.

She was tied to a wooden chair. Her hands were behind her, bound to the spindles of the seatback. Her ankles were bound separately, one to each of the chair's front legs. She was in the middle of a room; the walls and floor were made of rough-surfaced planks. There was a doorway leading to another room, and there was a window looking out on a dense woodland of old-growth pines, with no other buildings visible. The window was single-pane, the thin glass old enough to have ripples in it – real ripples, not just the sort her mind was whipping up right now.

Of the next room she could see very little. A bit of floor and wall visible through the doorway, nothing more.

Her captors called this place the cabin. She had seen only this single room – she'd been hooded when they brought her in – but she could tell there was at least a bit more to the place. There was an upstairs, she knew; she heard men talking up there sometimes, and heard the old beams groan when someone walked above her.

She had seen only three people all day. Two were the men who had driven her here from the Mojave. They were both thirty, give or take, and had a hard look to them. They reminded Claire of guys you saw on those prison documentary shows.

That left Cullen. Cullen was fortyish, and very big, and he had much more than just a hard look to him. Whenever she happened to meet his gaze, Claire had the impression she was looking into the eyes of a machine. Something with no concept of empathy or restraint. A crude simulation of a human being.

The three men had watched her all day so far, sometimes all three of them in the room, other times just one or two.

They didn't quite seem to know the correct use of this drug – they weren't being especially nice, and they sure as hell weren't baking cookies – but so far, at least, they weren't physically hurting her. Not yet.

Her wrists and ankles were sore from the bonds. She could feel abrasions on her skin, and her hands and feet were partly numb from cut-off circulation. She wasn't sure exactly how many hours she had been bound to the chair – keeping track of time was difficult with the drug in her system. There had been a single bright point in the day, some time ago now, like a star seen through a break in an overcast. One of her two original captors had been in a nearby room, talking on his phone. Claire had discerned a single line of the conversation, spoken louder than the rest, torqued by stress and confusion: *They had him zip-tied.*

She hadn't necessarily been at a peak of lucidity just then, but she had understood what it meant all the same. Sam was free.

Which was a silver cloud with a dark lining: If he was free, he was trying to find her. He was taking risks to do so.

Claire blinked and lifted her gaze. At the moment only Cullen was in the room with her. He was seated at a card table against the wall, playing solitaire. The deck of cards looked like it had been handled by a mechanic right after an oil change.

The other two were off in some other part of the place. Claire had heard them upstairs, maybe ten minutes ago.

The shimmers intensified. She watched them rise up off the floorboards like little ghosts. She knew what it meant.

The clearheadedness was leaving her again. Peak to trough. Down she went.

If there was any consolation, it was that this lucid spell had actually yielded an idea.

A very bad idea.

Maybe, but it was better than nothing.

The colors swam and churned against the muted browns of the cabin. Claire gave in and let her thoughts blur all the way out.

Another peak. Another lucid spell. How long had she been under?

Cullen was still alone with her. He still had the greasy cards spread out on the table, though at the moment he was watching her, smiling a little. The smile did nothing to ease the coldness of his features. Quite the opposite.

Claire looked away, but not before catching the satisfaction that rose in his expression.

'Afraid?' Cullen asked.

His voice was deep; his chest probably measured fifty inches.

Claire didn't answer.

Cullen flipped over three of his cards. His eyes roamed across his piles.

'What you should be is impressed,' he said. 'I'm a trusted guy around here. They trust me to do all kinds of things.'

'What things?' Claire asked. It was something to say.

'Killing people.'

Another three cards. Another search for moves.

'Who do you kill?' Claire asked. She could hear the drug in her voice. A matter-of-fact tone that might have been humorous on a different day.

'Anyone they tell me to,' Cullen said.

'Like who?'

'I killed a nineteen-year-old boy in Portland yesterday.'

'Who was he?'

'How should I know?'

'They tell you to murder some random kid, and you do it?'

'Who says it was random? They always have their reasons.'

'What reason could there be for that?'

Cullen shrugged and said nothing more. His attention stayed mostly on his cards.

Then he said, 'It gets you a little hot, doesn't it. Knowing what I do.'

He looked up again, and Claire met his eyes, and she thought, *He knows all about how the drug works. He knows about the side effects. The shimmers, and —*

And the other one.

The second side effect.

The technical term for it, in the interrogation manual, had been *arousal,* but that did it no justice at all.

As one of the docs had put it, way back, *It makes you horny like a high school boy feeling a pair of tits for the first time.*

She stared at Cullen and understood: He knew about that effect, and didn't realize *she* knew.

He was playing with her.

'It does, doesn't it,' he said. He laughed softly to himself. 'Makes you a little hot. Just a little bit.'

Claire looked down at her knees and didn't reply. She felt her cheeks flushing, which she supposed looked like embarrassment, though it wasn't.

She thought, *The technology is a month old, and these are the hands it's in.*

Not really a coincidence, she supposed. Life was just like that. The world was just like that. There was a kind of gravity to the way bad tended to win out. Like the world was an ant-lion's funnel, everyone sliding down toward some clicking, mandibled nightmare at the bottom.

She thought those things, and hated herself for thinking them, and hated Cullen for making her think them.

'It gets you wet,' Cullen said. 'I can tell. I can smell it.'

The fact that the last statement might be true, strictly speaking, sharpened her anger to a straight-razor's edge.

Cullen laughed quietly to his cards, and Claire clenched her fists behind her, and after a moment she felt the light-headedness taking her down again. Down and down and down.

'What if I am?' she asked.

Some amount of time had passed – a few minutes, she guessed. She was in the clear again, her wits more or less intact.

Cullen, still alone with her, looked up from his cards. For all his cold smugness, he looked surprised.

'What?' he said.

Claire glanced at him for only a second and then looked down at her lap. She let as much fear into her voice as she could.

'Turned on,' she whispered. 'What if I am?'

Even at the edge of her vision, she could see Cullen staring at her. She felt the dynamic of the room change.

Felt Cullen suddenly transformed into something all too human: a man whose libido had suddenly perked up, like a dog at the sound of the treat drawer sliding open.

While she waited for him to say something, she took in the silence of the cabin. The other two men were still upstairs somewhere. To her right – she compelled herself not to turn her head – was the window. The deep forest outside. The thin pane of glass separating her from it.

'Nobody's around,' she said softly. 'I can be quiet.'

She felt his stare even as she kept her eyes cast down. Another long stretch of time went by. Ten or fifteen seconds. Then Cullen stood and slid back his chair – quietly. He crossed to her and knelt to her eye level. He looked cold again. A taxidermied human face brought to life.

She watched him take stock of the chair and her bonds. Watched him mentally working out the mechanics of trying to have sex with her while she was tied up this way. It wasn't going to work. It was obvious he could see it for himself.

Claire kept her eyes down and waited for him to give up on it. To shake his head and go back to his card game.

Instead he took a knife from his pocket and clicked it open. 'You want to remember something,' he said. 'I weigh three of you, and I'm meaner than three of you, too. Understand?'

She bit her lower lip, allowed herself to shudder. 'Yeah.'

Chapter Forty

Dryden had expected Eversman to be a hard sell. Harder than Marnie had been. Harder than he himself had been, when Claire had first shown him the machine. He and Marnie had both encountered it only after witnessing things that would have been impossible without it. The trailer in the desert, in his own case; the predicted earthquake, in Marnie's. Events that demanded an outsized explanation, and laid the foundation for believing the machine was real. It was different with Eversman, just as it had been different with Cal Brennan: There had been no such impossible experience.

They made the most of the earthquake, the coverage of which was now getting much of CNN's airtime. There was a video clip running every few minutes, in which one of the workers from the construction site spoke of the stranger with the fake bomb threat – the man who had saved them all. The chyron text at the bottom of the screen read: SURVIVOR: 'HOW DID HE KNOW?' Between that evidence and the machine itself, open and running on the big granite island in Eversman's kitchen, they at least seemed to have the man's full attention. That the news was coming from an FBI agent probably helped.

He listened as they explained the system. He paced,

and sometimes sat, while they showed him the e-mails and the newspaper articles: his election, his murders.

When they'd finished, Eversman turned away from the island. He crossed the dining area to a huge set of sliding doors overlooking the rear yard. The grounds rolled away to the brick wall at the back, and the dense evergreens of the Carmel Highlands beyond. In the living room, CNN was now muted.

'Fenway,' Eversman said, almost to himself.

Marnie glanced at Dryden, then returned her gaze to Eversman.

The man turned from the glass doors and came back to the island. He picked up the printed article that detailed his election night victory. His speech to the crowd at Fenway Park in November 2024.

'FDR gave his final campaign speech there,' Eversman said. 'Not a lot of people know that, but I read about it somewhere, years ago.' He was quiet for a moment, his eyes drifting over the page in his hands. Then: 'I bet almost every president we've ever had spent his life dreaming about that job before he got it. Even the ones that seemed humble. I bet they pictured what kind of carpet they'd put down in the Oval Office, years before they ever ran. What color drapes they'd hang.'

He let the printout fall to the granite slab.

'I've had the thought of running for president in my head since my early thirties,' he said. 'For the record, I'd go with beige carpet with dark blue stars around the edges, and blue and white drapes. And I've known for probably ten years that if I ever really did it, I'd make my victory speech at Fenway Park. I've pictured it every time I've watched a Sox home game on TV.'

Somewhere else in the giant house, Dryden heard a phone ringing. He heard a small dog barking in response to it. Heard a woman answer the call, too far away for her words to be discernible.

'A thing like that,' Eversman said, 'I guess you can't stop yourself from thinking about it, even if you know it makes you an egomaniacal prick. What you can stop yourself from doing is ever talking about it. And I have. I've never mentioned the Fenway thing to another soul, and I've never written it down anywhere. So either this is real, or else you know someone who can read minds.'

Dryden made no reply to that.

'So you believe it,' Marnie said.

His eyes still on the printout, Eversman nodded slowly. Then he looked up, his gaze going back and forth between the two of them.

'Who else have you shown this to?' he asked.

'No one who's still alive,' Dryden said. 'Right now, you're it.'

Eversman seemed about to say something more when footsteps came clicking down the hallway that led into the dining area. A woman, maybe his wife, came to the stone arch at the hallway's end.

'Someone from corporate on the phone,' she said.

'I'll have to get back to them,' Eversman said.

'It sounds important.'

Eversman exhaled softly, then looked at Dryden and Marnie again. 'It'll just be a minute.'

'It's fine,' Dryden said.

Eversman followed the woman back down the hall, leaving the two of them alone at the island.

'Did I look that mindfucked when you told me about all this?' Marnie asked.

Dryden nodded. 'I'm sure I did too, when Claire told me.'

For a while, neither spoke. Dryden could hear Eversman down the hall, talking, his words dulled out to nothing by the distance.

Dryden looked at his watch. 5.40. Twenty minutes to go before the chopper would arrive to pick him up in a high school parking lot five minutes' drive from here.

'Do you love her?' Marnie asked.

Dryden looked up. 'What?'

'Claire.'

Dryden shook his head. 'It was never like that with us.'

He thought of asking why that mattered to her, but she spoke up again before he could say anything.

'I'd really like to know what you're planning to do in the Mojave.'

'It's better if you don't,' Dryden said. 'Better if no one does.'

'But these people, the resources they've got — for Christ's sake, they know the future —'

'They know *some* of the future,' Dryden said. 'They can get the answers to questions, if they can *think* of the questions.'

'That's a pretty good advantage.'

'There are ways around it.' Dryden thought about it a few seconds longer, then said, 'Can you stay with

Eversman? After you take me to the chopper, I mean. Keep the machine here; what happens with it after that point is up to the two of you. Whatever you decide, about going after these people.'

'You're not planning a suicide mission, are you?'

Her gaze was intense. Drilling into him, unblinking.

'If it works like I hope,' Dryden said, 'then Claire lives for sure. Possibly me, too.'

Her eyes stayed on him for another moment, and then a door opened in the hallway and Eversman's footsteps came toward them over the stone tiles.

'Sorry for that,' Eversman said. He crossed back to the island and the arrayed printouts.

'Does any of this stuff hit a nerve with you?' Dryden asked. 'It's one thing if they don't want you to be president – there could be lots of reasons for that. But why are they *not* killing you right now? Does that part tell you anything?'

Eversman thought about it a long time. He sighed, half smiling. 'Maybe they're big investors in one of my companies. Maybe they're worried about the stock price crashing if I die tomorrow.'

'That's actually not a bad thought,' Marnie said. 'How small of a suspect pool would it give us?'

Eversman offered the almost-smile again. 'Hundreds of people. And now that I think about it, it's not much of a theory.' He waved a hand at the printed documents. 'People with the kind of system you're talking about wouldn't be worried about money at all. They could play Wall Street like a video game.'

'What else, then?' Dryden asked. 'Why else would these people be scared to make a move against you in the present, but not later on?'

Eversman's focus stayed on the printed pages. The articles. The headlines. His death, by gunshot and plane crash and gunshot again, over and over. Finally he just shook his head.

'I don't know,' he said. 'I really don't.'

For a passing instant, Dryden found himself wondering if that was true. If the guy really didn't know, or if he was keeping something to himself. Something in his tone gave Dryden that impression, but it was there and gone so quickly he wasn't sure he'd really seen it.

'I intend to find out, though,' Eversman said, looking up at both of them. 'I've sure as hell got a vested interest in it.'

The hissing static from the tablet's speakers broke. Mama Cass's voice came through, singing about night breezes and what they seemed to whisper.

Marnie turned to Dryden. 'We should go.'

Dryden nodded. 'I need a disposable phone. We can get one in town.'

Twenty minutes later he was standing in the deserted parking lot of Pacific Grove High School, Marnie beside him and the FBI chopper coming in low over the city. The air-hammer clatter of its rotors shook the space over the lot, and then the ground beneath it. In the last moment before it touched down, Marnie turned to him. She looked like she wanted to say something, but knew he'd never hear her. Instead she just grabbed his hand. Not exactly a handshake – she simply held on tight for two or three seconds and looked into his eyes.

She mouthed, *Don't die.*

He nodded. Then she let go, and Dryden turned and jogged to the chopper as its skids settled on the blacktop.

Chapter Forty-one

The helicopter landed an hour and fifty minutes later in Palmdale, in the southwestern Mojave, half an hour's drive from the place where Dryden had last seen Claire Dunham. He had seventy minutes to get there, which gave him forty minutes to do what he needed to do in town.

He walked into the lot of a used car dealership and found the cheapest thing that looked capable of surviving the short trip: a 1991 Ford Ranger, its bed full of rust holes big enough that he could see its rear axle through them. It turned over on the first try, though, and ran steadily enough. The dealer wanted three hundred dollars for it. Dryden offered two hundred and didn't budge, and drove it off the lot at a quarter past eight, forty-five minutes from the deadline. He filled the tank halfway up at a station in town and headed out into the desert, where the shadows of Joshua trees stretched out in the long evening light. He had a Beretta tucked into his waistband, but didn't expect to use it. If it came to that, he would probably be in very big trouble.

Ten minutes before nine, northbound on 395, he passed the blank ground-level billboard he'd last seen in the predawn darkness, when he'd followed Claire along this road. A quarter mile past it he found the place where she'd led him off the pavement. Where they had parked and she had shown him the machine. Where the patrol officer had been killed.

There was little sign now that any such things had happened here. No yellow police tape. The shot-up cruiser was gone, as was Claire's wrecked Land Rover. Dryden parked and killed the Ranger's engine and got out, pausing to wipe his prints from the steering wheel and door handles.

He found the scoured earth where the Land Rover had skidded and flipped. The ground was discolored, and when he scraped it with his foot he smelled gasoline. He saw the drag marks where Claire herself had been pulled out of the vehicle.

He heard the drone of engines and looked up, and saw two black SUVs coming in from the north. Cadillac Escalades. He took the disposable phone from his pocket and walked back to the Ranger. He stood next to the driver's-side door, hands low at his sides, and simply waited.

The two vehicles rolled in and circled around and stopped directly west of him, twenty yards away. A pretty basic tactical move on their part: putting the glare of the sun at their backs, forcing him to stare into it when he looked at them.

Three men emerged from each vehicle. They looked more or less like the four who'd attacked him and Claire, and the two who'd abducted Curtis. Midpriced hired help, competent enough on a good day.

Five of the six held pistols, low and relaxed. The sixth

man, the driver of one of the Escalades, stepped around his open door and walked ten paces toward Dryden, stopping midway between the SUVs and the Ranger. He wore a black V-neck T-shirt and jeans.

Dryden didn't bother scrutinizing the Escalades for a sign of Claire inside. She wasn't here. That had never been a possibility.

'You're supposed to have something for us,' V-neck said.

'It's not with me,' Dryden said.

'Where is it?'

Dryden ignored the question. 'Give me a phone number for your employer.'

'It's not supposed to work like that.'

'It's going to,' Dryden said.

He turned away from the guy and leaned against the Ranger, staring off to the south. He studied the chaparral and the cool shadows growing beneath it, the rises and concavities of the desert landscape all picking up contrast. At the edge of his vision he saw V-neck stare at him a moment longer, then turn and walk back to the Escalade.

A minute passed. Then Dryden heard footsteps scrape, and caught movement at the corner of his eye again, and V-neck came back to his spot in the open space between the vehicles. He called out a phone number. Dryden punched it into the throwaway cell phone and waited.

On the third ring, a man answered. The voice was digitally scrambled to sound tinny and mechanical. For all that, a hint of an accent came through. French mostly, but maybe just a trace of something else mixed in. The man didn't say hello. He came right to the point.

'Tell me where you put it.'

'I want proof of life,' Dryden said. 'Put Claire on the phone.'

'That's not going to happen.'

'Then we've got a problem.'

'You've got a problem. You're alone, one on six.'

'I think we should talk about *your* problem,' Dryden said. 'It's a lot more interesting than mine.'

'Us losing track of that machine isn't such a problem. Wherever it eventually turns up, it'll make headlines. Or it'll be detailed in some official record. All of which we can run searches for, with our system. Whether the machine surfaces next month or next year, we'll know where it's going to be, and when. We'll get it back, sooner or later.'

'We'll see,' Dryden said. 'But that's not the problem I was talking about. You have a bigger problem than that. And I wasn't kidding when I said it's interesting.'

'Tell me,' the man said. There was an edge of sarcasm in his tone, though it sounded just a bit forced. Like a front.

'I spent some time in the military,' Dryden said. 'I ended up in a pretty unorthodox little unit. A lot of what we did was off the books, not all of it strictly legal. The nature of the work required us to have unusual ways to communicate. We had duress codes, and nonduress codes. We had a whole cobbled-together language only we knew. And we all still know it.'

The man on the phone waited.

'A lot of our codes were just people's names we made up,' Dryden said. 'So if I got a text message from one of my guys saying, 'Did you hear about Dennis Woods?' it meant there was new intel expected soon. Or someone might send one saying, 'I heard Aaron Newhouse was in town,' which really meant, *Drop everything and come talk to me, right now.*'

'Okay.'

'One of the guys from my unit ended up with the state police out here in California,' Dryden said. 'He oversees those alerts they plaster all over the TV and radio sometimes – flood warnings, emergency broadcast system notices, abducted kids.'

So far, every word of this was true. That was about to change, but the man on the phone would have no way of knowing.

Dryden said, 'This friend of mine, if I asked him to – and I have – he could put an alert on the airwaves that wasn't actually real. An abduction notice about a kid named Aaron Newhouse, for example. He could run it a few minutes from right now.'

From the other end of the phone call, Dryden heard a soft hiss of breath, alien-sounding in the digital distortion.

Dryden said, 'You know what I was doing ten hours and twenty-four minutes ago? I was listening to your machine pulling in signals. Which means I was hearing radio traffic from right now. And if my friend sends out that alert in a couple minutes, there's a very good chance I'd hear it, all those hours ago. Be on the lookout for

Aaron Newhouse. You can bet your ass it would get my attention.'

There was a long silence that told Dryden a great deal, and when the man finally spoke there was no more sarcasm in his voice. No front. Just naked fear exposed by the collapse of those defenses. 'You can't do this,' the man said.

'Of course I can,' Dryden said. 'And if ten-and-a-half-hours-ago me heard that name on a missing alert, I'd know for a fact it was my friend who sent that message. Then I'd do the math and know he sent it right now, around nine in the evening. I wouldn't know *why* he sent it, but that doesn't really matter, does it? What matters is that it would throw a wrench in the timeline. It would change the past, at least from our point of view right here and now. My past, and yours, too. Sending information back in time would change it, one way or another. And I could swear I heard somewhere that you guys are nervous about changing the past.'

'Listen to me,' the man said. Dryden pictured him gripping his own phone a bit tighter, as if that tension could come through the connection and emphasize his point. His accent had also sharpened, especially the French. 'What you're talking about is something we never do. We designed the system very carefully to avoid it. The computers send information back through time, but they send it *from the future*. From *our* future. This distinction is god-damned critical. We change our future, but we never change our past. For Christ's sake, we don't even know what that would feel like.'

'We're about to find out.' Dryden looked at his watch. 'It's a minute past nine o'clock. My friend executes the alert at ten after unless I call and tell him to abort.'

It crossed his mind to wonder what his friend was actually doing at that moment. Maybe having dinner with his family. Maybe walking the dog. Dryden hadn't spoken to the guy in months.

'Listen to me,' the man with the accent said. 'Listen. You are talking about a perfect unknown. Very smart people lose sleep thinking about this. *Nobody knows* what it would feel like, from our point of view.'

'You and I will, in nine minutes. Actually more like eight and a half.'

The man on the other end went quiet, except for the breathing. Dryden heard it going in and out, sibilant, as if coursing through teeth.

'This is a bluff, yeah?' the man said. 'You're lying to me.'

'Maybe. Why don't we stand around a while and find out?'

'You wouldn't risk this for yourself. You're smart enough to know better.'

'I'm fucked either way,' Dryden said. 'Like you said, I'm alone out here, one on six. Eight minutes now, by the way.'

Again the man went silent.

'Proof of life,' Dryden said. 'Put Claire on the phone.'

He heard the guy's breathing accelerate, but otherwise there was no response at all. No answer as the seconds drew out.

Dryden felt his own skin tighten and go cold.

There was no reason for these people to withhold proof of life. No reason unless –

Unless they had killed her.

The tightness in his skin spread down into his muscles. It set them pulsing, a vibration he felt to his core.

'I can't put her on,' the man said.

'Is she there with you?'

'She is, but –'

'Then put her on the phone.'

'She's under sedation. She's blacked out. I can't put her on.'

Everything in the man's tone said he was lying. It was obvious, even through the voice scrambler.

Dryden had experienced pure rage before. Feral anger, elemental, independent of thought or language or anything else that might temper it. He felt it blooming inside him now, a burst of red ink in water.

And then a thought got through it anyway. A possibility that shone like a search lamp in the pitch black.

He considered the idea. He thought he saw a way to test it. It would require an assumption, but not much of one: the belief that if Claire's captors had murdered her, they would still have the body with them. That they would not have dumped it in some random place where authorities might find it. If they did still have the body, it might be wrapped up in plastic by now. It might even be buried. But it seemed plausible that they could get to it, if they had to – if he was wrong about that, then this idea wouldn't work. There was nothing for it but to try anyway.

'You say she's there with you,' Dryden said.

'Yes.'

'Is she *right* there? In the room?'

'She's close by.'

That sounded vague. Which was good. Maybe.

'Okay,' Dryden said. 'She has a birthmark behind her left ear. Just under the hairline. It has a distinct shape. Describe it to me.'

No bluff this time. The birthmark looked like a sideways teardrop, its point aimed almost straight back toward the nape of her neck.

It was a question the man could answer in seconds, if Claire was really unconscious in the same building as him. Or he could answer it within a minute, if she was dead and bundled up in dropcloth. Or five minutes, if digging was required.

But if he couldn't answer the question by then . . . if he couldn't answer it at all . . . it might be very good news.

'Are you there?' Dryden asked.

No response. Except for the breathing. In and out. Hissing. And speeding up.

Dryden was focused intently on that sound, and so he didn't immediately notice when V-neck and his five men turned their attention away from him. They turned around and stared west, into the glare of the sunset. Dryden caught the movement just as the last of them pivoted. He saw them shielding their eyes against the hard light, and cocking their heads to listen for something.

Dryden heard it. The rattle of a chopper coming in, its shape still hidden in the sun glare.

An instant later there came another sound: the impact of a bullet against one of the Escalades.

Chapter Forty-two

The five men around the Escalades threw themselves flat, putting the vehicles between themselves and the helicopter. V-neck turned and sprinted back toward them, diving for the ground.

Dryden pressed the button to end the phone call. Keeping his eyes on the six men, he drew back to the Ranger's tailgate and ducked around it, using the truck as cover against both the chopper and V-neck's guys – though he found he wasn't very worried about the chopper.

He heard another bullet strike one of the two SUVs. One of the struts framing its windshield broke in the center and buckled inward. The windshield itself spider-webbed and caved in around the point of impact.

By then the sound of the rotors had begun to change – the helicopter wasn't due west anymore. It was angling south as it came in. Dryden leaned past the Ranger's back end and caught sight of it, a quarter mile out, hugging the desert at an altitude of fifty feet above ground level. It wasn't the FBI chopper he'd flown in. It wasn't anything official, judging by its markings. It was a Bell 206 or some close variant, blue and white with a tail number Dryden couldn't quite read. It was privately owned, whatever it was. A civilian aircraft.

The bay door on its side was open, and someone was sitting there, strapped in, holding a weapon. Dryden saw a muzzle flash from the end of it, and a split second later a tire blew on one of the Escalades. One of V-neck's guys started screaming, the sound full of pain.

By now the chopper was dead south, tracking around in a tight arc that would put it directly east of the vehicles. V-neck's guys were yelling and shouting; Dryden heard them scrambling to reposition themselves on the far side of the two SUVs, away from the chopper's line of sight.

The aircraft reached a position maybe two hundred yards east, then tilted back and checked its forward momentum. It settled into a hover, the pilot rotating the vehicle to give the gunner in the bay a clear angle.

The rifle's muzzle started flashing again and again, once every second or two. Dryden heard the bullets passing over him. Heard the impacts as the Escalades took hit after hit. Heard the men scream as the rounds passed all the way through the SUVs and struck their bodies, one by one. The rifle had to be .50 caliber.

On the breeze, coming from west to east, Dryden smelled tire rubber and gasoline. And gastric juices. And blood.

The shooting went on for more than a minute, broken only by quick pauses as the gunner reloaded. When the barrage finally stopped, none of V-neck's guys were screaming. There was no sound at all but the patter of liquid spilling onto the hard ground; both vehicles' gas tanks had surely been ruptured.

The chopper started moving again. It turned and

dipped forward and came in over the two vehicles, climbing as it did. From a height of two hundred feet it made a slow orbit of the Escalades, the man with the rifle staring down through a scope mounted atop it, taking stock of the dead. He was a big guy, bald and bearded, wearing an aviator's headset and a pair of sunglasses. Dryden had never seen him or the pilot before. After a moment, the gunner said something into his headset microphone, and the chopper wheeled around. It descended and touched down on the hardpan, a hundred feet downwind of Dryden. Its rotorwash kicked up a storm of dust, which trailed away in the wind, across the highway.

Dryden got to his feet. He realized he still had the throwaway phone in his hand. He cracked its cheap plastic case in half, found the battery and detached it, then pocketed the two halves and ran for the chopper. The gunner had already unstrapped himself from his shooting position at the open doorway. He held out a hand and Dryden took it, and the man hauled him into the bay.

'Dryden?' the guy shouted.

Dryden nodded.

The gunner said no more; he just handed Dryden another headset with a built-in microphone. This headset had a cell phone plugged into it. Dryden put it on. The big muffled earpieces drowned out most of the chopper's turbine scream.

'Hello?' Dryden said.

Marnie's voice came through the headset's earphones. 'Jesus, you're alive.'

'What the hell is going on?' Dryden asked.

'Claire got away from her captors,' Marnie said. 'At least we think so.'

'I do, too,' Dryden said. 'How did *you* find out?' Then, on the heels of that question, he said, 'Do you know where she is?'

'We don't know. I'll explain everything when I see you. I don't want to say much on the phone.'

She said good-bye and clicked off, and in the same moment the chopper's engine powered up again and the aircraft lifted off the desert floor. It climbed two hundred feet and pivoted to point itself northwest, but for a moment it made no move to accelerate forward. It held its hover, and the big guy in the sunglasses reached into a seatback compartment and came out with a flare gun. He aimed it out through the open bay door, down toward the two Escalades and the pool of gasoline soaking the ground beneath them. The gunner fired the flare, and Dryden looked down and saw a sheet of flame erupt beneath the SUVs.

At last the chopper tipped forward, climbing as it gained speed. Dryden turned in his seat and looked back, and saw both Escalades fully engulfed beneath a thick tower of black smoke.

PART FOUR

Saturday, 9.10 p.m.–
Sunday, 4.00 a.m.

Chapter Forty-three

The chopper flew for just under two hours. It carried Dryden northwest over the Mojave, crossed the Sierra Nevada, then turned and followed the range north, straddling the boundary between the mountains and the broad, flat expanse of the Central Valley. Dusk was falling by then. In the twilight, Dryden saw cities lighting up: Bakersfield and Visalia, like bright islands ringed by sodium-lit suburbs and the wide-open darkness of farmland beyond. He watched for a while, then settled back in his seat and shut his eyes, and fell asleep within a minute.

He woke to a change in the turbine's sound, its pitch dropping through octaves. He blinked away the sleep and looked out the chopper's window, and saw Hayden Eversman's estate lit up in the dark. Landscape lighting cast a glow under the trees that dotted the grounds and outlined the pool, tucked in close behind the main house.

The chopper went stationary, dropping toward an open stretch of lawn out front. As it did, Dryden saw Marnie step out onto the pavers in front of the porch.

She met him halfway between the house and the chopper, and gave him a quick hug. She looked excited to share what she knew.

'Claire sent a text to your phone,' she said. 'Your real phone, I mean. She sent it at seven fifteen tonight. I found out about it a few minutes after eight, when I turned my phone on to check for messages from my field office.'

'How did your phone show a text from Claire to me –' Dryden cut himself off. He knew the answer.

Marnie nodded. 'When I was tracking your vehicle this morning, I was monitoring your phone, too. Any call you made or received, any text, I'd get a notification.'

She took out her phone, opened the message, and handed it to him.

The text was from a phone number Dryden didn't recognize. He read the message:

Hey Sam its Jodi do you need me to stop over and give the cat her meds this week? I'm free today, but will be tending bar at Bond's starting noon tomorrow. See you.

Dryden lowered the phone. Relief soaked into him like cool water to a parched throat. He looked up and met Marnie's gaze.

'So it's real,' Marnie said. Her tone suggested she'd been close to sure of it, but saw proof in Dryden's expression now. 'It's really from Claire?'

'It's really from Claire,' Dryden said. 'She must have stolen someone's phone to send this.'

Marnie nodded. 'I figured she grabbed it off a table in a café or something. The number really belongs to somebody named Jodi.'

'Claire had to assume the Group might be monitoring

my phone. She wanted to tell me she'd gotten away, so I wouldn't risk my life looking for her, but she didn't want to tip them off in the process.'

He glanced over the message again. The part about the cat was meaningless; the rest was close to literal.

I'm free.

. . . will be tending bar at Bond's starting noon tomorrow.

'Bond's is a bar we used to hang out at, in Monterey, with a few of the guys from our unit. Only that's not the name of the place, it's just what we always called it. There used to be a bartender there who looked like Roger Moore – I guess between being twentysomething and drunk, we thought Bond's was a hilarious name for the joint, and it stuck. No one but Claire and a couple of our friends would know that.'

'She wants you to meet her there at noon tomorrow.'

'I'll be there.'

He handed the phone back to her. 'How did *you* know the text was from Claire?'

'I saw a few years' worth of your financials this morning,' Marnie said. 'Sorry. Anyway, no vet bills, no pet stores. Between that and the message itself, I gambled.'

Dryden nodded. He turned toward the house.

'There's a lot more to tell you,' Marnie said. 'Eversman wants to explain it himself.'

Eversman's wife and daughter were in the living room when Dryden entered. Dryden had seen the wife earlier, though only briefly; Eversman introduced her now. Her name was Ayla. She seemed nice enough, if a bit distant.

She spoke to them just for a moment, then took the daughter, Brooke, into a different room.

When they'd gone, Eversman said, 'I haven't explained any of this to Ayla yet. I can't think of how to begin.' He nodded down the hallway toward an open door with fire-light flickering from it. 'Let's talk.'

The room turned out to be a library. The fireplace was huge, flanked by comfortable-looking chairs. There was a bay window with a bench seat built into it, overlooking the grounds: the front drive and the trees and the distant helicopter on the lawn.

Nodding at the aircraft, Eversman said, 'I take security seriously, and I don't farm it out. My security staff are direct employees of mine, and I own the hardware. I keep a chopper in San Jose, and another one in Los Angeles; I have offices in both places. Tonight when Marnie found Claire's text, she called the FBI chopper that you'd flown in, but you'd already been dropped off by then – and we didn't have the number for your disposable phone. I sent my chopper from L.A. because it was all we could think of. I'll be honest; I didn't expect them to reach you in time.'

Dryden wondered how much longer his bluff would have kept him alive in the Mojave. A few more minutes, maybe.

Then he considered the whole encounter and shook his head. 'That shouldn't have worked at all. Just sending in a chopper and shooting those guys.'

'What do you mean?' Eversman said. 'Why wouldn't it have worked?'

Dryden thought of what Whitcomb had said in the scrapyard, right at the end.

'Because going into a situation like that,' Dryden said, 'the Group would use the system to look at future police reports and headlines. From the moment they scheduled that meeting tonight in the desert, they would have checked for any record of how it would turn out. Any kind of aftermath the police would discover out there, once it was over with.'

Marnie nodded. 'The Group would have seen articles about two shot-up SUVs being found, and a bunch of dead guys. Which would have told them the meeting was going to go bad for them. They would have seen that, way ahead of time. And they would have changed their plan.'

'They would have sent a bigger team,' Dryden said.

'Maybe they *did* send a bigger team,' Eversman said. 'Maybe that *was* the bigger team that you ran into. In some other version of the event, the first time around, it could have been just one SUV.'

Dryden considered that. It was a thought, but it didn't entirely wash. He had no better explanation himself, though – a fact that unsettled him more than he wanted to admit. He paced to the nearest bookshelf, thinking it all through, but got nowhere with it.

'In any case,' Eversman said, 'I mentioned my security because of the main point I want to make.' He turned from the window and faced Dryden and Marnie – but mostly Dryden. It was obvious Marnie had already heard all of this. 'I want to do exactly what this other man, Dale Whitcomb, meant to do. These people . . . the Group . . .

305

I want to eliminate them.' He frowned, unsatisfied with that wording. 'I want to kill them. And I'm damn well on board with erasing this technology, if we can do it. I guess my reasons are obvious enough.'

Dryden nodded. Hard to argue against that.

'Earlier this evening,' Eversman said, 'you asked if I knew why these people haven't tried to kill me in the present. Why they've arranged it to happen nine years in the future, instead. I didn't say it then, but I wonder if it comes down to firepower. Maybe they don't want to go up against my security resources in the here and now. Maybe they're worried that even if they got to me, my people would hit them back – which they would. Maybe the future feels safer to them.'

Dryden thought about it. 'I don't know. Still seems like it would be easier to pull off now instead of then, when you'll have Secret Service protection and the whole world watching you.'

'What do we actually know?' Marnie said. 'If you step back from it, we have exactly seven pieces of information. We know there's one future in which you become president of the United States. And we know there are six different futures in which you're killed, in the months before the election. There has to be a reason.'

'Any ideas?' Eversman asked.

Marnie could only shake her head. She crossed to one of the chairs near the fireplace and sat, resting forward with her elbows on her knees.

'What if they're planning to have their own candidate in the running that year?' she said. 'On the other ticket.

What if your rival in 2024 is one of them, one of the Group, and they set up your assassination, hoping their guy would win in the aftermath?'

'Doesn't explain why they had to find six different ways to kill me.'

'Actually it might,' Marnie said. 'What if they tried it the first time, and their candidate still didn't win? Say the newspapers from the future still showed their guy losing – to your VP nominee or some other last-minute replacement. If the Group saw that future, well, they could always just change their plan. Kill you a few weeks earlier, then check the headlines again and see if that changed the outcome. They could do it again and again. Maybe the sixth time was the charm.'

Eversman considered it. He looked impressed by the logic.

'You're talking about a sleeper,' Dryden said. 'A member of the Group running for the White House.'

Marnie nodded. 'Why not? It's clear they're thinking on that scale. And why couldn't they pull it off, with the advantage they've got? Their system.'

'I don't know if they'd get past the screening,' Dryden said. 'It's not so obvious to most people, watching an election play out, but a major party candidate for president gets a damn thorough once-over by the intelligence community. I knew guys who used to do it. They turn your life inside out looking for flaws. It's one thing if they learn about an affair with a co-worker ten years back, but if a person had something genuinely bad in their past . . . like a hidden loyalty . . . some secret motive for becoming president . . . the alarms would go off. Believe it. A candidate like that would be in real trouble, I think.'

'Intel really worries about that?' Marnie asked. 'A mole running for office?'

'It's their job,' Dryden said. 'And they're good at it.'

Marnie thought it over, then turned back to the flames. 'I agree,' she said. 'And I don't have any other guesses.'

For more than a minute, no one spoke.

'It's a moot point, if we stop them now,' Eversman said. 'None of it would happen anyway.' He laughed dryly. 'Maybe an hour before we broke down their door, all their searches would show them a future going back to normal.'

At those words, Dryden looked up sharply. A second later, so did Marnie. Her head spun toward Dryden.

She stared.

He stared back.

'Oh God,' she said. It came out as only a whisper.

Dryden said nothing. Just held her gaze. She had to be thinking exactly the same thing he was. The same idea, triggered by Eversman's joke.

Marnie started to say something, but couldn't form the words. All that came out was the same soft interjection as before. 'Oh God.'

Eversman looked back and forth between them. 'What?'

Marnie looked scared in a way Dryden hadn't seen until now. He wondered if he looked the same. Maybe.

'*What?*' Eversman said.

'We have a problem,' Dryden said. 'Maybe a big problem.'

Eversman waited.

'Our goal is to kill these people and destroy their system,' Dryden said. 'It's the only way we win. Right?'

Eversman nodded. 'Right.'

'But if we figure out how to do that, some plan that would actually work . . . then they'll know about it in advance.'

Eversman looked thrown. 'I wasn't serious about the headlines going back to normal. But would they? Is that what you mean?'

Dryden shook his head. 'The headlines wouldn't go back to normal. They'd disappear. *All* the data these people are getting from the future would stop coming through, if we were about to attack them and destroy the system.'

A flicker of understanding crossed Eversman's face. He said, 'When they use the system to grab information from ten years in the future . . .'

'It only works because their equipment *exists* for the whole ten years. Curtis called it a daisy chain. Like a video camera filming its own feed on a TV screen. That chain has to be unbroken the whole time. That's why they buried the equipment in the ground. If they want to see a decade into the future, the machinery has to keep running that whole time.'

Marnie stood and faced Eversman. 'They're going to see us coming. No matter what.'

'You're certain?'

Marnie nodded. 'Think about it. They suddenly find there's this weird cutoff – the system can grab information right up to some certain time, say seven o'clock tomorrow night, but it can't seem to get anything from beyond that time. They'll know what it means. They'll know the system gets destroyed at seven o'clock tomorrow night. They would *know* we're coming. Jesus, they'd even know when.'

Eversman frowned. 'Well, what if we . . .' He trailed off, his expression searching.

'There's nothing to think of,' Dryden said. 'There just isn't. By definition, *any* plan that beats them . . . also warns them.'

Silence fell. A whole minute of it. Hayden Eversman went to his fireplace and sat down in front of it. 'What the hell are we supposed to do?' he said.

Chapter Forty-four

The three of them sat up another half hour and hardly spoke.

At last, burned out, they left the room.

Dryden wondered if Eversman would direct them to the guesthouse, but instead he led them to a pair of spare bedrooms in the east wing of the main house. Each bedroom had its own full bathroom. Dryden borrowed a set of clothes from Eversman – khakis and a flannel shirt – then shaved and showered and dressed again. It was the first time he'd felt clean since the night before, walking the rooms of the gutted cottage in El Sedero.

He stood at the window in his room for a long time, staring out on the grounds of the estate. At midnight most of the landscape lighting went out, no doubt on a timer. Just a few lights out at the perimeter wall stayed on, leaving a relaxing darkness under the big trees that dotted the grounds.

Dryden stared at the canopy of the woods beyond the wall. This place wasn't all that far from where he would meet up with Claire tomorrow – maybe twenty minutes' drive. He took in the night and thought of her, alone somewhere right now – but free. She was as resourceful as any soldier Dryden had ever served with, and more so than most. She was also careful as hell. Right now she was probably asleep in a wheat field somewhere, as random and secluded a spot as she could find, and tomorrow at noon, hell or high water, she would be at a dive bar in Monterey called Myrtle's.

There was a soft knock at the door.

He crossed to it and opened it. Marnie stood in the hall, showered and wearing what had to be one of Ayla's spare outfits: a blue cotton blouse and white slacks.

'Feel like taking a walk?' she asked.

They went out the front door and wandered into the darkened grounds. The air was full of the smell of cedars and cut grass.

'You never finished your story,' Dryden said. 'What was simple enough that a ten-year-old would think to write it on a mirror? What did *COI* mean?'

It took her a long time to answer. They passed beneath a white pine, the night wind rustling its boughs.

'It wasn't supposed to be *COI*,' Marnie said. 'It was supposed to be *COP*. The bathroom door got kicked in before she could finish the last letter.'

Dryden thought of what Marnie had said in the car, all those hours before. The girl's mom dating her boss, the two of them taking the kid out to dinner a week before the abductions. Getting in some kind of altercation at the restaurant.

'The cop who showed up to settle the fight?' Dryden asked.

Marnie nodded. 'Once I saw what the letters meant, he was the obvious first guess. I got on the phone and started shouting, and there were black-and-whites at his place about five minutes later. He actually came out the door shooting. The responders took him down and went in, and found the mom and daughter in the basement. The mom was long gone – dead for hours. But the girl was still –'

She cut herself off. By her tone of voice, Dryden knew the next word in the sentence wasn't *alive*.

'She was warm,' Marnie said. 'The ME said she'd probably died about twenty minutes before those first units rolled up.'

She was quiet again for a while. In the faint light, Dryden saw her stuff her hands into her pockets.

'Six hours,' she said. 'Six hours it took me to understand what she meant. What she was counting on me to understand. If it would have taken me five . . .'

She didn't finish it. She stopped walking and just stood there looking away into the dark.

If there was anything consoling to say to her, she'd probably heard it fifty times from others, years back. Probably none of it had helped, even then. Dryden said nothing at all. He put a hand on her shoulder instead. She responded by taking her hands back out of her pockets, turning and wrapping her arms around him. He held her against himself, his jaw resting atop her head.

When she spoke again, it was in a whisper that sounded strained, like glass bent almost to breaking. 'Why someone would use those machines for anything other than good . . . What the fuck is wrong with people?'

Dryden held on to her and didn't try answering.

*

They went back inside five minutes later. In the hallway that led to their rooms, Marnie stopped and faced him.

She said, 'Eversman keeps choppers on standby. I wonder if he's got a security detail in the guesthouse.'

'I wondered the same thing.'

'I'd only feel a little safer if he did.' She paused. Then: 'Want to crash on my floor? Two guns are better than one, right?'

Tired as he'd been all day, sleep eluded him now. He lay on the floor beside Marnie's bed, with the pillow and blanket from his own room.

They actually had three guns – her Glock and Claire's two Berettas. Dryden had both of them loaded and ready on the floor beside him.

They talked for a while and then went quiet. In the darkness he listened to her breathing, wondering if she was asleep. He didn't think so.

Then she moved. She reached to the nightstand above him, and he heard the click of a latch and a plastic lid falling open. He saw the pale glow of a tablet screen, and then Marnie touched it, and the familiar static rolled out into the room.

She looked down and met his eyes. 'Is this an addiction?'

'Feels like one,' he said.

She nodded and reached to shut the thing off.

'Don't,' Dryden said.

'Why not?'

'Because you want it on. And so do I.'

She held her position for a moment, propped up on

one elbow, looking down at him. Then she rolled onto her back again, and Dryden pictured her lying there the same way he was, staring at the ceiling in the milky light.

Ten minutes later she really did seem to fall asleep.

Dryden didn't.

He lay awake for what felt like hours, listening to song fragments breaking through the static. He heard a news report about a traffic accident on I-80 north of Sacramento – no deaths, minor injuries. He heard a test of the emergency broadcast system, covering the townships of Jasper and Willis and the greater San Benito County listening area. He heard two minutes of live coverage of a tractor pull competition.

He thought of something Marnie had said earlier:

What do we actually know? If you step back from it, we have exactly seven pieces of information.

One future in which Hayden Eversman became president.

Six in which he was killed, time and time again.

Thinking it over, Dryden finally drifted away.

Chapter Forty-five

Mangouste stepped out the back door again. Into the night. He crossed to the rear of his property and passed through the gate, into the forest with its rhythmic sounds and its cool humidity.

He went to the clearing where the machinery was buried. Where the bass drone of its geothermal power supply hummed up through the ground, into his bones.

He stood there until the chill of the night had saturated him and set his muscles shuddering.

He thought of the problems that had plagued him for the past three days. Little steel burrs impeding the clockwork of his plans.

All those problems would be settled by tomorrow afternoon. Claire Dunham and the people she had turned to – they would be settled.

Mangouste smiled as the shivering became intense, and at last turned and left the clearing. Back through the gate. Back across the rear yard. Past the pool, dimly lit and rippling in the night wind. In through the back door of the giant brick house. His wife stood at the sink, getting a glass of water, her eyes heavy with sleep.

'Hayden, come to bed,' Ayla said.

PART FIVE

Sunday, 11.30 a.m.–6.30 p.m.

Chapter Forty-six

Claire Dunham steadied her binoculars and took in the front of Myrtle's from a quarter mile away. The place was open for business but was nearly empty. Half an hour before noon on a Sunday, all its regulars were probably still asleep; it wasn't the sort of establishment that drew tourists.

Myrtle's was perched on the waterfront of Monterey Bay, half on land and half sticking out over the water, held up by a forest of sea-weathered wooden pilings. Claire had been watching the place and its surroundings for more than an hour already. To its left was a shallow parking lot wedged between Del Monte Avenue and the bay. To its right was a kayak rental place. Beyond both of those were public beaches, but only a few people were on them; the day was sunny but unseasonably cool.

There was no sign of anyone unpleasant staking out the area. It didn't mean they weren't there, of course.

No sign of Sam, either, though Claire had already known she wouldn't catch sight of him. He would be every bit as cautious as her, watching the place from concealment and distance. If he was coming, he was probably at least as far from Myrtle's as she was, studying the building and all its approaches.

Claire lowered the binoculars and set them beside her

on the passenger seat. The vehicle was an old Geo Tracker she'd borrowed from a Walmart parking lot at four in the morning, after catching a night's restless sleep in the woods at the edge of a cow pasture. She'd borrowed the binoculars, too, from a sporting goods store here in Monterey. She meant to return both as soon as possible.

She leaned back and closed her eyes and exhaled deeply.

'Be here,' she whispered. 'Be alive.'

Dryden looked at his watch. 11.32. He raised the binoculars he'd borrowed from Eversman and stared through them for thirty seconds, sweeping them slowly left to right, then back.

'No sign of her,' Dryden said. 'There wouldn't be, though. She'll keep her distance until the minute she goes in.'

He was sitting in the second-row seat of a black Chevy Suburban, one of three identical vehicles Eversman had brought to Monterey, along with a clutch of his security personnel. Whether they'd come from the guesthouse or not, it wasn't clear; they'd been parked in the drive and ready to go when Dryden first saw them.

Marnie was sitting next to him on the bench seat. She was wearing the coat she'd worn yesterday, her Glock once more in its shoulder holster beneath it. Dryden had one of Claire's Berettas in his waistband.

Up front, Eversman was in the passenger seat. One of his security men, a stocky guy named Collins, sat at the wheel. All eyes were focused on the decrepit little bar, five hundred yards away; Dryden had given Eversman its name and location this morning.

The other two Suburbans were much farther back, stationed out of sight on side streets, four men in each vehicle, heavily armed. Eversman had insisted on bringing a significant force, in case things went badly. Dryden's only demand had been that the other two SUVs keep their distance; from Claire's point of view, anyone but Dryden himself would look like a hostile. If she got spooked, she would vanish.

Marnie looked at him. 'You okay?'

Dryden nodded but said nothing, keeping his gaze on the distant bar.

Marnie kept hers on him. Up front, Eversman and Collins turned and glanced back at him, too.

'We only get one shot at this,' Dryden said. 'I don't want to take any chances.' He nodded toward the bar. 'I don't like the sight lines we've got from here. I want better coverage on the left and right.'

'I can move up the other two vehicles,' Eversman said.

'No,' Dryden said. 'I'm going to get out and go closer on foot.' He looked at Marnie and indicated the cross street in front of them. 'Do me a favor. There's a café two blocks to the right on that street. You can't see it from here, but you'll find it. From there you should have a clear angle on the right side of the bar. Just . . . watch for anything that looks wrong. If anything sends up a flag, come back here as fast as you can and tell these guys.'

Marnie stared at him, her features suddenly taut. '*Are* you worried about something?'

Dryden shook his head. He managed a smile. 'Abundance of caution.'

He clapped her on the shoulder, nodded to the two men up front, then shoved open the door and stepped out of the vehicle. He headed off in the direction of the bar, and a moment later heard Marnie's door open and close behind him.

When Dryden was a block away, still visible, Eversman took out his phone and switched it on. He called the driver of one of the other Suburbans. The man picked up on the first ring.

'Slight change, but nothing serious,' Eversman said. 'The woman, Calvert, is at a café two blocks downhill from me on Sixth Street. After Dryden connects with Claire Dunham, Collins and I will pick them up. When that happens, you'll get Calvert and meet us at the third team's location.'

He ended the call, his eyes still tracking Dryden as he moved closer to the bar. The guy's movements were casual; he wandered along a street of storefronts, looking in some of the windows, glancing up every so often to study the target location. At last he came to a little ice cream shop with a few metal tables and chairs out front. He bought something – it looked like a sundae, but it was hard to tell – and took a seat, watching the bar from maybe two hundred yards' range.

Eversman opened the glove box and took out a silenced .45. He turned and mentally rehearsed how things would play out, the moment Dryden got back into the vehicle with Claire Dunham.

It would be fast and brutal, no fucking around. It would

also be invisible to anyone outside; the windows in back were heavily tinted. And when the three vehicles rendezvoused, Marnie Calvert would be dealt with in the same manner.

Eversman was more than confident it would work: He knew. He had already used the system to verify it. He had already seen the headlines to come.

Chapter Forty-seven

11.53.

Dryden was still sitting at the metal table in front of the ice cream shop. Someone had left a Best Buy flyer on a nearby chair, and he was leafing through it, raising his eyes to the distant bar often enough to keep tabs on everyone approaching it.

Which wasn't many people. It was clearly not a popular lunch spot, at least on Sunday. Probably not on any day.

In the past ten minutes he'd seen only six people enter the bar. A young couple. A college-aged girl. Three men.

11.54.

He set down the flyer and simply stared at the place.

Claire gave the bar one last scan with the binoculars, then set them aside and started the Tracker. She considered driving right up to the building, parking in the narrow lot along the waterfront, but discarded the idea. If things went bad, there would be no time to get back in the car, start it, and drive off. There might be time to simply run, in which case it would be better to have the car hidden somewhere in the blocks close to the bar. She might be able to lose pursuers in a foot chase, then make her way to the car unseen.

She still had the Tracker in park. She stared at the distant structure, thinking.

The way she went into the place might matter. It would be impossible to go in undetected, but there were ways to make it less obvious who she was. Anything that could make potential observers less certain was worth doing.

She exhaled softly and shut her eyes. The whole logistical calculation felt wishful. *Was* wishful. If the Group was somehow watching, it would be game over a few minutes from now.

Nothing to do but try.

She put the vehicle in gear and pulled out of her space.

11.56.

Eversman was holding the binoculars Dryden had used earlier. He was leaning forward, bracing his elbows on the dash, training the binocs alternately on Dryden – still sitting at the ice cream shop – and the bar.

Eversman found his thoughts already wanting to move on, past all this. Like the attention of a child nearly finished with his schoolwork, thinking ahead to free time. With the cat-and-mouse game wrapped up, he would use the system for its real purpose again. Even now, his subordinates were back at it, tucked away in their little haven, tapping at the keys. Scouting the world to come. Finding the pivot points on which decades and centuries could be tipped. The future was filled with those, just like the past was. How many times had the track of humanity been shifted by some one-off event, some unheard-of person? Like Gavrilo Princip. Like Vasili Arkhipov. The future was no different. History was a surprisingly workable medium, before it was written down.

He thought of his superiors, too. The higher ranks of the Group, back in the old countries. Their ideas for what the world should be – what it should have been for seventy-plus years now. A world set to strict but beautiful standards. Clean architecture and infrastructure. No muddy backwaters full of shanty towns and hovels. No slums laced with graffiti and broken windows. Clean people, too. Better people. Better stock. He thought of the movie star, decades back, sitting at the fireplace in that Italian villa, rubbing the haunches of a Rottweiler at his feet. *We bred filthy wolves into these things. Why in God's name wouldn't we refine ourselves?*

Eversman agreed with most of those sentiments still – the big picture, if not every brushstroke. None of it would happen overnight, of course, even with all the advantages the system offered. It would be the work of decades. It already had been. His whole life had been a preparation, in the hope that this technology would end up in his hands. Positioning himself in the best possible way to make use of it, if it ever arrived – every decision had been made toward that end.

Renewable energy had been just one part of all that, a long political bet: that by the middle of the 2020s, voters' hearts and minds would favor the greenest candidates. He hadn't needed a machine to tell him that; the curving trendlines had been obvious even by the late '90s, and were only more so now. It was a smart way to place himself, no more or less.

Even the presidency would only be another link in the chain. So much more would need to be done to trigger the changes the Group had in mind. He would need their help soon enough, though for now, he had not even told them about the machines or the system. That could wait a bit. When he'd fortified his position, when he'd set enough in motion that there was no going back, when his control was incontestable, then he would let them in. Everything in its time.

He swung the binoculars from Dryden to the bar. Watched the place for ten seconds. He was just about to swing them back when he saw something:

Three people approaching the bar on foot. Two were a couple, probably in their fifties. Close behind them, jogging a bit to catch up, was a woman in her early thirties. Under other circumstances, Eversman might have guessed it was a party of three, the older couple and the younger woman going in together. Then he swung the binoculars and saw that Dryden had already stood from his chair and set off walking. Fast.

'He's identified her,' Eversman said.

Collins turned the key in the ignition and reached for the gear selector.

Eversman held up a hand. 'Hold here for now. Let him get inside first. Don't spook her.'

Claire stepped across the threshold and found the interior of Myrtle's disorientingly dark, after the harsh sunlight outside. Even the windows along the back wall, overlooking the harbor, didn't help much; they seemed to offer more glare than light, leaving the rest of the place deep in gloom.

She crossed the entryway, the ancient wooden floor creaking beneath her feet. As her eyes adjusted, she swept her gaze down the row of booths along the left wall, and the line of bar stools on the right. The place was dotted with the handful of people she'd watched drifting in over the past half hour.

She crossed to the nearest booth, which was empty, and sat facing the front door.

Eversman watched Dryden cover the last fifty yards. Watched him cross the street and the front lot, reaching the bar's entrance maybe two minutes after the woman had gone in.

'Let's go,' Eversman said.

Collins put the Suburban in drive, and Eversman turned his phone on again, tapping the number for the team that would pick up Marnie Calvert.

Dryden pushed the front door inward and stepped through into the dark space of the bar.

A college kid in an apron looked up from a table he was clearing.

'Welcome to Silver's,' the kid said. 'Is it just gonna be you?'

Dryden nodded. 'Just me.'

Chapter Forty-eight

12.00.

Claire watched the door for Sam, her pulse already thudding in her eardrums.

Something was wrong.

She'd been here three minutes now. More than enough time for Sam to have reached this place, after seeing her walk in.

If he'd seen her.

If he was anywhere nearby at all.

If he was alive.

Footsteps outside, scraping the blacktop in front of the building. Someone moving fast, almost running.

For an instant her mind drew a picture of men with pistols in hand, swooping in to get her. The end of the line, just like that.

She was unarmed. There wasn't a thing she could do.

Then the door swung in and a woman came through. Dark hair to her shoulders, dark eyes. She was winded, like she'd just covered serious distance on foot. The woman blinked, taking in the dim space of the room, scanning it quickly. When her eyes found Claire, they stopped.

Marnie saw her. The only woman alone inside Myrtle's – which was decidedly not the location Dryden had named hours earlier, before the two of them had saddled up along with Eversman's people.

The place Dryden had directed them to, Silver's, was twenty blocks away from here.

Marnie let the door fall shut behind her and took three steps toward the woman in the nearest booth.

'Claire Dunham?' she said.

The woman, who'd gone dead still the moment Marnie locked eyes with her, only stared now.

'Who the hell are you?' the woman asked.

'Marnie Calvert. Sam Dryden sent me to find you. He said to tell you Biscuit was still a weak name for a dog, and that you should have used Chet, like he recommended. As in Chet Baker.'

The woman – Claire, beyond a doubt – seemed to register three or four different emotions all at the same time. Relief and confusion were chief among them.

Strictly speaking, Dryden hadn't *told* Marnie to say that. He'd written it down on a piece of notebook paper – along with a great deal more – and folded it into a tiny square lump. A lump he'd pressed against her when he'd clapped her shoulder in the Suburban, then allowed to fall out of sight behind her. She'd pocketed it unseen before leaving the vehicle herself.

Then she'd gone to the café and stood outside it, reading the message on the page, each sentence pushing her a little closer to a nervous breakdown.

Claire slid out of the booth and crossed to Marnie. The competing emotions in her expression fell away, leaving only intensity. There was a distinctly military edge to it. It reminded Marnie of Sam.

'Where is he?' Claire asked.

'It's complicated.'

'Then uncomplicate it.'

'He has a plan,' Marnie said. 'He wrote it down.'

'What plan?'

Marnie stared at her and thought, *You're not going to like it. I already don't like it.*

Eversman kept his eyes on the front door of Silver's as he and Collins pulled into the lot. The Suburban rolled to a stop thirty feet from the entrance. He expected Dryden and Claire to emerge immediately. Expected them to be watching at the door for the vehicle's arrival and to come running the moment it stopped.

The bar's entrance stayed shut. No one came out. No one was even looking through the strip of glass in the door.

Collins shoved the selector into park, and the two of them sat staring at the place. Five seconds passed.

'Go take a look,' Eversman said.

Collins got out and crossed to the door at a fast walk. He went through it. Another five seconds went by, and then he shoved it back open, leaned out, and waved his arm for Eversman to come.

'What the hell is this?' Eversman said.

He opened the passenger door, stuffed the silenced .45 into his waistband, and rounded the Suburban's hood. He broke into a run and grabbed the front door of Silver's and hauled it open. Collins had already gone back inside – Eversman could hear him yelling at someone.

'Was there a woman?' Collins shouted.

Eversman's eyes adapted to the low light. He saw Collins ten feet away, leaning in on one of the servers, a guy in his early twenties.

'Dude, what the fuck is your –'

Collins dropped his volume but managed to sound more intense at the same time. 'Did you see him with a woman? She'd be about thirty.'

The kid shook his head. In the same moment, Eversman's eyes took in three people in a booth to the left: the fiftyish couple and the younger woman who'd jogged to catch up with them on the way in. Party of three, after all.

Collins turned from the waiter and crossed toward Eversman. 'Kid says Dryden came in, and then he was gone a minute later. He didn't see where he went.'

Eversman's mind raced. He and Collins had maintained visual on the bar the entire time they were driving up to it. Dryden had not come out the front door.

'Check the restrooms,' Eversman said. 'Both of them.'

Collins nodded and moved off. Eversman crossed to the back of the barroom, where a screen door led onto a dining patio. Beyond the patio's railing was a three-foot drop to the ground: a shallow lawn that led to the edge of a pine forest. The bar's property was butted right up against the woods, a forested hillside rising along the edge of town.

Eversman called on his own mental picture of the

wooded slope, as it had looked from his stakeout position five hundred yards away.

The hill was a forested circle, maybe half a mile by half a mile, some kind of protected wilderness land. There was city sprawl on this side, the north edge, and probably farmland beyond the hill's southern boundary.

If Dryden had entered the woods here – however in God's name he had *known* to do so – then he could come out anywhere.

At that moment Eversman's phone rang. He answered and heard the driver of one of the other SUVs. 'We're at the café. The Calvert woman's not here.'

Eversman heard a door slam somewhere behind him. He turned and saw Collins coming from the ladies' room, shaking his head.

Eversman's thoughts felt as scattered as a crowd running from flames. What was happening? And why? He let the panic stir for two seconds, and then he clamped it down and spoke into the phone. 'Look at the wooded hill behind the bar. Dryden is somewhere in those trees. Collins and I are going in from the north. I want you and the other team to go in from the southeast and southwest. Fan out, don't miss him. Call the other team and coordinate it.'

By this time, Collins was standing next to him. He didn't need to be told anything. Eversman shoved open the screen door, crossed the patio, and dropped over the rail to the grass. As he sprinted for the treeline, Collins beside him, Eversman thought of Dryden's background. He had researched the man during the night – had tried to, at least. His résumé was impressive, most notably for the fact that six years of it were invisible. But even that work, whatever it had been, was now eight years in Dryden's past. He had to be a bit rusty. He was also one against ten.

Crossing into the cool space of the forest, Eversman drew the .45 from his waistband; beside him, Collins took a SIG Sauer from his shoulder holster.

Chapter Forty-nine

Dryden was only a little winded when he reached the top of the hill. He had moved as quickly as possible through the trees, seeking the high ground in the middle of the woods. Now he stopped and held still and let his pulse slow. He turned in a circle, listening. To the north – it was easy to keep track of direction, because the bay was visible through the pines – he heard someone slip and catch himself on loose soil. The sound was hundreds of yards away.

In almost the same moment he heard another sound: a heavy engine running hard, then braking and shutting down. It was somewhere to the south and west. Dryden had no sooner processed that than he heard it all over again – racing engine, skid of tires, shutdown – this time south and east of his position.

Eversman and his men were coming into the circular woods from three equally spaced points along its edges: the corners of a triangle laid over it. Eversman and Collins were entering at the top of the triangle; the guys in the Suburbans – four men per vehicle – were starting from the two bottom corners.

They would all fan out. Like hunters driving prey. What they thought was prey, anyway.

Dryden took the Beretta from his waistband. He had

only one of Claire's two pistols, but he had both magazines. One of them was loaded into the weapon, full with fifteen 9mm Parabellums. The other magazine, in his pocket, held nine. It was missing the two that had gone into Harold Shannon in the Mojave, and the four that'd gone into Dale Whitcomb in the scrapyard.

Ten adversaries. Twenty-four shots.

He heard vehicle doors open and shut at the lower corners of the triangle. Heard footsteps on concrete, and then nothing.

He looked down and considered his clothing: the khakis and flannel shirt he'd borrowed from Eversman last night. Not quite what he'd worn during wilderness training, fifteen years back, though at least the flannel was black and green.

He heard the trickle of a flowing stream, a spring breaching the slope somewhere downhill toward the west.

He moved. Fast and silent. He covered fifty feet and found the stream. It was hardly more than a mudslick, like someone had left a garden hose running in a flowerbed.

Good enough.

He crouched and set down the pistol. He took handful after handful of the mud, smearing it on the cream-colored khakis until a fine layer of it was ground into the fabric, rendering it brown. He smeared more of it on his face and neck. Then he wiped his palms on his shirt and picked up the gun again.

He moved thirty feet from the stream and listened.

Nothing.

It was tempting to find cover right there and wait, but

the location was wrong. Too close to the center of the woods. Too likely to be a convergence point where he might encounter all of Eversman's people at once.

He turned and faced southwest, toward where he'd heard the first Suburban stop. He got moving, staying in the cover of ground vegetation as much as possible. Staying quiet.

He stopped again after a hundred yards. He found a dense spot of brush and got low in it, facing the direction Eversman's men should be coming from, and settled in for the wait.

He felt his heart rate drop, felt his breathing go silent – all of it happening automatically. The primordial psychology of waiting for game.

A minute passed.

Two.

He heard something.

The faintest rustle of movement – dry pine needles on the sandy ground, yielding to the pressure of a footstep.

Somebody moving – but not in front of him. Off to his left somewhere, outside his field of vision.

Someone close by, and coming toward him. Less than ten feet away.

Dryden held perfectly still. Even turning his head right now might give away his position.

Another footstep. Closer.

Dryden had the Beretta in his right hand, his left braced flat on the ground, his whole body coiled like a spring, tense and ready.

The guy would either spot him or he wouldn't. If he

didn't, then Dryden would take him easily – either the moment the guy stepped into his view, or after he'd wandered off just far enough that Dryden could turn without being heard.

If the guy did spot him, then things were going to get complicated in a hurry, and hundredths of a second would suddenly matter: the sharp little fragments of time in which he would hear the man's breath catch, and the sound of the guy's feet scraping the soil as he flinched and turned. After that it would be a race, decided by fast-twitch muscle fibers, the geometry of firing angles, the momentum of arms swung fast and checked fast. And luck.

Another step. Closer still.

Dryden breathed shallow and waited.

Eversman was halfway up the hill when he heard the first gunshot. A flat *crack* cutting through the trees, followed half a second later by a rapid salvo of three or four more shots, and before the echoes had faded he heard someone shouting, high and shrill: *'I hit him! I hit him! Move in on me, I hit him, I fucking hit him!'*

Eversman heard a flurry of motion in the southwest quadrant of the forest, over the hill from where he stood. Men running, breaking through thin branches, kicking up ground cover as they raced in toward the voice.

Eversman cocked his head, listening as the shouting went on.

Which of his men was that? The voice could have belonged to almost anyone, yet he could just about pin down –

He sucked in a breath as understanding hit him.

The voice didn't belong to any of his guys.

He turned and cupped his mouth to shout something – maybe it would have been *Stop* or *Wait* – but before he could make a sound, another series of shots erupted. They came from right where the first volley had been, though these were far less spastic and rapid-fire.

The shooting sounded careful this time. It sounded aimed.

Three seconds later it stopped; everything else stopped with it, the footsteps and the breaking branches. In the silence, Eversman found himself sure of only one thing: He had just lost the entire crew from one of the Suburbans.

Dryden took stock of the dead – all four of them – as quickly as he could; time was not in abundance.

They were down for good: head shots and torso shots, shirts soaked with blood.

He found a Steyr M40 on the first body, with two spare magazines in the guy's pocket. He stuffed the weapon in his waistband and took the mags, and didn't bother checking anyone else's firearm. He was looking for exactly one thing, and he found it in the front pocket of the third body: the keys to the Suburban.

Even as he took them, he heard men shouting to each other, far away. He thought he heard Eversman's voice among them, barking orders. Dryden didn't need to hear what the orders were; it was obvious enough. They were coming for him. Fast.

His own best move was obvious, too.

*

Eversman was running. Sprinting and calling out to Collins and the other four men. Screaming for them to run for the Suburban at the southwest edge of the forest.

What else could Dryden be doing but simply running for that vehicle? There was nobody to stop him from getting in and driving away.

Eversman ran. He crested the hill somewhere west of the peak, and then he was moving downslope through the trees, brush twigs scraping at his face and arms, the .45 in his hand. Running downhill was practically a guided fall; you could maintain something near sprint speed without tiring. Off to his sides he could hear the other men crashing through the woods, keeping pace with him.

Then he heard the big SUV's engine turn over and rev hard.

'Get on him!' Eversman screamed. 'God *dammit*!'

The vehicle wasn't far ahead. Another fifty yards, maybe. Eversman could just make out the edge of the forest now, the gaps in the trees filled with the bright surface of a gravel road and a wheat field beyond.

He heard the Suburban's drive gear engage. Heard its tires spin and bite into the dirt road surface before it lunged forward.

Three seconds later he heard it crash. The sound was unmistakable. Steel on wood. Glass shattering and sprinkling onto metal.

Eversman broke through the treeline and saw the wreck, thirty yards to his left. The Suburban had veered off the road and hit a tree dead center.

Directly in front of him, Eversman saw the place where

the vehicle had been parked. There were deep impressions where its tires had dug into the gravel when Dryden gunned the engine.

There was also blood. A thin, spattered trail of it, leading from the wood's edge to where the driver's door would have been.

'He's hurt!' Eversman shouted. 'He took one!'

His men were breaking from the forest now: Collins to his right, all four of the guys from the other Suburban to his left. The gravel road formed a perfect boundary between the pine forest to the north and the wheat field stretching away far to the south. There was thick, humid air rolling off the field. There was no other vehicle anywhere to be seen on the road.

The men had their weapons leveled on the crashed SUV. They began moving in on it now, a loose cluster, fanning out just enough to give themselves clear shooting angles. Eversman stood back and left them to it.

At twenty yards they opened fire – Collins and the other four. The storm of bullets blew out the vehicle's remaining windows. Punched holes through the quarter-panels and the doors, high and low. One by one the men ran dry and reloaded and kept shooting. They were still at it when the top four inches of Collins's head came off in a burst of blood and gray matter.

Eversman flinched and jerked and looked around; the other men didn't even notice what had happened. Their eyes were trained dead ahead, their peripheral vision full of muzzle flashes, their ears full of nothing but gunfire.

The next three seconds unfolded like a slow-motion

nightmare scene, Eversman screaming in vain, unable to hear even himself over the shooting. The men took their hits one after the next, left to right like empty beer cans on a fence rail. Only the last one sensed anything wrong. A spray of blood hit the side of his head, and he turned just in time to take the last bullet through his eye.

Silence.

Eversman heard himself making a low mewling sound, doglike. He still had the .45, but it hung low at his side. He turned his head and scanned the trees, and then he felt an impact like a nightstick smashing into his right forearm. He felt the bone snap, and a split second later he heard the gunshot from the woods.

He looked down. He had dropped the .45 in the dirt. He was bleeding all over it from the wound in his arm. By the time he looked back up, Dryden was there, rushing in on him, shouting for him to get down flat, arms and legs out.

Dryden didn't appear to have suffered any gunshot wound. He looked just fine. He had his Beretta in one hand and some kind of bunched-up rag in the other.

Eversman dropped to his knees, then went flat, hands outstretched. Dryden dropped the rag in the dirt, and Eversman saw what it was: somebody's shirt, saturated with blood, but twisted now like a wrung-out washcloth.

He felt Dryden drop onto him, ramming a knee into his lower back. Felt his arms wrenched painfully behind him. Then Dryden grabbed the bloody shirt again, and Eversman heard him tear off one of its sleeves. A moment later the length of cloth was looping around his wrists in a figure eight, over and over, before Dryden tied it off tight.

'You could have just gotten away,' Eversman said.

'I didn't want to get away,' Dryden said. 'I wanted to talk to you.'

For another moment he left Eversman lying there while he searched the pockets of the dead men nearby. On the third man in the line, he found the keys to the other Suburban, the one that was parked at the southeast edge of the forest.

Dryden came back to Eversman. He took the silenced .45 from where it had fallen, and tucked it into his own rear waistband. Then he reached down, grabbed Eversman by the upper arm, and hauled him to his feet.

'Let's go,' he said, and stiff-armed Eversman forward, off the road and back into the deep shadows of the forest.

Chapter Fifty

'You would have killed all three of us,' Dryden said. 'Me and Claire and Marnie.'

They were just into the woods, moving east, roughly paralleling the curved gravel road fifty yards south of them.

'That's how it would have gone,' Dryden said, 'if I hadn't known better. You would have driven us out to some place like these farm fields and shot us. Or maybe you would have done it right inside the SUV. Is that what the silencer was for?'

Eversman didn't answer.

Dryden kept them moving forward, toward the other SUV on the far side of the woods. He had his left hand clenched around a fistful of Eversman's shirt in back, his elbow locked, propelling the guy step by step.

'I would have lived through it,' Dryden said. 'One way or another. I would have survived and even gotten away.'

'Confident thing to say,' Eversman said.

'No. It's just true. I already know it.'

'How would you know a thing like that?'

For a second Dryden didn't answer. He forced Eversman forward over a knee-high fallen trunk.

Dryden said, 'Marnie asked me yesterday if I would ever change the past. Would I change it if something

344

happened that I wanted to undo? Something I couldn't live with.'

'We never change the past,' Eversman said. 'It's too much of an unknown. We can't even imagine what it would feel like from our point of view.'

'That scares you guys,' Dryden said.

'It should scare anyone. It should scare you.'

'It does,' Dryden said. 'And when Marnie asked me whether I could do it, I said I didn't know. But now I do, and it turns out the answer is yes. If something bad enough happened, I would change the past to fix it.'

'What are you talking about?'

'I've got a buddy who oversees missing child alerts that go out on the airwaves, and emergency broadcast messages.'

Eversman said nothing.

'I got a message from him last night,' Dryden said. 'Three or four in the morning. I was lying on the floor in Marnie's room, and we had the machine on, and I heard an emergency test for the townships of Jasper and Willis. But those aren't townships. They add up to a person's name.'

'Jasper Willis? Am I supposed to know who that is?'

Dryden shook his head. 'He's nobody. The name is a shorthand code we used in my unit, way back. We'd send it to someone as a text message, like, "I heard Jasper Willis got transferred stateside." All that mattered was the name itself, and what it meant. Which was "Don't trust your contact. You're about to get screwed."'

Eversman stayed quiet. From Dryden's position,

behind and to the right, he could only see the man's face in profile, but it was enough to see his expression go slack.

'Three or four in the morning,' Dryden said. 'Add ten hours and twenty-four minutes to that, and it's a couple hours after noon – after the meetup here in Monterey. The timing works out just about right. If things went bad here, but I survived, I'd have time to get in touch with my friend and get that message on the air. And I would have already known Marnie and I had the machine on, ten and a half hours before that. I would have known I had a decent chance of actually hearing the warning.'

Eversman's face remained blank as Dryden shoved him along, though at least an edge of disbelief seemed to show there.

'I would have been scared shitless to change the past,' Dryden said, 'but I guess I was mad enough to balance out the fear. You must have really pissed me off.'

They crossed over a muddy stream like the one Dryden had used to darken his pants and face.

'The warning from my friend last night got me thinking,' Dryden said. 'All those different futures. One in which you become president. Six in which you get killed before that. It never made sense. Why would the Group kill you six times? And then I saw it.'

Eversman made a sound like a dry laugh. A nasal breath. Derision, bravado. Dryden ignored it.

'You're part of the Group,' Dryden said. 'And in 2024, *you* would have been the sleeper running for the White House. The intelligence community would have done its background check on you, and they would have found something, wouldn't they? I told you, they turn a candidate's life inside out. And if what they learned about you was bad enough, what would they do about it? My guess? They'd kill you.'

They were midway across the woods now, crossing the swell of the hill, far south of the highest point in the middle of the forest.

'I bet you weren't lying when you said you'd always wanted to be president,' Dryden said. 'I bet the part about Fenway wasn't even bullshit. And when you and your people got the system up and running, and you could read headlines from the future, I bet I know the first damn thing you searched for. Your name in 2024, to see if you were going to win the election. But you weren't going to win. You were going to get shot to death, because someone in intel figured out what you really were.'

They crossed another mudslick. Far ahead, to the east, Dryden could make out a hint of light through the trees. The opposite side of the forest.

'When you saw those headlines,' Dryden said, 'you knew what to do about it. You scoured the future to find out exactly which intel people were going to figure you out. Maybe some article from far, far ahead in time, twenty years from now, when the names had been declassified and the stories told. You found out who was going to bust you . . . and you had them killed – right here in the present. Some of them were probably still college kids, weren't they?'

Eversman didn't reply.

'Then you checked the 2024 headlines again,' Dryden

said. 'See if you survived this time around. But you didn't – because in that altered future, there would just be *other* intel people filling those job positions. People just as capable of nailing you. So you killed them too, and checked the headlines again, rinse and repeat the whole goddamned thing until you got the future you wanted. Right?'

No response.

'Marnie and I had it backwards from the start,' Dryden said. 'We thought the original future was the one where you were elected president. We thought the Group changed that future six different times, killing you in six different ways. But the Group wasn't killing you. They were saving you. Shuffling the deck by eliminating the people who would find out the truth about you. And finally it worked. Finally there was a future in which you lived all the way to Election Day.'

Eversman looked up into the treetops, as if pretending to be interested in something there. He said, 'You sound like you know everything. Why even ask me about it?'

'Because there's more I need to know, and you're going to tell me.'

'Why would I say anything to help you?'

'I'll just go ahead and ask anyway,' Dryden said. 'We'll see how you respond.'

Eversman only shook his head. He glanced upward again, just briefly.

'Some parts are obvious,' Dryden said. 'When Marnie and I showed up at your place in Carmel yesterday, you must have thought you'd won the lotto. The Group was turning over heaven and earth to find us, and we rolled right up to your gate and pushed the buzzer. When we finished telling you our story, one of the first things you did was ask us who else we'd talked to. I should have picked up on that, but I didn't. I imagine, in that moment, you thought all the loose ends were tied off. Marnie and I probably would have been dead inside the next five minutes, but then you got a phone call. Something so urgent you had to take it. Let me guess: That was the news that Claire had gotten away. Just like that, you still had a loose end out there. But you also had a sure way to get her back. You had me. The one person Claire would try to contact and meet up with.'

Ahead in the direction they were walking, the light through the trees was brighter. They were maybe two hundred yards from the east edge of the woods and the SUV parked there.

'So everything after that was bullshit,' Dryden said. 'The meeting in the desert had already been planned, so that still had to take place, but since it was your own people I was meeting out there, you could easily arrange for me to survive it. The fact that Claire sent me that text message offered a perfect reason, but you would have come up with something. I wonder: Were you the guy on the phone, during that meeting? Were you the scrambled voice with the accent?'

Eversman didn't answer.

'I wondered last night why the chopper attack in the desert worked,' Dryden said. 'Why the Group didn't know about it in advance and prepare for it. Now I understand.

349

The whole damn thing was staged anyway. Sure, the six guys of yours that you killed in the Mojave weren't in on it, but I don't imagine you care about them.'

'What exactly do you still need to know, then?' Eversman asked.

'Two things,' Dryden said. 'First, the system. The buried unit. It's at your estate, isn't it.'

Eversman's reaction was complex, a sequence of different emotions in the space of a second. Surprise, annoyance, then an attempt to maintain composure and hide both of those responses. Too late.

'You're never getting near it,' Eversman said. 'So why do you care?'

Dryden ignored the comment. 'I want to know how it works. The system itself is buried in the ground, but there have to be keyboards and monitors somewhere. There have to be people sitting at them, running the searches and looking at the results. But you know what I think? I think there are as few of those people as you can possibly make do with. Because those people are liabilities. Any one of them could start getting ideas of their own, with that kind of power at their disposal. If I were you, I'd have a skeleton crew at those keyboards, and I'd keep them all in one place where I could watch them like a hawk. I'd make them live there. I'd probably keep them right in that guesthouse on the estate.'

Another little spike of surprise and annoyance. Another score.

'Nobody else knows a damn thing about it,' Dryden said. 'Do they. Not your superiors in the Group, wherever they are. Not the guys who just tried to kill me in these woods. Not the people you send out to commit murder. They know the bare minimum they need to. Why would you tell them anything more? I bet your wife doesn't even know about the system.'

Eversman rolled his neck as if to work out a kink, but the movement looked fake – like his real purpose was to take another good look at the sky through the trees. Dryden looked, too. Nothing there.

'So how many in the skeleton crew?' Dryden asked. 'Five? More than that? Is it –'

'Three people. Plus me.' Eversman's tone was calm. Even proud. 'Yes, they live in the guesthouse. Yes, I keep an eye on them. Yes, they're the only ones in the world, besides me, who know anything about the system. Do you know why I'm not afraid to tell you this?'

Dryden waited, still pushing Eversman forward through the trees.

'Because you and Marnie were exactly right,' Eversman said. 'Any plan that could destroy the system would also tip it off. And it hasn't been tipped off. So none of this is worrying me.'

They were a hundred yards from the east edge of the forest now.

'What's the second thing you want to know?' Eversman asked.

Dryden said, 'Why am I pointing a gun at you? Why do I have your hands bound?'

'You're asking *me*?'

'What I mean is, how did I outplay you here? You and

351

your people could have used the system to see how this would turn out. And you must have.'

Eversman nodded. 'We must have.'

'So why did I win?'

Eversman laughed; he seemed to catch himself off guard by doing so, as if he found something about the moment genuinely funny.

Then he planted a foot, bringing himself and Dryden to a hard stop, and turned in place so that the two of them were suddenly eye to eye.

Eversman's wrists were still tied behind him. Dryden was still holding the Beretta. There was nothing Eversman could do to change the dynamic.

Yet the guy's expression was all confidence.

'Who says you won?' Eversman asked.

Before Dryden could reply, Eversman cocked his head, listening for something.

Five seconds later Dryden heard it.

The rattle of a helicopter coming in.

It was somewhere to the north, beyond the wooded hilltop, the terrain and the trees masking its sound. It was already very close – thirty or forty seconds away at most.

Eversman smiled. 'I told you last night, I keep one stationed in San Jose. I called for it to lift off as soon as Collins and I entered the woods.'

Dryden looked around, painfully aware of how little cover the forest would offer against an airborne attack. Someone looking straight down from a hundred feet up would see through any of the ground cover, and even through most of the tree boughs.

'I bet you instructed Marnie and Claire to stay away from here,' Eversman said. 'Didn't you. I also bet they're going to ignore that. In fact, I know it.'

Dryden looked at him. 'What are you talking about?'

'My people and I did use the system to see how this would turn out. We checked this morning. You know what we found? Headlines about you and Marnie Calvert disappearing. You were last seen alive in Los Angeles two days ago. She was last seen Saturday morning in Santa Monica. The two of you end up linked forever, because apparently she was tailing you at the time you both vanished. We found true-crime write-ups about you two, published as much as five years from now. You're one of those oddball little stories that sticks in the public consciousness. Claire Dunham ends up missing, too – no one connects her disappearance to yours, but either way, she vanishes. So there you go. If no one ever sees you three again, what else could it mean? We're going to bury you. All of you.'

The clatter of the rotors was much closer now, just over the summit of the tree-covered hill.

Dryden stopped looking around and leveled his gaze on Eversman.

'You didn't check for headlines about anything strange happening in Monterey today,' Dryden said. 'Did you?'

'Why would I? You three weren't going to disappear from Monterey. There wasn't going to be any record you'd been here at all. What headlines around here would I have looked for?'

'That's why you didn't know I was going to kill your guys,' Dryden said. 'Because you never checked. You saw the stories about us missing, and you figured that told you everything.'

'It told me we'll accomplish the part that matters. It told me enough.'

'What else didn't you check for?' Dryden said. 'Did you search for headlines about your own death?'

Eversman's confidence remained intact. He held Dryden's stare.

'You three disappear because we kill you,' Eversman said. 'I take that to mean I win. That I live.'

On the last word, the sound of the incoming helicopter suddenly intensified. Dryden looked up and saw it through the pines, just passing over the hilltop, flying no more than twenty feet above the trees. It wasn't the same chopper that had broken up the meeting last night in the Mojave, but it was similar enough. The setup was the same. Open bay door in back. A gunner strapped in place and leaning out with a big rifle. Probably another .50 caliber.

In the half second Dryden was distracted by the aircraft, Eversman moved – far more quickly than Dryden would have guessed. The guy lunged forward, bending at the waist for a headbutt. Dryden dodged it by spare inches, throwing his own head sideways and taking the impact as a graze against his cheekbone. He pivoted and shoved Eversman hard, meaning to send him sprawling, but the guy caught his balance and came on again, all adrenaline and desperation.

Dryden swung the Beretta toward him and fired. Three shots, a tight group centered in Eversman's chest. Three little rips in his shirt fabric, instantly soaked with blood.

Eversman stopped as if he'd hit an unseen wall. For another second he stayed on his feet, his eyes wide and staring at Dryden. His mouth worked soundlessly; he looked like he was trying to say *How?*

Then he fell where he stood, probably dead before he hit, and Dryden forgot all about him. He spun toward the oncoming chopper – it was making straight for him, though he couldn't possibly have been visible to the pilot yet. Dryden looked down at Eversman's body and understood: The guy's phone must have been relaying its GPS coordinates to the chopper, calling it in like a beacon. It would have been the easiest way for Eversman to guide it here from San Jose in the first place. Dryden turned east, toward the nearest edge of the forest, and ran.

Chapter Fifty-one

He knew already that escaping in the other Suburban wasn't an option. Even if he could reach it unseen, it would be suicide to get into it and try driving away.

He ran toward it anyway, east through the forest, simply to move away from both Eversman's body and the chopper itself. He tried to stick to the densest clusters of trees, the best visual screens available.

Fifty yards from where Eversman had fallen, Dryden stopped. He turned and crouched as low as he could in the brush. He watched the chopper slow and take up a hover directly above the corpse.

The gunner in the bay door leaned farther out and looked straight down. Dryden could see some kind of bulky headgear on him. A helmet with a scope built right into the front of it. Probably a FLIR camera. Thermal vision. Even in daylight, it would make child's play of searching for a human target in a forest like this. The shaded ground could be no more than sixty degrees. Dryden was thirty-eight point six degrees warmer than that. Not even the sunlit canopy of pine boughs overhead would be that hot. Not on a brisk day like this. Not even close.

The chopper stayed in its hover, the gunman staring down and taking in Eversman's corpse. The FLIR scope would make it obvious the man was dead. There would be body-temperature blood seeping out in a big puddle, contrasting starkly with the cool dirt.

If the pilot took the chopper a little way to the west, the gunner would see the bodies of the first four men Dryden had taken down. There would be more puddled blood there, and the bodies themselves might have already cooled noticeably. The same would go for the other five out at the southwest edge of the woods, on the gravel road that bordered the wheat field.

The chopper didn't do any of that, though.

Instead the gunner looked up from Eversman's corpse and swept his viewpoint over the surrounding woods in a quick, efficient arc.

He saw Dryden almost immediately.

There was no question the guy had spotted him. The low brush Dryden was crouched in was useless. A two-foot-wide tree trunk would have helped, but there was nothing like that within sight.

For three seconds the gunman just stared. Dryden held still and considered his options. He couldn't play dead; he was already upright in a crouch. He couldn't stand his ground and fight; he would be outgunned and outmaneuvered to a degree that would be comical to anyone but himself. He couldn't flee the woods to the nearby south or east side; there was only open farmland in both of those directions.

He could escape to the north. Out of the woods and into the city sprawl.

If he could get that far – the northern edge of the forest was almost half a mile away.

He was still thinking about that when the gunner's mouth moved beneath the bulk of his FLIR scope. Instructions via headset to the pilot. A second later the chopper tilted forward and left its hover. It banked as it did, coming around in a shallow curve that would put the gunner right above Dryden's position.

Dryden broke from the brush and took off in a sprint, straight north.

For the first thirty seconds he didn't look back. He didn't look anywhere but straight ahead, jumping deadfalls and low stands of brush. He heard the chopper's rotors and control surfaces making rapid adjustments behind him, the sound chaotic through the trees. Dryden had flown helicopters before; it had been part of his training. He could picture the pilot moving the cyclic control left and right and forward, second by second, using the pedals to whip the tail this way or that, anything to give the gunner a good sightline as the aircraft skimmed the treetops and raced north, gaining on him.

He heard the first zipping whine of a bullet, somewhere just above him in the boughs, half a second before the sound of the gunshot crashed down around him. He didn't stop.

Another bullet – this one buzzing through the airspace five feet in front of him. It left a ragged line of cut-loose pine needles in its wake, a ghost of the bullet's path. Dryden ran right through it a split second later.

He heard Eversman's words in his head:

I bet you instructed Marnie and Claire to stay away from here.

I also bet they're going to ignore that.

In fact, I know it.

The third shot passed close enough that he felt its heat across his forehead, as if someone had waved a lightbulb two inches from his face.

If no one ever sees you three again, what else could it mean?

The chopper was above and to his left now, somewhere around his eight o'clock, and close by. The last two shots had come down on high, steep angles.

Dryden ran another five paces, until half a second before his internal stopwatch said the next shot was coming.

Then he jammed a foot into the dry soil and pulled up short, and heard the zip and the gunshot almost in unison, the bullet ripping through the base of a sapling three feet in front of him. He pivoted and lunged sideways, passing directly beneath the chopper, coming out on the gunner's blind side ten seconds later. Then he turned and sprinted north again, the chopper now above and to his right. He heard it once more making adjustments, correcting its position. He imagined the gunner shouting into his headset, scouring the woods as the aircraft came around.

Dryden kept running. There was no other move.

The edge of town was still impossibly far north, given the circumstances. Somewhere between a half and a quarter mile – more than a minute's run for a world-class athlete on smooth asphalt. Already he could hear the chopper settling into another favorable flight path for the gunman, this time taking into account the maneuver

Dryden had used. The chopper would stay farther off to his side now, far enough that it would be useless to try dodging beneath it again.

Running hard, ducking branches, darting past clumps of pines. Cresting the flank of the hill now, the ground dropping away in a shallow grade before him, helping just a bit with his speed.

Another bullet cut through the air, spare feet behind him.

And another, just above his scalp.

At the edge of his vision he saw something; his body reacted to it as much as his brain did. He turned without stopping and sprinted on a diagonal from the line he'd been running on. A bullet splintered a thin branch six inches from his face. Scraps of bark stung his cheeks; his lungs filled with the smell of pine tar.

He reached what he was running toward three seconds later: a knotted old tree with a trunk twice as wide as his body. He slammed to a stop against it, putting it between himself and the chopper.

For ten seconds the gunner held his fire. Dryden drew back from the tree, slowly, ten inches and then twenty. Enough to catch sight of the chopper's tail, past the trunk's left edge. Enough to keep tabs on the aircraft as it circled, and to keep himself shielded by the tree no matter where the chopper put itself.

He could circle this tree all day; the chopper couldn't. It had only so much fuel, and only so much time before some motorist found the bodies near the wheat field. The guys in the chopper wouldn't want to hang around once police started showing up in the area.

The aircraft's tail was slipping away to the right. Dryden eased himself clockwise around the tree, keeping just the last two feet of the tail in view.

Easy.

Then the chopper went stationary, and turned sharply to the right, a move that would point the gunner entirely away from him. Why? Dryden risked leaning out past the trunk to see the reason.

He saw.

Forty yards away from him stood Marnie and Claire. Marnie had her Glock in hand, held low. The two of them stared up as the chopper rotated to point the gunman at them. Then they bolted sideways — and away from each other — as a rifle shot ripped through the space where they had been standing.

Dryden lost sight of Claire. He managed to keep his eyes on Marnie as she moved roughly toward him.

The gunner kept his eyes on her, too. Another bullet cut through the pine boughs, missing Marnie by a foot at most.

Dryden drew the Steyr M40 he'd taken from one of the dead men. It was the first time he'd had a clear angle on the chopper without the .50 caliber rifle being pointed at him.

He raised the pistol and aimed it high, compensating for the chopper's altitude and distance, and opened fire.

There was no way to see what he was hitting inside the cockpit. A direct hit on the pilot would be ideal. A ricochet that winged him with a bullet fragment would be almost as good. All he had to do was make the guy flinch at the controls. Make him lose focus for half a second. That would be enough.

361

Flying a helicopter was difficult as hell, and holding in a hover was the hardest part by far. You needed both hands and both feet engaged at all times. You had to manage drift and altitude and yaw, each one a separate task, and any correction to one of them threw off the other two. You had to focus.

Dryden saw at least one bullet hole open up in the aircraft's thin metal skin. Saw one of its side windows blow inward.

The pilot lost his focus.

The chopper's tail dipped and slewed to the left. Through a window in the back, Dryden saw the gunner reach frantically for a handhold. A second later the aircraft tilted deeply forward, as if to bow at the conclusion of its performance. As it did so, its main rotor clipped the top of a pine tree; the chopper reacted as if an invisible giant had reached up and slapped it sideways, hurling the craft into the highest boughs of a nearby grove. The rest of the rotor assembly tore itself apart against the tree trunks, at which point the helicopter was essentially a falling minivan. Loaded with aviation fuel.

It slammed into the earth beside the grove, its tanks rupturing and detonating in the same instant. Dryden felt the radiant heat flash out and warm his skin.

He turned and saw Marnie staring at him. A second later he saw Claire; she stepped into view past a screen of brush, twenty feet away.

Claire Dunham. Alive and well. She looked healthier than when he'd last seen her. She'd slept, at least.

An ugly thought came to Dryden; he realized he had

suppressed it for most of the past twenty-four hours: Deep down he had not expected to see her again.

She stepped past the brush and came toward him. She drew a folded sheet of paper from her pocket; it was the note he'd given Marnie in the Suburban. Claire unfolded it as she crossed to him, stopping two feet away. She held it up, her expression somewhere between amused and pissed.

She said, 'Your plan is for all three of us to vanish off the grid for the rest of our lives? You really expect us to do that?'

'We did do that,' Dryden said. 'Would have, anyway.'

Marnie came up beside them. 'Do we still have to?'

Dryden shook his head. 'The girls in the trailer didn't have to stay dead. We don't have to stay missing.'

He turned in place, got his bearings, and faced southeast. The intact Suburban was down there somewhere, parked along the road beside the forest.

'We need to go back to Eversman's estate,' he said. 'Right now.'

'Why the hell would we go back there?' Marnie asked.

'Because the system is there. And I know what to do about it now.'

Marnie's eyes narrowed. 'What about what we said last night? There's no way to beat it without warning it.'

'There is,' Dryden said. 'Whitcomb was about to tell us, yesterday. He had it all figured out. Come on.'

He led the way east, sprinting through the trees.

Chapter Fifty-two

'Think very carefully,' Dryden said. 'When we met Eversman's wife, did he introduce you as an FBI agent?'

They were in the Suburban, rolling out of Monterey and into the hills, twenty minutes from the estate. Behind them, the city was dotted with police flashers streaming in from all quarters toward the crash site in the woods – amid much else they would find there. During the run to the SUV, Dryden had stopped to relieve Eversman's corpse of its wallet. With any luck, that would buy a bit of time before authorities identified the man and descended on his home. He had taken the guy's cell phone, too.

Dryden was at the wheel. Marnie rode in the passenger seat, Claire behind her on the middle bench.

'No,' Marnie said. 'He just used my first name. And yours. Maybe he didn't want her remembering us, if we ended up on the news after we disappeared.'

'Maybe,' Dryden said. 'I don't think she was in the loop on anything. She didn't know about the system. I doubt he was ever going to tell her.'

'Why does it matter whether she knew I was an agent?' Marnie said.

'Because we still need her to forget us. Or at least not remember us well enough to point the authorities in our direction. And she won't.'

Claire leaned forward. 'Why does any of that matter?'

Dryden explained what he planned to do. By the time he'd finished, Marnie and Claire looked noticeably pale.

'If there's any other way,' Dryden said, 'I'd love to hear it.'

All that followed was silence.

When they reached Eversman's estate, they drove past it. They followed the switchback residential road as it turned and climbed. They stopped half a mile farther on, where a gap in the trees offered a view down onto the distant brick house. They could see Dryden's Explorer still parked in front.

Dryden took Eversman's phone from his pocket, switched it on, and pulled up the contact list. Ayla was near the top. He opened her contact page and tapped SEND MESSAGE. He typed:

> Ayla, take Brooke and get out of the house right now. Pick a hotel in town. Don't talk to anyone. I will call and explain soon.

He pressed SEND.

They waited. Twenty seconds later, Eversman's phone rang. Ayla. They watched the mansion as the ring tone trilled on and on. It was still going when one of the house's garage doors began to rise, and a moment later a sleek red SUV – a Porsche Cayenne, Dryden thought – lurched out and sped down the driveway.

Dryden put the Suburban in drive, made a U-turn and headed back down the road toward the estate. At the last curve before the entry drive, he slowed and stopped, three hundred yards shy of the big iron-and-wood gate. He nosed forward just far enough that he could see it while mostly keeping the Suburban hidden from view. The gate was already swinging inward.

The red Cayenne burst through the opening, fast enough that it nearly clipped the concrete wall on the far side of the road before it could turn. Then it was pointed downhill and accelerating away, and a second later it was out of sight beyond a curve.

Dryden stepped on the gas. He pushed the Suburban to 60; it felt like 90 in the boxed-in canyon between the property walls. He braked hard and turned in at Eversman's drive, the gate just beginning to swing shut again. He steered around and past it, and twenty seconds later he rolled to a stop in front of the guesthouse.

He turned and looked at Marnie and Claire.

Pale again, both of them. Breathing a little faster than normal.

'We're not the bad guys,' Dryden said.

He opened the door and got out, Eversman's silenced .45 in his hand. He crossed to the guesthouse's front door and simply knocked.

From the moment the door opened, the violence that followed took less than a minute. There were three men in the guesthouse, as Eversman had said. They weren't armed. They weren't expecting trouble to show up. They were, in fact, certain that it wouldn't.

When it was over, Dryden found the door that opened into the garage. There were two stalls, both empty. He pressed the wall-mounted button to raise the big single door, then waved for Marnie to drive the Suburban inside. She climbed over the console to the driver's seat and put it in gear.

Dryden wiped his prints from the .45 and set it on the concrete floor. Its suppressor was hot to the touch.

Marnie braked, killed the engine, and got out. Claire stepped out behind her. The two of them stood staring through the entry into the house.

'The computer room is downstairs,' Dryden said. He punched the button to lower the garage door again, then led the way back inside.

Before seeing it, Dryden had imagined the computer room would look like a scaled-down, slapped-together mock-up of the war room in every movie version of NORAD. Giant flat screens everywhere, a kind of digital nerve center with data streaming in from all over.

Instead it had a single computer. It was a desktop unit that might have cost five hundred dollars at Best Buy. It had a case and a monitor and a keyboard and a mouse, all sitting on a plain wooden counter against one wall of the room. It had a printer on the carpet nearby.

The monitor currently displayed a black screen with a blinking white cursor at the top. Nothing else.

Someone had stuck a Post-it note on the edge of the keyboard, with a line of text scribbled on it:

EXAMPLE QUERY: (YEAR)(MONTH)(DATE)
search term goes here

Farther down the length of the counter were three chairs, each with a cluttered workspace in front of it: stacks of paper arranged in haphazard order, notecards pinned to the drywall above, photos and computer printouts everywhere. Dryden made his way past them, taking in details.

There was a card with bullet-point notes written in a neat hand:

- Mark Squires is 31 as of Apr 10, 2026 (date of Newsweek interview)
- Would have been 20 as of this past Apr 10
- Attended Ohio State (*NYT* interview)
- 2 students with this name enrolled there now
- Lived in Atlanta during grade school age (*NYT* interview)
- Figure out which Mark Squires at *OSU* used to live in Atlanta

'Look at this,' Claire said.

Dryden turned to her. She was standing before a long folding table butted up against the end wall of the room. There were short stacks of paper on it, orderly and squared, forming a row that ran the table's length.

Dryden went to her side, along with Marnie.

For at least a minute none of them said a word. They only stared.

Each stack was topped with a black-and-white photo on regular printer paper. All the photos were of people, ranging in age from the midteens up to fifty. Each had a line of text written in red pen at the top: *DOB* followed by a date. Date of birth. Judging by the dates and the images, these were all pictures of the subjects as they appeared in the present day. They were the kinds of photos that could have been found on each person's Facebook page, or in an employee or student directory online.

Every photo also had a red *X* across the face, with the word *DONE* written below it.

Claire exhaled slowly. Dryden thought he heard a tremor in the sound.

He moved to his left down the row, looking at each picture in turn. One stopped him: a woman in her late twenties, beautiful but with eyes that looked troubled somehow. Dryden slid the photo off the stack, and found beneath it a printed screenshot from a Facebook timeline.

The woman's name was – had been – Aubrey Deene. Twenty-eight years old. Postdoc at Arizona State. She had attended high school in South Bend. The person with the red pen had written two words diagonally across the sheet, in big letters: *DEFINITELY HER*.

Dryden slid the printout aside and saw a text document below it. It was a newspaper article, formatted like the ones in Curtis's binders. The headline read: DEENE CONFIRMED, HIGH COURT BALANCE SHIFTS TO 7-2.

The article was dated October 9, 2033.

'Oh hell,' Marnie said softly.

Dryden looked up. At the far end of the table, Marnie had raised a hand to her open mouth. Dryden followed Claire to where she stood.

The last four stacks in the line were all topped with photographs of college-aged girls. All four had the same date of birth written at the top, which would have made them all nineteen years old. All four were *DONE*.

Marnie had slid each picture halfway off the sheet beneath it, revealing three screenshots from Facebook and one from a Twitter account.

All four of the girls had the same name – first, middle, and last.

On each of the four social media printouts, the same scribble appeared in red ink:

1/4 CHANCE IT'S HER

The hand Marnie had raised to her mouth began to shake. She made a fist of it and dropped it to her side. For a long moment she remained quiet. Then she turned to Dryden, her eyes hard.

'Tell me,' she said. 'Tell me how we got this far without alerting these guys that we were coming. What was Whitcomb going to tell us?'

'He was describing how they buried the system in the ground. How the power supply doesn't need maintenance. They designed the whole thing to be future-proof. They needed it that way, because to get headlines from ten years in the future, the machine has to keep working that whole time. They had to guarantee it would, no matter what changes came along over the years. So that's how they built it. Buried and self-sufficient. They said it would keep running, even if, in the future, everyone in charge of it died. It would just sit there in the ground, all by itself, working away. I said that was pretty clever, and Whitcomb said it was very, very stupid. It was their biggest weakness. The way we were going to beat them.'

Marnie's eyebrows drew toward each other. She was putting it together.

'We thought they'd know when we were coming,' Dryden said. 'They'd be able to tell, because all of a sudden their searches wouldn't work past some certain point in the future. The time when we would show up and destroy the system.'

Marnie nodded. 'So the way around that is . . .'

'Don't destroy the system.'

She stared, thinking it over.

Dryden nodded to the work counter. 'We'll take the computer they were using to access it. We'll cut the data line where it comes through the wall. There's no one left alive who knows about any of this stuff. If someone later on tries plugging into that line, they won't know what to make of it. They won't have the software these guys had. But none of that matters anyway, because nobody *will* try plugging into it.'

Claire looked at him. 'What do you mean?'

'You'll see.'

'But the system itself,' Marnie said, 'buried somewhere on this property . . . we just leave it running? That's why these guys didn't know we were on the way?'

'They looked pretty surprised to me.'

They hauled the computer up to the garage and put it in the Suburban. They gathered all the paperwork and took that up, too. They made a fast, thorough sweep of the guesthouse and found three other crude models of the original machine, hooked up to tablet computers, like the one Claire had first shown Dryden. They took all three to the Suburban.

They wiped their prints from the doorknobs and light switches, then raised the garage door again and drove across to the main residence. Inside, in the bedroom Dryden and Marnie had slept in, they found Claire's machine where they'd left it on the nightstand. They wiped their prints from the obvious places they could think of in the main house, but only as an abundance of caution; neither house on the property was going to yield a hell of a lot of evidence to the authorities.

Dryden entered the big garage the red SUV had come from, and found both things he wanted within thirty seconds. The first was a remote for the front gate, clipped to the visor of a BMW convertible in the second stall. The second was a five-gallon container of gasoline.

Three minutes later Marnie was at the wheel of the Suburban again, Claire riding shotgun. Dryden crossed the motor court to his Explorer. Passing the back end, he saw Dale Whitcomb's blood still covering the license plate. It was dried brown and flaking at the edges. It looked like dirt. If there were security cameras with coverage of this driveway, no one would ever be able to identify the vehicle's owner. That was assuming any data from a video system would survive – which was assuming a lot.

He started the Explorer, nosed around in a sharp turn, and followed Marnie down the driveway. He glanced in the rearview mirror as they rolled toward the opening gate. At every main-floor window of both houses, flames capered.

They reached El Sedero just after six in the evening. They skirted the town and drove into the hills a few miles inland. Ten minutes later they parked the Explorer and the Suburban on an overgrown two-track way up in the evergreens, the land pitching steeply up on one side and steeply down on the other, toward a brush-choked pond thirty feet below. They positioned the Suburban nose-first at the edge of the dropoff.

They destroyed the computer they had taken from the guesthouse. They pried open its case with a tire iron and smashed everything inside. They left the pieces scattered on the Suburban's floor.

They hauled the four machines out and set them in the dirt – the three from the guesthouse, and then Claire's machine, last in line.

They took turns on the first three machines, using the tire iron. They smashed through the outer cases, shattered and snapped the delicate components inside – circuit boards and strangely shaped arrays of wire and plastic and even glass.

Claire went third, and when she'd finished, she sat crouched there, still holding the tire iron.

With her free hand she shoved the wreckage aside, and dragged the last machine in front of her. Her machine.

Dryden raised his gaze and traded a look with Marnie. Claire looked up at both of them, then unlatched the plastic case and opened it.

She stared down on the machine. The red LED glow shone out from inside it, stark in the shadows of the overhanging pines.

Claire lowered the steel tool until it rested on the machine's surface. She dragged it lightly across the slats where the light bled through. In the still air, Dryden could just make out the low cyclic hum from inside the thing.

With her other hand, Claire reached down and switched on the tablet computer. She tapped the icon to open the machine's control program. Four simple buttons: ON, OFF, RECORD, STOP.

She pressed ON.

The cyclic hum sped up. The red glow turned green.

Static. Soft and steady. It might have been the sound of wind pressing through the boughs.

Then it faltered. Receded. A woman's voice came through.

'– *spokesperson for the L.A. County Sheriff's Department said there is no suspect at this time. The victim's father told reporters –*'

Claire swung the tire iron down onto the machine as hard as she could.